FATHER
JUNIPERO'S
CONFESSOR

FATHER JUNÍPERO'S CONFESSOR

A NOVEL

Nick Taylor

HEYDAY, BERKELEY, CALIFORNIA

Library of Congress Cataloging-in-Publication Data

Taylor, Nick, 1976–
Father Junípero's Confessor : a novel / Nick Taylor.
pages cm
ISBN 978-1-59714-261-8 (paperback : alk. paper)
1. Spain—History—18th century—Fiction.
2. Franciscans—Missions—Fiction.
3. Conversion—Catholic Church—Fiction.
4. California—History—To 1846—Fiction. I. Title.
PS3620.A95945F38 2013
813'.6—dc23

2013014771

Cover Photo: Sudhakar Chandra
Cover Design: Lorraine Rath
Interior Design / Typesetting: Joe Lops
Printing and Binding: Worzalla, Stevens Point, WI

Orders, inquiries, and correspondence should be addressed to:
Heyday
P.O. Box 9145, Berkeley, CA 94709
(510) 549-3564, Fax (510) 549-1889
www.heydaybooks.com

10 9 8 7 6 5 4 3 2 1

To

Jessica

and

Violet

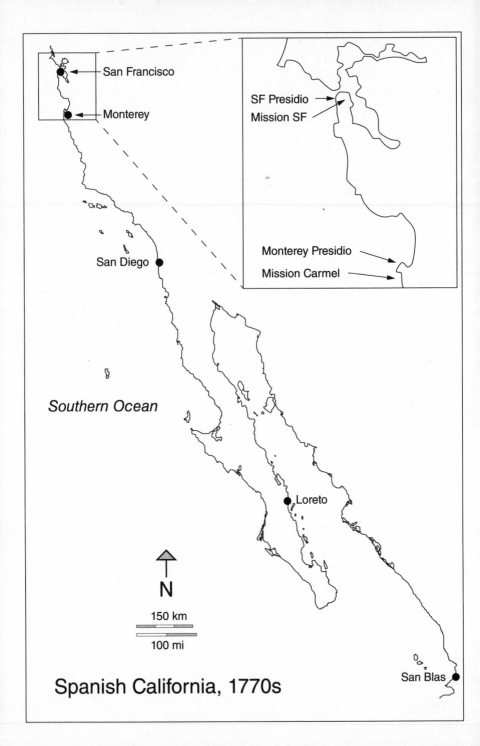

San Francisco

Monterey

SF Presidio
Mission SF

Monterey Presidio
Mission Carmel

San Diego

Southern Ocean

Loreto

N

150 km

100 mi

San Blas

Spanish California, 1770s

For from the year 1740, when he received me as one of his students, until the year 1784, when death separated us, I was the object of his very special affection, an affection we always mutually shared, more than if we had been brothers in the flesh.

—FRAY FRANCISCO PALOU, *Life and Apostolic Work of Fray Junípero Serra* (México City, 1787)

ONE

NUEVA CALIFORNIA, 1784

I ROSE AT DAWN a humble conqueror. Here, a thousand leagues north of the landfall of Cortés, the Bay of San Francisco was alive with birds, giant flocks passing before the sun like veils. The briny aroma of the marshes rose to the window of my lodge, along with the cloying odor of acorn porridge.

The Earth's newest Catholics were stirring.

I had convinced the neophytes of the rightness of tortillas at supper, but their allegiance to *atole* in the mornings was unshakable. To me it seemed cruel, not to mention unwise in a time of uncertain provision, to forbid such an innocuous privilege. I myself had sampled the acorn gruel, and to the best of my knowledge it was not intoxicating, nor poisonous in any way. The taste was another matter. The acorns were ground and reground on the women's stone *metates* until the tough fibres of the acornmeat gave way to coarse meal. My children used no herbs in seasoning the dish, nothing but creek water.

That morning I selected two neophyte boys to serve as runners and translators on the journey to Carmel. Neither gave even the slightest hint of pleasure when I called his name, for it was the habit of this tribe to suppress all outward signs of emotion. In the two years I had lived among them, I had only on rare occasions seen a smile, and then only from a baby.

After breakfast we waited for the last member of our traveling party, a soldier from the presidio. I had no reason to expect that we would be bothered on our journey, particularly with the two neophyte boys in my company, but custom required that we be attended by a soldier. The King's soldiers were dull men, deficient always in some way, for why else would one be posted here at the wildest frontier of all Christendom? As we waited for the tardy soldier, I joined with my companion, the Reverend Fray Vicente Santa Maria, in singing a Mass for the safe completion of our travels and the healthful recovery of Fray Junípero.

"Kiss the hands of His Reverence," implored Fray Vicente, "and assure him that the work goes well in this quarter."

"That news will cheer him more than a thousand kisses," I said.

My companion nodded knowingly. The little bird-boned Galician was right to anticipate that Fray Junípero would ask first about the mission. I would be lucky if His Reverence gave me five words about himself, so fully did our work consume his thoughts.

"But you will kiss his hands for me?" Fray Vicente's brow creased above his weak gray eyes.

"I will, Brother."

The soldier arrived just as the boys finished saddling our mule, and we four joined the trail before the sun had burned the dew from the grass. While arduous, the fifty leagues' journey between my mission on the bay and Fray Junípero's at the edge of the great Southern Ocean was a tonic for my nerves. The hills were dry at this time of year, and in every direction they rolled out like golden waves, studded here and there with live-oaks, manzanitas, prickly pear cactuses and other camels of the plant kingdom, each guarding its hoard of water deep within the Earth. In some places, there had been no rain since Easter. But even arid land provides fodder for the senses: there was the sage and anise scent of the chaparral—like the *maquis* of my native Mallorca—clinging to the grades too steep for the oaks. There was the rustle of oak leaves, stiff as fish scales, in the breeze. Hawks screeched on their high circuits, waiting for the rustle of the serpent or the vole. And always the steady clop-clop of the mule. His plaintive snort, the soothing words of the boy holding his rope. The grunt of the soldier on his horse, stomach aching from last night's tipples. And my own breathing, always in my ear, the only constant companion all these years.

In the great valley south of the bay, the air was warm and dry. Extending my arms on either side of the trail, I brushed the whiskers of yellow sunburned grass. Before the governor forbade it, the Indians burned the hillsides once a year to clear away the dead grass and flush out game. In spring, fresh shoots would grow, turning the hills green for a while. The oldest Indians said that the hills were never as green as they used to be, as though we Spaniards, with our unfamiliar tongues and customs, had brought curses rather than the light of Christ.

These people, the *costanoans* as we called them, were kin more to the beasts of field and forest than to the European man. They compared unfavorably also with their southern cousins, the descendants of the *aztecas* and *mayas,* who had been, when Cortés found them, skilled with tools and accustomed to rule by monarch. These northern tribes lacked even the most rudimentary understanding of human society. Agriculture, pottery, stonemasonry, metallurgy—all of these were as foreign to them as the Spanish tongue. Without crops of any kind, they lived an irresponsible life, gathering acorns and various wild grains, relying on the vagaries of nature for their sustenance. Their poor nutrition made them ugly, short, lumpish, and ungainly. The women went about in skirts made of rabbit skins laced together by sinew thread. The men and children were altogether naked. To mask their physical shortcomings, or perhaps to distract the looker, they marked themselves—men and women—by smearing pigments into wounded skin. We forbade scarification among neophytes residing at the missions, but the practice continued beyond our perimeters. Some pagans had even adopted the cross into their designs—a development which cheered Fray Junípero even as it horrified the rest of us. "The skin is only the beginning, Paco," Junípero had said. "Soon the Holy Cross will be etched into their hearts. All is progress, my son! Love God!"

The first day's travel was routine. The only excitement came when the neophyte boys spotted on a distant hillside a small flock of *cierdas,* which are a kind of antlered deer found in this country. Being well provisioned and impatient to reach Carmel, I denied the boys' request that we stop and hunt. We spent the night at the southernmost reach of the valley, laying our mats under an oak as wide as the apse of a cathedral. I spent a restless night worrying about the condition of my master, and after a breakfast of cold *tamales,* I could wait no longer for news: I sent the two neophyte brothers ahead to Monterey with instructions to return like Noah's doves with news of His Reverence.

Thus I was alone on the trail that second day with only the pitiful young soldier, my escort, for company. Astride his sweltering horse, he scratched his groin constantly and complained too often of thirst. Several times I tried to engage him in conversation but gained only that he had been raised in the diocese of La Mancha. The dolt lad had no thoughts on God, art, or politics. I resolved that we would walk in silence, and I occupied myself in imagining that the ridgelines of the hills were the spines of giants buried beneath the earth. "Cervantes would have loved this country," I said out loud, trying one final time to engage the young man. He said nothing, being either unwilling or unable to reply.

We followed the trail over the crest of the coast range onto the sandy plain formed by the delta of the Río de Monterey. The river had been named San Elizario by Fray Juan Crespí—may his soul rest in Christ—but had been changed subsequently to match that of the nearby presidio, which served as the administrative capital of New

California. The fog normally enshrouding the basin was out to sea that day, and late in the afternoon I was able to see our returning messengers some distance down the trail. They called when they saw my mule inching gingerly down the slope.

"*Amar a Dios,*" I replied in the usual fashion. "What is the news of Fray Junípero?"

Pánfilo, the elder of the brothers, gave the report: "When we arrived, he was seated at a workbench outside his cell, cutting a bolt of cloth with . . . scissors." The neophyte spoke carefully measured Spanish, pausing only briefly at the end before remembering the word for the odd cutting implement, *las tijeras.*

Watching the boy struggle with the Castilian tongue, I recalled how Rigoberto, my first neophyte son, had once described the unfamiliar sounds of our language: "The Spanish tongue is like a minnow, father, snapping insects from the surface of the pond." Like these boys, Rigoberto had once gone ahead. But he had never come back.

Pánfilo's younger brother could not contain the thrill of finally laying eyes on the famed Fray Junípero Serra. Switching to his native tongue—which I spoke only haltingly but understood well—he said, "There was a line of women, Father, waiting to receive the cloth. Some had been baptized in Christ, and some not. Some were heathen women from the villages. But it did not matter—His Paternity made each kneel and hear a prayer to Our Lady."

I knew that if a heathen woman came to Fray Junípero on any feast of Our Lady, he would allow her the same amount of cloth as a baptized woman—so long as she knelt and listened to a prayer sung over her by the matron of the convent. I pictured these women clearly: they would be dressed as Spanish peasants in loose-fitting robes, sun-bleached linen blouses, *huaraches,* and wide straw hats. Their unbaptized cousins stood in their rabbit waist-tunics, waiting patiently to see the friar who required only that they hear a song to receive his gift of woven cloth, a commodity more dear to these people than gold.

The report of His Paternity engaged at his usual work gave me hope that he had been premature once again with his boding. Indeed, when we arrived at Carmel around dusk, he came all the way to the road to greet us. With him were Father Fray Matías Noriega, his companion at the mission, and a crowd of not less than one hundred neophytes, or nearly all the population in residence. They trailed behind their father in perfect discipleship, bearing candles and boughs of fragrant cedar. It was a clear evening, and the sun was just then setting over the ocean, bathing the scene in a warm orange light. As always, Fray Junípero beamed with the favor of Christ, arms spread wide in welcome. My soldier escort was so moved by the sight that he spurred his horse so that the beast would not tarry on the last decline.

Our animals' feet churned up an unfortunate cloud of dust. Taking a lungful, Fray Junípero began to cough: a bitter, painful noise. He lifted an arm to cover his face. I ran to his side and was joined there by Fray Matías and Junípero's boy, Juan Evangelista José. Junípero pushed us all away, preferring to make his own way, unaided, back to the dormitory. We remained in the road, careful not to move for fear of stirring up more dust. When His Reverence disappeared inside, Fray Matías touched my arm.

"Fray Francisco, I apologize for not contacting you sooner, but the Father President insisted that I keep his secret."

"You should have written."

"I beg your pardon, but he reads my correspondence."

I had known Fray Matías many years and had always found him candid and trustworthy. All of our band of missionaries agreed that he was an exemplary friar. Indeed, that is why Fray Junípero had chosen him to replace our friend Fray Juan Crespí—may he rest peacefully in Christ—as his companion at Carmelo. Now, though, I wished Fray Matías had been perhaps less exemplary in his devotion. I resented what the soldiers might have called his "weak spine."

"You could have sent word another way," I said. "A runner, perhaps."

"He is much changed since Fray Juan passed."

"That was two years ago, Brother."

Fray Matías bowed his head. Though a decade younger than I—not yet into his fiftieth year—his head was entirely bald, save for a gray corona at the rear. "I only know what I have seen, Your Reverence. I have prayed many times for God to give Fray Junípero the strength to mourn, but I assure you his grief persists unabated. I know I could never replace Fray Juan, but it seems as if there is an obstacle in his heart."

"Fray Juan will never be replaced," I said, measuring my words like a chemist mixing a powder. "Even so, you must not burden yourself with Fray Junípero's suffering."

The idea of anyone bearing the suffering of our Father President—this man who beat himself with iron chains, who smashed stones against his breast until his skin was torn and bleeding—was sufficiently inconceivable that it struck both Fray Matías and me as a kind of joke. He smiled and said, "I suppose you are right."

It was now nearly dark. The neophytes had gone back inside the walls of the mission, and the gate would soon be locked for the night. Fray Matías and I were alone in the road, feeling a change in the air. Mission San Carlos Borromeo is located on a bluff above the Río Carmelo, and in the evenings, the fog rolls onto the marsh below the bluff, filling it up like a lagoon.

"He wrote also to the brothers at San Antonio and San Luis Obispo," said Fray Matías. "But he asked that I hold the letters until you arrived. I was not to tell anyone the extent of his suffering."

We walked together as far as the door of Junípero's cell, where I asked Fray Matías to leave me alone to compose myself. I had a sudden feeling of dread, caused not by the failing health of my dear beloved friend, but by an old jealousy, something I thought I had put behind me long ago.

I took a deep breath and knocked. A moment passed in silence, and then came the familiar voice: "Who is there?"

"Your Reverence, it is Fray Francisco."

Another pause. "Come in."

I had not been to Mission San Carlos in over two years—not since Fray Juan's requiem Mass. Much had changed at the site since then, most noticeably the construction of the stone church building, which was now nearly three-quarters complete. Fray Junípero's cell was exactly as I remembered it: four bare walls, unplastered so that one saw the pebbles and bits of straw in the adobe bricks. The earthen floor was neatly swept. There were no furnishings but a wooden bed frame, a stool caned with tule reeds, and a low table for writing. A single candle burned in a pewter cup on the table.

Fray Junípero sat on the stool, fingers clasped about his rosary. He made no effort to rise as I entered, but only said, in his usual high-pitched, grating voice, *"Amar a Dios,* Brother."

"Always," I replied.

He looked, in a word, diminished. His eyes had retreated into their sockets, and his mouth turned down slightly at the corners. Although short in stature—never more than five feet, crown to sandals—Fray Junípero had always maintained an unyielding posture. Now he was hunched like a cobbler. Both sleeves of his habit, I saw, were crusted with mucus from coughing. Around his neck hung the usual wooden crucifix, an enormous object, one of the only possessions he had brought with him from Mallorca those many years ago. At bedtime he removed the crucifix from its cord and placed it on his chest, where the horizontal beam stretched nearly the width of his breast.

I stood awkwardly for a moment, before my Father pointed to the bedstead, indicating for me to sit. "Oh, Paco," he said, "would you please close the window? I am so cold."

I went to the far wall, where a portal about the width of a man's forearm opened onto a garden of roses and pink gillyflowers. I myself had planted this plot, before the founding of Mission San Francisco called me north. In my time at Carmelo, I had never had the pleasure of witnessing the roses in full bloom. I could not see the colors in the darkness, but the smell confirmed success.

I pulled the casement shut.

"Thank you, Brother. Please sit."

There was no mattress, only a thin wool blanket spread over the slats. Many years ago, I had wondered how a man could sleep on such a pallet. That was before I discovered that His Paternity did not sleep.

"I came as soon as I received your letter," I said.

"Remind me, Brother, which letter is this? I have sent you so many. And each time . . . each time you remained at your mission."

"Your Reverence, I am here now."

"I suppose you want to discuss the supply ship."

"As you wish."

"One never knows when there will be a supply ship. You recall the time at San Diego when Governor Portolá was ready to march us all back to México? And he would have, were it not for the intercession of Santa Barbara. On the ninth morning of our novena, there it was—the blessed supply ship cleaving the mist in the harbor. Do you recall that, Brother?" As Junípero spoke, his fingers continued to move slowly along the beads of the rosary.

"I have heard the story many times, Your Reverence."

He looked up suddenly. His eyes met mine, and I felt the hair stand up on my arms. "Ah, but how careless of me! It was Fray Juan, not you, who was in San Diego with me. How thoughtless of me to confuse you!"

There was a long pause as Fray Junípero's fingers continued along the beads. He did not move his lips as he prayed, and he did not look down at his hands. Instead, he searched my face with his eyes— those hard owl eyes, which had penetrated the souls of heathens and viceroys alike.

When his fingers reached a decade on the rosary, he spoke again: "If you would be so kind, Father, I should like to confess my sins."

I had been Junípero's confessor for thirty-four years—since 1750, when we left Mallorca for New Spain. The sacrament came easily between us. This time, however, I made much of my preparations, arranging the candle on the table, the blanket on the bed frame, and asking God to give me a gentle ear, as if the penitent were yet a stranger.

"Have you seen the church, Fray Francisco? My children have been busy."

With great trouble, His Paternity rose up from the stool. Quickly removing myself from the bedstead, I offered my arm, but he refused to take it.

"If the Lord wants me in His house," he said, "He will give me the strength to walk there."

The neophytes keeping vigil outside Fray Junípero's room scrambled away when I opened the door. A choir assembled in the plaza began a low *Te Deum* as they saw His Paternity emerge from the cell. On the side of the yard nearest the church, a neophyte man in a simple blouse and trousers fussed over a torch, trying to light a candle from its flame. As we approached, I saw an *ofrenda* from the heathens in the nearby village—a collection of pine-bough torches arranged like flower petals above a small altar. Brightly colored baskets adorned with feathers and beads steamed in the evening cool. I smelled acorn gruel.

Two boys stood by with baskets of rose petals, which they cast on the ground before us as we walked.

The church loomed as a shadow against the sky. Its walls were composed not of adobes but of massive stone blocks the neophytes had quarried nearby. The church was already as high as four men; I wondered how much taller it would get before the carpenters raised the roof.

Inside, the moon shone directly onto the floor. As a boy, in Palma, I had played in the ruins of a Roman countinghouse not far from my family's home. The unfinished church put me in mind of that place—though of course this building was at the opposite end of its life. We stepped around a water-trough. A line of masonry tools hung neatly along its lip. On the other side of the trough, I tripped over an oak branch lying on the ground. The noise frightened a hen sheltering with her chicks under the trough. Without turning around, Fray Junípero clucked softly under his breath, and the chicks returned to their mother. Soon enough, they were silent. The mellow tones of the choir came to us on the breeze.

Midway down the nave, Fray Junípero paused at a tall wooden box and began examining the ornamentation along its edges with his fingers. This would be the new confessional. In the old wooden church next door, confessions had been held in the open, with the penitent kneeling behind a screen. I waited for His Paternity to finish his examination and step aside, so that I might enter the booth and resume my preparations.

Instead, Fray Junípero motioned for me to follow him to the far end of the structure. In the spot where the sanctuary was to be located, the earth was surrounded by a rope. Looking down, I saw that a grave had been dug in the dirt floor.

"I want you to bury me here," he said, "beside Fray Juan."

Fray Juan Crespí had been buried in the sanctuary of the old wooden church. Presumably his remains would be moved when the stone church was done.

I said nothing.

"This is my final wish, Fray Francisco. Do you understand?"

"Yes, Father."

I followed His Paternity back to the confessional. Again Junípero fingered the curls and filigrees carved into the wood. "The love of God will save these people," he said. "Look at what He has done for them already." Turning to me, he exclaimed, "Why, Brother—you have turned pale!"

"Forgive me," I said, trying to hide my eyes, which surely betrayed me.

"Was it my instruction? I have also sent orders to the carpenters for a casket, you should know." He paused and stared at me. "Let us be clear about one thing, Paco. It is not for you or me to know when I shall pass from the Earth. It is for God alone to decide. When He is ready, He will take me."

"I understand, Father, but—" I stood at the door of the confessional, poised to step inside and hear what would likely be my dear friend's last earthly reconciliation with his Lord. All of a sudden, it seemed as though all of my sixty-one years—and especially the forty-four spent in the Seraphic Order of San Francisco—had been but a prelude to this moment. This was the act for which I had trained all my life.

Yet I could not step inside. The moonlight shone directly in my face. I could not hide my tears. "It will be done, Father. You shall be buried as you wish."

His Reverence stepped into the light. I could see that his eyes, too, were filled with tears. He reached out to touch the confessional, so that his arm formed a gate between me and the door of the confessor's chamber.

"Francisco, *mi condiscípulo*." He took my hand. "Paco—"

"Yes, Father?" I stood as straight as I could, fighting the trembling of my legs.

"My friend—perhaps we should switch places."

TWO

MALLORCA, FORTY-FOUR YEARS EARLIER

AS THE STROKE OF midnight decayed into the cool air over Palma, I rose with my fellow novices, a half-dozen teenaged boys with bleary eyes, wiping off that warm, dark slumber which the Lord in his mercy spreads over the adolescent soul. Somehow we found the pegs where we had hung our cassocks just four hours before. The garments flew over our heads, the cords cinched around our waists. Following the boy in front of me, I marched from our cell to the convent chapel, down a passage paved with smooth, foot-worn stones. Had I been of clearer mind, I might have taken inspiration from the feet that had trod this path, how many brothers and uncles and great-uncles and great-great-uncles and all the other sons of this sun-bleached Mediterranean rock had been called to the perfect life of San Francisco. But at this hour I felt lucky just to know my right foot from my left and to remember those Latin phrases which would secure swift passage back to my bed.

The master of novices, Fray Rafael Verger, was already in the chapel when we arrived. A thick, burly man with eyebrows the exact size and texture of the hairy caterpillars which plagued our island every spring, Fray Rafael was the youngest son of a respected olive-growing family. His pedigree alone would have commanded our respect even if he had not been our master. Huddling us together in the cave-like subterranean chapel, illuminated by the glowing white candles on the altar, he began the Night Office with a hymn. When the time came for our reply, we mangled the Latin syllables like a newly conquered tribe. But Fray Rafael was of no mind for remediation at that hour. He pressed on, verse after verse, psalm after psalm. Finally he gave his blessing, turned, and knelt before the altar. This was our sign to return to our cells, and we wasted no time in doing so, for we knew that the bell would toll again in four hours for Matins, at which time we would return to this same candlelit cave to pray until the sun rose.

That night, the return march to the dormitory was made lively by a rumor, first whispered only the day before, that we were to have a new professor of theology. The new man was rumored to be, like Fray Rafael, just a few years older than us. We wondered what a man of that age could possibly profess. Only in the lives of the saints did there exist such precocious learning. My classmate Narciso Nadal, a printer's son who published every thought in his head, ventured that the new teacher had been sent from Rome by personal dispatch of the Pope. In fact, he said, the new Father Lector was none other than a sacred spirit, risen from the dusty bones of both Our Seraphic Father San Francisco *and* the Most Blessed Doctor of Scripture, San Buenaventura.

When we reached our cell, another novice pulled the wooden door shut. Young Moisés Sabio, who among us all was the most interested in the mystic qualities of our new faith, asked, "But how is it possible that a man should rise from two saints' relics?"

"I do not know, Brother," said Narciso. "The cook overheard a conversation between Fray Rafael and the Father Guardian. Before this, I had only known about risings from a single saint's bones. But this is the magnitude of our new professor. This is tremendous, brothers—do you understand? This is *Seraphic!*"

Our cohort had been in seminary only a few months at that point, and we were all just struggling to comprehend the complex rules and hierarchies of monastic life, not to mention the theological subtleties and unique nomenclature of our Order. "Seraphic," for instance, was an adjective reserved only for San Francisco and a few other superlative friar-saints. Young Narciso surely only sensed the weight of the word and had no idea of the mild blasphemy he was committing.

One member of our group was not so confused. "You ought to think before you speak, Brother," said Juan Crespí. "You ought to retract your words, all of them, right back to the bit you whispered in the passage. And further, I expect that you should apologize to San Francisco—and report the transgression to Fray Rafael. Or I shall do it for you."

Juan Crespí was a tall, pale-skinned boy, whose blue eyes suggested that he had, in addition to his Mallorcan lineage, some blood from northern Europe. Juan and I hailed from the same district of Palma, the parish of Santa Eulália. Our heads had been submerged in the same baptismal font, our blessings sung by the same bishop. We had been tutored together Sunday afternoons in the rectory, sung hymns in the same choir. Our older sisters had married twin brothers, so we were even related to some degree. Juan was a year older than I, but I had always felt like his protector because of his shyness. Most of the time he was timid and deferential, but issues of faith had a tendency to raise his hackles. His unusually strong devotion had already earned him the nickname *Beató,* or Blessed One.

"Listen, *Beató,*" said Narciso, "I only know what I heard from the cook."

"We must not bear false witness," Juan explained.

"False witness? Do you know it is false? Do you correspond with the Pope?"

Juan shook his head, frustrated that he should be subjected to such a fatuous debate. "You do as you wish," he said. "But I shall tell Fray Rafael." And with that, he crawled onto his bed, took the rosary up off the pillow where he had left it, and began to pray.

The other boys were not ready to retire the subject.

"Do you know in what manner the Father Guardian received the news?" asked Moisés. "Did this new Father Lector appear to him in a vision?"

Narciso stroked his hairless chin. "I would not be surprised if there had been a vision."

"Gentlemen," I said, "we shall meet the Father Lector soon enough, and then we shall see with our own eyes whether the cook has good advice."

I could tell that Narciso wanted to continue the debate, but even he realized that our time was best spent in recuperation. He rubbed his eyes with a fist.

Another boy blew out the candle, and we crawled into our bunks. For a few minutes there was the rustle of sheets, and then only the pulse of measured breathing. The two o'clock hour tolled softly from the tower. I could not find my way back to sleep. In my head, I practiced Latin verbs—a sure passage to slumber—but my thoughts drifted back to the new Father Lector, the young man who was to teach us the wisdom of Saint Bonaventure. In my imagination he was a child sitting on a swaddling cloth, holding a brightly colored rattle in one hand.

Was this a vision? Certainly it was not the first time I had beheld in my mind's eye a thing I had never seen before. My father, who worked on the wharves in Palma harbor, had once promised me a gray parrot for my birthday. He described this bird as the most talented mimic in the world—capable of holding a conversation in any tongue you could name. I had never laid eyes on a gray parrot, but when I imagined one he had a clever smile and a mouth full of fine white teeth. Had that been a vision too, or was the term reserved exclusively for revelations of a spiritual nature?

I turned onto my side. Whispers rose from Juan Crespí's bunk. Pressing my ear to the slats, I heard the click of beads as his fingers worked over the rosary: "*Ave Maria, gratia plena. Dominus tecum . . .*" Between decades, Juan voiced intentions: "Holy Father, most merciful God," he whispered, "take pity on my brother Narciso. And San Francisco, most perfect servant of the Lord, please forgive Narciso, your humble disciple, for his transgression regarding your special title. *Ave Maria, gratia plena . . . "*

His words devolved into a stream of air and sibilance as I finally drifted off. I had no dreams that night, nor any visions. When I woke for Matins three hours later, Juan Crespí was already dressed and standing by the door, his fingers still worrying the beads.

IF NARCISO WAS correct, and the new Father Lector had been created from the bones of saints, then God was playing a joke on us all, for no one could have devised a less divine form than Fray Junípero Serra. I had once seen a family of dwarves at a traveling circus, but outside of such novelties, the tiny friar we found in the library the next morning was the smallest man I had ever encountered. Painfully thin through the neck and jaw, he looked like a starving dog. When we entered the room, we found him with his head bowed in prayer, and I noticed that the stubble under his tonsure was rather sparse, considering his supposed youth. I wondered if he were perhaps older than we had been led to believe.

In fact he was twenty-six, an extract from the hot and dusty center of our island. His village, Petra, was known as one of the few places in the Balearic Isles where the Castilian tongue had still not taken root—this after several hundred years of Spanish rule and numerous treaties binding us to the mainland. He was a paradox made flesh: a young man who looked old; a small man with enormous ambitions; a deeply pious man who would, at the height of his influence, hold more temporal power than anyone in New Spain but the Viceroy himself. He was a man one could know, but never fully understand.

Even before he had spoken a single word, I understood that I was in the presence of greatness. Despite his small stature, he commanded the room. He was a lodestone, a charged rock. I could not swing my attention away from him any more than a compass needle can diverge from north. At this point I did not fully understand the mechanism of his attraction, the special alchemy that distinguished Junípero Serra from an ordinary professor of theology, from an ordinary friar, from an ordinary missionary. All I understood was that he was no ordinary man.

"*Amar a Dios,*" he said as we moved around the table. There was no special urgency in his voice—it was the tone of a priest casually calling a group together. A few of us murmured replies ("*Amar a Dios, Frater,*" etc.) but otherwise we kept our heads down. As I moved closer to my new master, I noticed on the floor a pail of water—the same pail we novices used to scrub the walls and floors of the convent. I wondered if the new Father Lector did not yet realize that we did our chores in the afternoons.

Then suddenly Fray Junípero rose to his feet, sending his bench hurtling backward against the wall. "My brothers!" he exclaimed. "If you do not love God, I cannot help you. No one can help you!"

We said nothing. Those of us who had not yet taken our seats remained frozen in place, half bent over, reaching for the benches in front of us.

He began to walk around the table. I was closest to his right, and he approached me first, pressing so close that our sandals touched. I had to look down to meet his gaze, for I was at least a head taller than he. For a while he said nothing, but only searched my face with his hard, dark eyes—pupils as dark and deep as gun barrels. Where his eyebrows came together over his nose, the hairs bristled out like thorns. I imagined myself becoming trapped there, like an insect, pressed as close as possible to the Father Lector's face so that he might examine me better.

"Tell me your name, Brother."

Though utterly terrified, I somehow managed the correct response. "Your Reverence, I am Francisco Palóu."

"And how old are you, Brother Francisco?"

"Your Reverence, I am seventeen."

"Seventeen years old." He took a step back and surveyed me head to toe. "Let me ask you a question, Brother. Do you think we ought to expect more from those who take the name of Our Seraphic Father San Francisco?"

I hesitated. Francisco was, after all, only the name my parents had given me. I doubted I would have chosen a different seminary if my name had been Dominic or Ignatius. "I beg your pardon, Father, but what more might one expect?"

"Some extra measure of piety, perhaps? A special commitment to learning. It is just a theory I have, nothing more. Tell me, Brother Francisco, do you love the Lord?"

"Your Reverence, of course I love the Lord."

Without pause, he shot back, "And *how* do you love the Lord, Francisco?"

Luckily I recalled the Gospel: "With all my heart, Your Reverence."

He stepped closer. I was the fly. "And how else?"

"With all my soul, and with all my mind, and with all my strength. I love Him every way that is possible, Your Reverence."

"Then why did you not leap with joy when I greeted you?"

"I beg your pardon?"

But he had already gone on to the next boy. In turn he examined us all in the same manner, asking our names, and also sometimes our places of origin. I noticed that his questions for no two boys were the same. He asked Narciso why the sun rose in the east and not the west, and whether we could draw some truth about God's love from that phenomenon. Poor Narciso was flustered, which I expect was precisely Fray Junípero's intention, the boldest students being the most difficult to unbalance. He wanted us all in that state so he could more readily glimpse our souls.

At least two of our number went to tears under the questioning. One of these was Juan Crespí.

"Where is your parish, Brother?" Fray Junípero asked Juan.

"Nearby, Father. I was raised here in Palma."

"Your family must be pleased that you are still so close."

"I have not seen them since I entered seminary, Father."

"I see—so you might have gone to seminary in Madrid, for all you've made of the proximity."

This was too much for poor Juan to bear. I knew he had several times passed up opportunities to visit his parents, whose home was only a short walk from the convent. Each time he had opted to devote his free hours to Latin, Greek, or any of the other subjects that came to him with such difficulty.

The Father Lector instructed us to sit. "I have neglected to introduce myself. Doubtless you have heard my name. And here you see my face. You may come to know that my father was a farmer. That my singing voice, while lovely to God's ear, is actually plain. But what do those markers tell you of me? Nothing of substance. Nothing of the contents of my heart."

Here he took up the pail of water from the floor.

"Remove your sandals."

After each dip into the bucket, he squeezed the rag as though wringing out sin. He said not a word as he traveled around the room washing the feet of his students, twelve novices in turn. When all were clean and dry, he went to the window and poured the dirty water into the courtyard. Then he returned to his bench, lowered his head, and began to pray. We sat in silence around that long oak table for another hour. Finally Fray Junípero raised his head and said, "You may go."

Not one of us dared to move.

HIS REVERENCE'S THEOLOGY class, held every morning but Sunday in the little seminar room, quickly become the highlight of my days. Until I met Fray Junípero, I had thought of theology only in abstract terms—elegant explanations about the love of a God I had never seen. I had always been attracted to the logical puzzles of Catholic dogma, the mystery of the Holy Trinity and so forth, but the parish priests who gave me my early instruction lacked the imagination to bring the dogma to life. In Fray Junípero's hands, theology was no longer a theory described in chalk on a slate—it was an explanation of life itself! From his hands, the calf-bound *Lives of the Saints* fell open to reveal another hero on every page. It delighted me to know that so many of these soldiers of Christ had been members of our Order: San Antonio of Padua, for example, was not only a Franciscan but a scholar. I was able to imagine myself one day emulating these famous men—for was I not training in the Friars Minor and studying theology with all my energies? It was a practice that would never have occurred to my parish priests—imagining oneself as San Antonio—but Fray Junípero supported it and even encouraged it, for in his mind emulation of the saints opened our hearts to receive the grace of God.

But I was only one of many students in his class. I tried to distinguish myself through erudition (or my sophomoric imitation of erudition), but I never managed to earn the Father Lector's praise. Then one day an oratory contest was announced to the novices. Each of us was to prepare a short sermon on a topic of his choice, containing relevant scriptural citations with lessons clearly demarcated for the unsophisticated ear. The winner of the contest would be allowed to leave Matins an hour early every day to help prepare for morning Mass. It was a small favor, but I was determined to win because Fray Junípero would serve as judge. This was my chance to make myself known to the master.

At once we began poring over the writings of San Buenaventura, Blessed John Duns Scotus, and all of the Franciscan theologians who now seemed like members of our own community, thanks to the enthusiastic introductions of Fray Junípero. I chose to study the teachings of San Bernardino of Siena, who together with his friend and contemporary San Juan of Capistrano preached devotion to the Holy Name of Jesus in fifteenth-century Italy. But

I had trouble distilling a suitable lesson from my fascination. I had plenty of lovely thoughts, but no arguments. After several fruitless weeks of research, my sermon consisted of a single bland exhortation: "We must venerate the Holy Name of Christ."

Meanwhile, at the other end of the long seminar table, Juan Crespí happily filled leaf after leaf with his meticulous black script. Though Juan had trouble with spellings, he had none with the act of writing itself. In fact, the prolix novice kept a journal under his mattress in which he noted every day the name of the saint whose feast it was, and what prayers he had said to honor that saint. (Narciso Nadal had browsed the book surreptitiously and judged it uncompelling.)

Juan's sermon was to be an examination of the doctrine of the Immaculate Conception—the notion that the Blessed Virgin was conceived in her mother's womb without the stain of original sin. Unlike his prayer journal, his sermon-in-progress was kept always on his person, rolled into a tube and tucked next to the rosary on his waist-cord. The other novices might have found this odd, but I knew that Juan had a good reason to guard his text: he had a terrible memory, an affliction which would follow him throughout his career. Indeed, in the forty-two years we shared the habit of the Friars Minor, I would never see Juan Crespí deliver a sermon without the aid of written notes.

The contest was to be held in the private chapel where the Franciscan community gathered for Mass. In its outward aspect on the Plaça de Sant Francesc, the chapel appeared rather plain: a tall, unadorned wall of camel-colored sandstone, crowned with terra-cotta tiles. Even the oculus window above the door hid its face behind unassuming stonework. But the staid exterior belied the richness within: the magnificent gilt altarpiece, its monstrance reaching nearly to the vaulted ceiling. At the center stood the Holy Reverence of Assisi, Patriarch of the Stigmata, and at his sides San Buenaventura, San Luis Rey de Francia, Santa Clara, and Santa Catalina de Bologna. The Baroque grandeur of the high altar and its *reredos,* or side altars, seemed at first a violation of the austerity espoused by our Order. But the senior friars assured me that all of the materials used in construction, including the gold leaf and red Binissalem marble, had been given as alms by wealthy Balearic families in honor of kin who served in the humble example of San Francisco.

By the afternoon of the contest, the faces of my young brethren were showing the effects of several consecutive sleepless nights. I had finally managed, just before the call for Matins, to complete my sermon on the Holy Name. My technique was rudimentary but effective: I went through the writings of San Bernardino and kept a tally of how many times he used certain phrases. It was decent student work; I hoped Fray Junípero would applaud my effort, if not the finished product.

The entire community, four dozen friars, nattered in the pews when we entered the chapel. In the sanctuary, the superannuated Father Guardian sat on a dark wooden bench beside Fray Junípero. When the novices were seated, Junípero rose and welcomed the congregation.

"*Amar a Dios,*" he began, his diminutive stature exaggerated in contrast to the Gothic arches soaring four stories above him. "I shall ask that the novices draw lots amongst themselves to determine the order of presentation."

Our group came together nervously. Moisés Sabio began ripping threads from the hem of his robe to use as "straws." Suddenly, I felt a hand on my shoulder and turned to find Juan Crespí. His face had gone pale.

"Francisco," he said, "I have made a grave mistake."

"What is it, Brother?"

"I have forgotten the draft of my sermon in our cell. I don't know how I could have allowed this to happen—you know how I rely on drafts."

"You have time to fetch it," I said. "Run, and I will draw your lot for you."

"Do you think there is enough time? Why don't you go instead? You are much faster than me."

This was true. Juan had stamina—as his service on the long expeditions of Portolá would later attest—but he was as slow as a tortoise and as awkward as a foal.

"I will go," I said, "but you must draw for me."

Juan agreed and explained that I would find the roll of paper under his pillow, where he had left it momentarily while helping another boy that morning.

"Thank you," he whispered. He was so shamed by his mistake, and by the necessity of asking his friend to help correct it, that he could not look me in the eye.

Outside the chapel, I removed my sandals so that I would not slip on the staircase. The stone felt cool and solid on my bare feet. My footfalls made no noise. The only sound was my breath and the rattling of the wooden rosary on my waist-cord. I was proud of myself, recalling the prophet Isaiah's response when the Lord asked for volunteers: "Here am I—send me!"

The novices' cell was in the basement of the old convent. Having only a single clerestory window, our cell was not well lit, even by the afternoon sun. But I did not need much light; I went directly to Juan's bunk and lifted the pillow, sliding my hand underneath to retrieve the sermon. To my surprise, I found no roll of paper. I slipped my hand under the mattress and located Juan's prayer journal. I had the correct bed.

I grew anxious. What if I were unable to find the sermon? Juan would surely have to forfeit. I began to tear at the bedclothes on the other cots. Before long, it looked as though a cyclone had swept through the cell. Blankets were draped haphazardly over bedposts and pillows lay scattered on the stone floor.

Was it possible that Juan had prepared another copy? Leaving the cell in disarray, I raced upstairs to the library. A wall of leaded-glass windows allowed long, lazy rays of afternoon sun to settle on the seminar table in a pattern of quadrangles. Motes of dust floated through the air. Half an hour later—or more, who could tell?—I closed the last bookcase. I had found nothing. My fingers ached, and my nose itched from dust. I was loath to leave empty-handed, but what choice did I have? Juan's sermon was lost.

I returned to the chapel by a side door so as not to distract the speaker, but then I stopped. I recognized the voice at the lectern. It was Juan Crespí. My brother stood in the pulpit, eyes cast down as he spoke, reading from a curled leaf of paper.

"And so, brothers, when the angel Gabriel said to Nuestra Señora, 'Fear not, for thou has found favor with God,' he showed us that God filled her with grace as a maid fills a bucket with milk."

After another paragraph or so, Juan looked up briefly. I was standing at the end of a pew, approximately halfway down the nave. Our eyes met for an instant before he returned to the page.

I felt sick to my stomach. It did not occur to me to sit down, so I simply stood at the end of the pew. When he finished, there was tremendous applause. The noise surprised me—the audience had been so much in Juan's thrall that none had made even a rustle while he spoke. Juan bowed to the Father Guardian and Fray Junípero, then returned to his seat. The senior friars murmured amongst themselves. I overheard almost unqualified praise for my friend's oration.

Now Fray Junípero went to the pulpit. When he preached, Junípero normally stood on a block in order to reach the lectern. But the block had been removed on account of Juan Crespí's height, and the little friar had to stand on his toes to be seen.

"We have a visitor," he announced, looking directly at me. "Brother Palóu, it is good of you to join us this afternoon, however tardy. Unfortunately, your colleagues have all finished their sermons. A shame that you missed them—we heard an excellent program this afternoon."

"Father, I apologize," I said. "I was on an errand for a friend."

I spied the first pew, where Juan Crespí was seated with his back to me. All the other novices in the pew had turned to listen.

"I am ready with my sermon, Father," I said.

"That is a shame. Your colleagues drew lots to determine the order, and I believe Brother Crespí's was the last. Is that not correct?"

"Father, I left instructions for someone to draw on my behalf."

"Is that so? Let me give you some advice: leave your instructions in writing. God did not *tell* Moses his commandments."

A few of the older friars chuckled.

"But Father—"

"And what's more, on top of your other transgressions, you have the poor sense to set foot in the Lord's House without so much as a pair of sandals on your feet?"

I looked down. In my haste to return from the library, I had forgotten to retrieve my sandals.

I looked to Juan, waiting for him to stand up and end this humiliation. But he did not turn. All I received for my sacrifice was the back of his deceitful head.

TWO WEEKS LATER I was back in the same chapel, waiting for my turn at confession. Our confessional was the simplest of structures: two thin olivewood doorframes hung with canvas curtains, with a third curtain on a rod between the chambers. The penitent slid the curtain open or closed according to his preference. A surprising number of my colleagues said their confessions in full view of their confessors. Narciso, for example, had remarked that he found the sacrament more "purgative" with the curtain open.

I myself preferred to keep the curtain shut. Even at that age, my relationship with God was deeply personal, more intimate than I felt comfortable discussing even with my closest friends and family. I was never one to demonstrate my faith through public declarations or bold actions like Fray Junípero. Indeed, that may be one reason why I was so attracted to him: our manners of worship, and later our ministries in the missionary field, were natural complements to each other. My first experience with faith came when I was nine years old. That year my mother, who worked as a laundress and piecework tailor, fell from a ladder and sustained a painful injury to her spine. Afterward she could not move any part of her body below the neck. Like an infant, she had to be fed by spoon, carried to the latrine, and bathed. Our father had no time care for her—the family needed his longshoreman wages more than ever—so the responsibility fell to me and my two sisters. I missed every third day of school. Two months into her convalescence, our mother saw that her condition had not improved, and she asked to see the priest. He came to her bedside and administered last rites. I had no Latin at the time, so I did not know what he was saying as he swung the censer and dabbed oil on her forehead. When he explained the meaning of the ritual, I was horrified. I ran out of the house and hid in my secret place, an alcove at the foot of the old city ramparts. I closed my eyes and asked God to make my mother whole again. She had children to look after, I explained, and a husband with no instincts for child-rearing. I had never asked God for anything, not even in the casual way children do. I had always felt that requests to the Lord should be reserved for the most dire circumstances—otherwise one risked exhausting God's favor.

But this circumstance was as dire as any I could imagine. Mother herself was preparing for death. So, huddled there in the dark beneath the ancient stones, I pleaded with the Lord to grant her health. Not to take her to Heaven just yet. I do not know what kind of reply I expected—a burning bush, perhaps?—but I recall that I was disappointed when I returned home. Mother was still in bed, still crippled and helpless. But slowly, over the next several weeks, her condition began to improve. She became able to move the fingers on one hand, and then the other, and then her toes. Six months after the fall, she was able to walk again, albeit with a limp. A month later she was up on her ladder, happily pinning sheets to the line.

I was young, but I understood the lesson: the favor of the Almighty was the most powerful force in existence, but it was not to be summoned lightly. My mother's recovery had vindicated my caution. I told no one about my prayers. To do so would have compromised the confidence of my Lord. I resolved never to make a spectacle of my faith, a promise I reaffirmed when I joined the Franciscans.

I took this modesty very seriously. To see a face—any face—as I recited my sins would be like staring into the sun. Although the sacrament is commonly called "confession," with the priest administering the sacrament the "confessor," the actual transaction is not between sinner and priest but between the sinner and God. The master of novices, Fray Rafael, was fond of reminding us that when he heard our confessions, he was not the accuser but the mediator; reconciliation was between the sinner and God. It was our duty to accuse ourselves of our sins.

Nevertheless, Fray Rafael was uncommonly skilled at squeezing sins from novices. In Rafael's strong hands, we were the halves of an orange, giving up every last drop of juice to the bottomless cup of the Lord. He did not tolerate ambivalence. "Tell God what you did," he would say, "tell it straight." At even the slightest pause, he would say, "Are you sure that is all?" Inevitably it was not, and I continued until I could finally say that I was empty—a dry, sinless pith.

Waiting in the lacquered pew, I scrutinized the events of the past week. I let my thoughts drift up and out through the high windows into the cool morning air. I imagined Palma as only a bird would see it, the bustling capital of Mallorca becoming smaller as I soared into the clouds, finally just a cluster of clay-tiled roofs along the sea cove. The rugged mountains in the north would rise like teeth in the watery mouth of the Mediterranean. I examined my soul like a milliner buying lace, noting the tiniest flaws, cataloguing them, but all the while avoiding the gaping maw at the center, the sin I was beginning to feel I could never put behind me. There was really only one thing I had to confess, and that was the same as what I had confessed the previous week and the week before that.

Soon Moisés Sabio emerged from the confessional looking very much like an exhausted fruit. He did not catch my eye, nor anyone else's, but continued to the farthest pew, where he began to recite his penance. Being next in line, I rose up from the kneeling board and slipped behind the curtain. Inside was a short stool. Moisés had left the divider between the cells drawn, so I had no view of my confessor.

At once, the familiar voice of Fray Rafael came through the curtain. *"In nomine Patris, et Filii, et Spiritus Sancti. Amen."*

I began the act of contrition. *"Deus meus, ex toto corde poenitet me omnium meorum peccatorum . . . "*

As I said these practiced words, there came a noise from behind the curtain—a scraping of the stool against the stone floor, as if Fray Rafael were adjusting his position. I heard muffled voices, and then Fray Rafael said through the curtain, "Brother, I beg your pardon."

There was more scraping, then the tingle of curtain rings. I heard breathing and murmured prayer. Then a new voice cried out, *"Amar a Dios!"*

My heart seized. I restarted the act: *"Deus meus, ex toto corde poenitet me omnium meorum peccatorum, eaque detestor—"*

"Of course you detest your sins," came the familiar voice. "Otherwise you would not be here."

Though we were not permitted to address our confessors by name, we always knew the identity of the man behind the curtain. Ours was a very small community.

"Father," I said, "I forgot the feast of Santa Ynéz last week. I ask God to forgive me that regretful omission and allow her perfect soul to rest in peace."

Fray Junípero said nothing to this.

"And also, I regret a singular trespass in my seminar on theology"—this I hoped would catch his attention, for this was his own seminar—"though I have struggled diligently for a fuller understanding of the doctrine of Christ's Holy Name, I regret that I have not yet accomplished it. The notion hovers in my mind, you see, but has not revealed its truth."

Fray Junípero brushed this away like so much dust on a bookshelf. "What truly burdens you, my son? There must be some other thing."

I had good reason to be scared. It was rumored that Fray Junípero beat himself like a savage to repent for certain sins. I knew there would be no hiding from him, so with a difficult swallow, I began, "Father, I have been injured in the most grievous way by a close friend and companion. This person, in fact, I have known since birth."

The chair on the other side of the curtain scraped the tile floor as Fray Junípero rose to attention. "Tell me more."

"It occurred on the day of the sermon contest. You recall that I was absent for most of the afternoon. I did not lie when I said that I was helping a friend."

"This is the friend who injured you?"

"Yes, Father. He pretended to have left his sermon in our residence so that I would retrieve it for him and miss my turn at the pulpit."

"I see. But why did your friend not retrieve his own sermon?"

"I volunteered," I said, feeling proud as the words left my mouth. Surely the connection to Isaiah would not be lost on the learned Father Lector. "I knew that I could make the trip more quickly, so I volunteered to go. But I could not find the lost paper, and when I returned to the chapel, I was horrified to discover that he had tricked me—"

Fray Junípero cast the divider aside with a swift, hard stroke, nearly ripping the fabric off the frame. He held me with his eyes. When Christ returns to judge the living and the dead, I cannot imagine He will appear more grave than Fray Junípero Serra appeared at that moment.

"You can stop this right now!" he said, not bothering to whisper. "I have no use for this kind of accusation, and neither should you!"

"But it is true, Father."

"Does that change anything? Was Our Savior not falsely accused?"

"That is precisely my point, Father—it is not a false accusation. Fray Juan did injure me in the way I describe. That is a fact."

"I abhor facts! This kind especially. What good is it to report your brother's transgressions to me?"

In class, I had grown accustomed to Fray Junípero's style of inquiry, but I felt as though a fearsome weapon, one that I had always admired for its strength and potency, had finally been turned against me.

"I scarcely need to tell you, Brother Palóu, that you have great promise as a lector—far more than the other novices, if you care to know the truth. You have the ability to grasp even the most abstract conceptions and pull them down out of the clouds for all to see. The Holy Name is not a difficult concept; you are right to understand it in simple terms. And your mastery of the temporal world—the world of facts and dates and circumstances—is just as impressive. It is the other side of your development that concerns me, for instance your lack of judgment in situations where the rigid application of *fact* subverts our larger cause."

"That was never my intention, Father. I only meant to explain my struggle to forgive this injury."

"Is that so? And what exactly are the consequences of this injury? I would imagine they are small. Ambition can be a dangerous thing, Paco." He used the diminutive I had heard all my life—*Paco*—the origin of which, I had learned since entering seminary, was an abbreviation of *pater comunidalis,* father of the community, one of San Francisco's many appellations. "Naturally," he said, "it is essential to have ambition if we are to accomplish anything of substance during our time on Earth, but there are consequences for reaching too far. You remind me so much of myself at your age."

Was this a compliment? From any other professor I would have thought so. But there was something about Fray Junípero that made me doubt he thought very highly of himself. I had noticed, for example, that at meals he divided the food on his plate into two portions—one large and one small. He ate exclusively from the small portion, and invariably offered the larger share to a table mate. After seeing him do this many times, I wondered why he bothered to serve himself more than the tiny portion he actually ate. Finally I realized that he relished the temptation. He derived more pleasure from denying himself that extra measure of food than he did from eating it. Only a deeply unhappy man, I thought, would torture himself in this way. And then there were the rumors of self-flagellation . . .

Comparison to a young Junípero Serra was a dubious honor at best.

"Your Reverence, thank you," I said. "Though I am not worthy of your praise."

"Is it praise? Listen to me: Brother Juan is a simple young man. Do you know he had tears in his eyes when he told me that you two, as babes, were baptized by the same hand?"

"Did Juan come to see you, Father? Surely his confession corroborates mine."

His Reverence's countenance turned grave once more. He gave a snort, reached up, and shut the curtain.

"Father?"

There was a rustling of fabric and a scrape of the stool on the tiles. A moment later, Fray Rafael's voice returned: *"In nomine Patris, et Filii, et Spiritus Sancti . . . "*

· · ·

I PUSHED OPEN the heavy wooden doors to exit the chapel. There on a bench in the passage sat a very surprised Juan Crespí.

"Why are you not in confession?" he asked me.

I looked both ways down the passage to make sure we were alone. I tried to stifle the rage throbbing in my chest. "From any other person, I would expect an apology, but from you, Beató, I would expect even more. Penitence certainly, but also a public display of shame. Instead, I learn that you have been to see Fray Junípero, only to continue your deception!"

Young Juan raised his head. Tears pooled in his wide blue eyes. "All of this is true, Brother," he wailed. "I have sinned against our Lord. I have ignored the most holy example of San Francisco. And most importantly of all, I have dishonored our shared history. My brother, I do not expect that you will ever forgive me, but I ask that you at least have mercy on my soul."

This was not what I expected to hear. For a moment, I watched my brother weep into his hands. Finally I said, "Mercy is not mine to give."

"Yes, of course. Of course." He sniffed and wiped his nose with the back of his hand.

I was appalled at how easily he broke down. With just a few strong words, he went to pieces. "I am confused," I said. "You must have known your sermon was good enough to win."

"I am so sorry, Brother . . . "

"Yes, I understand and accept your contrition. But I need to know why you did this to me."

Now Juan's sorrow gathered strength. He sobbed loudly, covering his eyes with one arm.

His weakness infuriated me. "There must be some reason," I said. "Look in your heart and tell me."

Juan wailed, "I cannot find a reason, Brother."

"I refuse to accept that. Make a conjecture. I deserve at least that much."

Juan uncovered his bloodshot eyes. "Yes, you deserve an explanation. But I cannot give it to you, because the Lord has not given it to me."

Disgusted, I left the convent and spent the afternoon walking in the hills above Palma. Water trickled in the stone flumes, bringing life to the thirsty orange trees. I had always loved the smell of citrus, from blossom to rotting windfall. But today the orchards brought me no peace. Even my favorite creatures of those hills, the little white butterflies who danced on the wild rosemary, failed to lift my spirits. Hours of walking covered my sandals in a fine layer of almondine dust. My cassock, soaked with perspiration, clung to my back like a second skin. Returning to the convent three hours later, I felt exhausted but no less angry. I was not sure when I would be able to forgive Juan Crespí. Certainly not right away.

I had always absolved ills freely. My heart had never before lingered on trespasses. When I was five years old, my sisters convinced me that our parents had disowned me on account of bad behavior. They said I was to leave the house at once and never return. They let me walk almost half a league down the road, wailing uncontrollably, until they fetched me back. All of this I had forgiven in due course. But now my heart was recalcitrant, refusing to move forward even with the goad of an apology. Whence had come this reluctance to forgive?

I had never despised Juan Crespí. But the arrival of Fray Junípero had upset the uneasy balance between us. In the weeks that followed I would attempt to push away my rancor. Perhaps hidden from sight it would reduce, like a boil sometimes shrinks of its own accord, without the aid of the lancet. But I would soon discover that a bitterness suppressed only turns more bitter with time. The diving leviathan is only gone until it surfaces again, showing all the world the scars and barnacles accumulated during its long, dark night in the abyss.

THREE

I DO NOT KNOW precisely when the rumor of the mystery missionary came about, but there reached a point in the late summer of 1748 when it seemed to be the only subject in every conversation around the convent. Naturally, I heard it first from Narciso.

"The cook took me aside to impart an interesting piece of news," he said to a group gathered after supper. "It seems that there is a restless friar among us who has notified the Father Guardian of his wish to leave Mallorca immediately for a missionary assignment in America."

Moisés raised a brow. "Who is he?"

Gossip was to Narciso Nadal as gold is to the miser; the pain on his face was evident. "Tragically," he admitted, "I do not know."

"But you must!" cried Moisés.

Narciso bowed his head in shame, but we did not fault him. I sensed already that a young man like Narciso might serve God to greater effect as a layman. My intuition proved correct, for at the end of our novitiate, at that time when a member of our Order must finalize his vows to God, Narciso chose to leave the Friars Minor. He disappeared for several years, leaving Palma on a Catalonian merchant boat. I heard not a word about him until one day some years later, when I received in America a letter from our friend Fray Moisés reporting the establishment of Mallorca's first newspaper. It was printed only monthly, but the publisher had plans to expand to fortnightly if interest held. It was rumored, Moisés wrote, that the publisher was not concerned with profit, because he had made a fortune on the Spanish mainland. Apparently it had always been his dream to provide news to the people of Palma. The man's name, of course, was Narciso Nadal.

"I asked all my sources, but this mystery friar has cloaked his identity like Satan. Brothers, I am sorry for failing you."

"Cloaked like Satan?" Fray Juan spoke for the first time all evening. "A member of our holy community? Do you realize what you are saying?"

"Oh, Beató, I did not mean it in that way . . ."

"In what way did you mean it then, Brother?"

Narciso shook his head in frustration. "Forget I said anything at all."

I pitied Narciso, and I wished to allow him the escape of our forgetting, but how could we forget this news? Much more was at stake than mere intrigue. In the rules of our Order, San Francisco stipulated that friars must never live alone. This edict we interpret strictly, so that nowhere on Earth, not even in the remotest corners of savage countries, will one find a friar without a companion. So highly does this requirement figure on the minds of our superiors that the question of companionship must have occurred to the Father Guardian right away.

Thus this news was, in effect, a challenge to each of us: would we consider leaving Spain for the Great Unknown, in the company of this mystery missionary? Our convent had produced several distinguished missionaries to the Americas. One had even been companion to San Francisco Solano, the Franciscan saint credited with establishing our Most Holy Faith in Perú. Indeed, from the moment the *conquistadores* planted boots in the New World, there had been a constant and unremitting need for missionaries. By the Royal Law of the Indies, all colonial expeditions were required to include both temporal and spiritual components—soldiers and clerics—in order to protect the bodies and the souls of new subjects. This had always posed a challenge for the King because it constrained the expansion of his Empire to the number of missionaries he could enroll for service. Soldiers were never the problem: any boy can be made a soldier with a few months of drill. The making of a priest, on the other hand, is a quiescent task. It takes patience, and no amount of money can speed up the effort—particularly not in mendicant orders such as ours.

One wonders, perhaps, at the paucity of volunteers. What was Christ, you might ask, if not a missionary? Did He not say in the Gospel of Luke, "Foxes have holes, and birds of the air have nests; but the Son of Man has nowhere to lay his head"? To find his answer, the reader might turn the question on himself: how sits with him the proposition of sailing thousands of leagues across a violent ocean? The call to travel must be so strong, so undeniable, that the hearer disregards the sacrifice involved. One can imagine there are few men who hear such a call.

And yet there is the possibility of rebirth through missionary work. One hears all the time of laymen setting sail to start their lives anew—to escape the demons of shame, loss, lust, passion, madness, and a hundred other ills. Let me suggest that such men exist in the religious sphere as well. My own dragon had at the end of his serpentine neck the angelic, blue-eyed countenance of Juan Crespí. This beast did not breathe fire, but benedictions. He had no claws, but prayers. No roars, but hymns.

As it happened, I had been entertaining the possibility of leaving the convent. I knew that I could find work on the Palma wharves with my father. But that type of work was for men like Fray Rafael—men built for drayage. My physique was not designed to heft any tool but a pen. I might become a clerk if I left the service of God. The thought did not thrill me.

And then into this climate of uncertainty came news of the mystery friar. Suddenly a new prospect appeared before me. I knew I could never become a charismatic orator like Fray Junípero, nor would I achieve the level of pious devotion that Juan Crespí appeared to enjoy. I was an ordinary man, but surely in the New World there was a need for reliable, constant young friars?

It was an expansive notion, the idea that in one stroke I might break free of my young life's disappointments and assume a new direction full of meaningful and dignified work. In fact even if I left the convent in Palma, I would hardly call my time there a failure. Was that not the root purpose of seminary—to find one's true calling?

I mulled over the idea, giving rein to my wildest ideas about America: the ignorant, God-starved natives; the impenetrable jungles; the innumerable mountains and rivers and oceans, many still unnamed. I had never considered myself adventurous, much less an explorer, but the prospect of America did have an certain allure. More than anything, I felt sure that America would give me purpose. After my mother nearly died I remember standing by in consternation as she resumed her old life, unchanged in body or spirit. She made meals, kept the house, took in laundry. She changed nothing as a result of her brush with death. That is not to say she took God's gift of life for granted; she attended Mass with the same fervor as before and gave proper thanks for all the material blessings our family enjoyed. But part of me felt that she failed to take full advantage of the opportunity God had given her. She did not, for example, raise funds to renovate our parish church, nor did she make a pilgrimage to Fatima or walk El Camino de Santiago. She did not join the Lay Third Order of San Francisco. My mother could not have left Spain for America; she had a family to care for. But I did not. My family was the brotherhood of this ancient cloister—a brotherhood that had given me the gift of theological training but could not be said to require my continued presence. To borrow a term I would use much later, when I was responsible for staffing missions—I was a supernumerary. An extra friar. San Francisco said there must be two; he did not say there must be three, or four, or forty. Just two. Any more than that was a kind of waste when your currency was friars.

I am not a man upon whom ideas arrive like tongues of flame. I take time to consider, to ponder, to weigh. I am careful and deliberate—qualities which would serve me well in the missionary field. But I was not called to that life in the normal way, by an angel or a vision from Heaven. Rather, the Lord planted a seed in my head, gave me time, and waited for the shoot to push out. For all I know of the workings of the Lord, the seed might had been planted years before I heard about the mystery missionary friar—perhaps as far back as that afternoon in the rampart wall, when I made a rare request for His aid. All I know is that a seed was sown by God. And a rumor made it grow.

ONCE THE IDEA was rooted in my head, I resolved to work quickly. I stole into the library at night after evening prayers and drafted letters to the Father Guardian. *Most Reverend Father Guardian,* I would begin, *after much prayer and deliberation, my heart has grown wings to fly to New Spain.* I cringed at the dreadful imagery—hearts with wings? Was this a worthy demonstration of my fitness for rough duty? Weeks passed like this. My confidence ebbed. The mystery friar still had not revealed his identity, but I feared that the opportunity would expire before I gathered the courage to deliver my intentions to the Father Guardian. Night after night I crept back to my cell with nothing to show for my effort but a headache and a tired hand.

I decided to seek the advice of Fray Junípero. He could be severe, I knew, but he was always truthful. He would tell me whether I was being foolish. I rolled up the latest draft of my letter and left the library. Reaching the Father Lector's door, I knocked softly.

"Hello, Your Reverence? It is Francisco Palóu."

I found my master lying on his cot. He held an enormous wooden crucifix to his chest with his folded arms. He did not open his eyes when I entered, but instructed me to sit. There was no stool in the room, so I crossed my legs and sat on the floor. The stones were cold against my ankles. I rocked back and forth to find a comfortable position.

"*Amar a Dios,* my son," said Fray Junípero, still not opening his eyes.

"*Amar a Dios,* Father."

We enjoyed a moment of silence, during which I saw, in what moonlight filtered into the cell from the window, my master's lips moving in prayer. My tutelage in the classroom had continued apace. If I may say so humbly, I had become an accomplished student of theology. Together with Fray Junípero, I had written a paper tracing the influence of Augustine on Bonaventure, which His Reverence had presented at a Franciscan college in southern France. I had also completed a history of our convent and was working on a *Catalan* translation of Bonaventure's *Commentary on the Gospel of Luke.* I felt that I had earned Junípero's respect in the scholastic arena, but I still worried about what he called the "other side" of my development, the ability to abhor facts. I hoped that my news would persuade him I was making progress there as well.

"It is late, Paco," he said finally.

"I know, Father. I came to seek your advice about an important personal matter. It concerns the mystery missionary."

Here, to my surprise, Fray Junípero rose up quickly, taking care to place the crucifix gently on the cot. His eyes flickered, but his voice was steady. "What it this about a missionary?"

Had he really not heard? The news of the missionary had been the talk of the convent for weeks.

"There is a friar among us who has told the Father Guardian that he desires to go to New Spain. Forgive me, but I expected that you had heard this rumor."

"I hear many rumors."

Hearing the word "rumor" on the Father Lector's tongue, it occurred to me for the first time that I might be altogether mistaken, that there might be no mystery friar at all. "I ought not heed rumors," I said. "I know."

"I did not say that. I only said that I hear rumors. I may even have heard the rumor of which you are speaking."

"I doubt it, Your Reverence. Forgive me for bothering you."

I stood up to leave, but before I could stop him, Fray Junípero snatched the rolled-up letter from my hand. He walked to the window and held it aloft to read in the moonlight. He required less than a minute to absorb the entire script. When he was finished, his eyes gleamed with tears.

"Brother Francisco," he said slowly, "allow me to make a confession. Just over a month ago, I had a terrible headache at supper. I excused myself and returned to my cell, where I began to meditate. Soon I noticed certain patterns forming on the wall. Do you see how the plaster presents an unblemished surface? Well, in this instance, the wall was alive with many sparkling designs and patterns, like the ones that sunlight projects on the bottom of a fountain. All this time my head continued to trouble me, as though there were long needles poking my brain from all sides. I continued praying to God, asking him to deliver me from this torment. And then all at once my pain ceased, and the patterns on the wall coalesced into the shape of a man. He wore the robe of our Order and carried a long wooden cross in his right hand. A violin lay at his feet."

"San Francisco Solano," I said.

"Yes. You know my devotion. As I watched, San Francisco Solano pointed his cross first at me, then off to the side, where more of these dancing auras had formed a raging sea and a tiny ship. The ship rolled on the waves like a floating cork. His Sainted Reverence said nothing to me, and just as soon as he had appeared, he vanished. When he was gone, my head was finally clear, but my eyes were sore from the vision. I rubbed them with the hem of my robe. Later I found that the cloth was stained with blood."

I became aware that I was shaking.

"So you see," His Reverence continued, "I did not sleep that night. I remained on my knees, praying for God to send more instructions. In the morning I went right away to see the Father Guardian. He heard my story and confirmed that I had been called to higher duty. 'My son,' he said, 'although this province will lose its most ardent juniper, I know that by its fertility that lone tree shall engender a forest of such junipers in the New World. And for that I give God all thanks and praise.' He said he would take immediate action to pair me with a suitable companion from another province. But I stopped him: 'Your Reverence,' I said, 'I know that the authorities of our Order could easily pair me with a missionary from a convent elsewhere in Spain—but what if there were a friar in this very place who has been similarly called by God? Let us wait to see if any other man has seen the same vision.' The Father Guardian dwelt on this and saw the wisdom in it. He preferred, though, that we not put out a general call, but instead craft a rumor and see who came forward."

My heart swelled. This was beyond any result I had dared to imagine. At last I would have the kinship with Fray Junípero that I had so long desired, the kinship I knew I deserved, but which had been denied to me by ill fate and the mendacity of my peers. His attentions here in Palma were spread amongst his dozens of students, and though he assured me I was among the best, the sheer number necessitated that his love be spread thin. In New Spain, that most needful vineyard of Our Lord, we would labor together, just we two, master and pupil.

"So you see," concluded Fray Junípero, "I am the mystery friar."

At last I would be able to prove my worth to this great man! In the end, I realized, I had not needed to win a sermon contest—my great opportunity was yet to come. All it had required was patience. I was so filled with the pleasure of this happy discovery that I began to laugh.

"I am delighted, Paco, that you will join me. And since you did not know my intentions, and came here through no prompting by me, I know that it is God's will."

He smiled and took my hands in his.

"And," he continued, "I have a surprise for you as well. I have heard from another of your cohort. Just last night he came and sat where you are now. It seems he too was blessed with a vision of San Francisco Solano—the same vision I saw. Tell me, Paco, how generous is the Lord, to give me not one but two *condiscípulos*?

"To be sure, it is God's will," I said. "But you must tell me, Father, who is the third member of our party? Do I know him?"

"I should think so," said my master. "You shared the same baptismal font."

NORMALLY A MODEL of faithful attendance, Fray Junípero Serra occasionally disappeared from our convent for several days at a time. He would give no warning of his impending departure, nor any indication where he was to be found. It was generally assumed that he stole away to a retreat somewhere north of Palma, perhaps to a cabin hidden in the gray-green hills of olive orchards.

A week before our departure for America, I learned that our guess had been half correct; Fray Junípero's retreat was indeed located in the hills, but it was not the cabin we imagined. Instead it proved to be a type of grotto hollowed into a granite hillside. After a grueling six-hour walk from the convent, this was to be our Porciúncula, the plotting-ground for our missionary works.

Fray Junípero mopped his brow with the sleeve of his cassock and exhaled loudly. He delighted in exertion, finding it physically and morally rewarding. Seeing the fatigue on our faces, he warned Fray

Juan and me, "If this walk tires you, brothers, I fear the path ahead may be your death."

Fray Juan in particular looked worse for wear; he had neglected to bring the extra skin of water I urged on him before we left the convent. Juan insisted that Junípero himself planned to carry nothing but a small bag of stale bread and oranges.

"Would you prefer to die of thirst?" I had countered.

Juan had struggled with the decision. He wanted to emulate our master in any way that he could, but two hours into our walk, pink-faced with exhaustion, he was forced to accept a drink of water from the extra skin he had refused.

When we finally reached the retreat, Fray Junípero threw his sack down in the dust and knelt before a crude cross of unhewn olive wood. It was perhaps four feet high, the crossbeam held in place with hemp twine.

"Is this your retreat, Father?" Juan asked.

His Reverence finished his prayer, crossed himself, and brushed the dust off the front of his cassock. He showed no sign of thirst, nor any fatigue. In fact, his eyes shone with excitement.

"This place has been my secret until now," he said. He looked wistfully about the premises. There was a small fire ring, a stack of kindling, and a few half-burned logs. I saw no signs of bedding, nor any cooking utensils. "I will miss it," he said finally. "But it is well; it has always felt like an extravagance."

Juan and I exchanged looks, as we had several times that day while we followed the tiny, hare-like friar up the mountain. In the weeks since Fray Junípero had revealed himself as the mystery missionary (and the two of us as his companions) Juan and I had been forced into each other's company often. At first I feared these meetings, but over time we had discovered, to my happy surprise, a kind of kinship in bearing witness to the Father Lector's eccentricities. These were many, and they ranged from the benign (such as his refusal to sleep more than two hours at a stretch) to the questionable (testing the sharpness of table knives by making small incisions on his palm). Neither of us, of course, deigned to judge our master, but we shared a kind of tacit, bewildered awe of him. It was a flimsy truce, but it was preferable to the rancor that had flavored our relations for so long.

En route to the retreat, Junípero never paused, nor even slowed his pace when the breeze died and the sun's glare grew intolerable. Because we did not stop for lunch, I was ravenous when we arrived at our destination. I had eaten nothing since breakfast. Now, in the late afternoon, I was ready to help myself to the bread and cold meat the cook had given me for our lunch.

Already thinking ahead to supper, Juan asked if he might gather wood for a fire.

"That will not be necessary," Junípero said, gesturing toward the meager pile of kindling—a single arm's load of twigs and green branch-ends. Then, tossing aside the notion of wood-gathering (and cooking, and all such mundane tasks), he said, "Come close, brothers. We have much to discuss."

We did as we were told, leaning our packs against the rock wall at the rear of the grotto. I noticed that the wall was damp; we could at least put our thirsty lips to the rock, I thought miserably, if it came to that.

"I brought you here so that we would not be disturbed. We must have absolute concentration to prepare for the journey ahead."

As the sun fell behind the mountain, we sang Mass, consecrating as host a bread crust from Junípero's tiny sack. I must admit that it was a liturgy of singular beauty, as we perched above the city of my birth, watching the lamps twinkle on in the houses—and beyond them, the lights in the harbor. I realized that it might be years before I saw this place again. Despite my readiness to leave, it was a bittersweet thought. This city, this island, was my home.

When Mass ended, His Reverence gave us each an orange. He sat with legs crossed, still half-immersed in meditation, and peeled his fruit. Juan and I ate our oranges, along with two more from my pack. Then I brought out a quartered chicken.

"Leave that aside, Paco," said Junípero.

"But we are hungry, Father. We have walked all day."

He exhaled loudly through his nose, making a wheezing sound in his tiny nostrils. "It is one day, my son. There will be hundreds like this. We shall have to put aside much more than chicken."

Juan and I nodded solemnly, trying not to let our thoughts rest too heavily on food.

"Look down there," Junípero said, his words gaining strength as he slipped into his professorial persona. "Do you see the lights in the city? Let us divide those lights into three parts, one for each of us. How many would you say there are in total, Juan?"

Juan hesitated, as though considering whether to attempt to count them. Then he said, "Several thousand, Father. Maybe five thousand."

"Very well. If we were to divide them evenly, how many would that be for each of us?"

"Sixteen hundred and sixty-six," I volunteered, "with one remaining."

"Thank you, Paco," said Junípero. "Let us imagine that each of us goes forth with the burden of sixteen hundred and sixty-six souls who cannot possibly travel to America. Think of yourself not as one Catholic man but as the tip of a spear, backed by the strength of thousands allied in Christ. When we sail for New Spain, we shall carry the intentions of our people, the commingled hopes and prayers of all *mallorquíns*. Look at those lights! One of every three depends on you."

I cannot know why, but at that moment my attention fell on Juan's face. His eyes searched the darkening sky anxiously. The idea of taking responsibility for thousands of our countrymen did not sit well with him.

"We go with many purposes," Junípero went on, "not only to enlarge the dominions of Christ, but also to ensure that the realm of Satan never expands to these shores. My sons, before you dismiss such a notion, recall that it has happened before. This island has not always been safe for the faithful. For hundreds of years the Moors reigned here, and before them the pagans of Rome and Carthage. It is the burden of the scholar to know these things, to remember what has happened and to prevent it from happening again."

Juan spoke hesitantly. "These people, Father—do they understand what we are doing for them, that we are defending them from harm?"

"Some do," Junípero said. "But we are no less obligated to those who do not."

"Of course not; I did not mean to suggest it. However, when we return from our missions, will we share our intentions with them? Not for the sake of glory, of course, but only to communicate that the Kingdom of Heaven has been enlarged at the expense of Satan, and that by their combined prayers they had a role in the victory?"

Fray Junípero drew his lips tight over his teeth. He said, "We would certainly share such news, Brother, if we were ever to return."

"Are we never?" Juan had not expected this turn in the conversation. Nor frankly had I. There had been no discussion of the length of our journey. I had assumed we would be absent from Spain several years—not much could be accomplished in less time, especially when one considered the lengthy voyages to and fro—but I never guessed we would be leaving forever.

"It is God's will that we work fresh soil," His Reverence explained. "America is a vast continent of virgin lands, rife with souls in the thrall of Satan. Even if we were three thousand missionaries instead of three, our work would never be finished to the satisfaction of the Lord. To that end, we should assume that we will never return to Europe."

We sat silent, Juan and I, stunned in equal measures by hunger, fatigue, and this news. The sun was gone, retired behind the hills, and darkness rolled down the mountain like an advancing army. In the distance the lights of Palma twinkled ever more brightly.

"Should I share this with my family?" Juan asked.

"That is your choice, Brother."

"And what about our brothers at the convent? What should they expect?"

"They can expect correspondence."

"That is all? Correspondence?"

Junípero frowned. "The life of the missionary is not a surprise, my son. It is well documented."

"To be sure, Father, I have read missionary stories in the *Lives of the Saints*, but—"

"Why should our lives be any different?"

And there it was, finally. This was the standard by which our journey would be measured. I should have seen it when Fray Junípero described his vision. Recall that his messenger had not been Christ, nor the Blessed Virgin, nor even the Seraphic Father. Had any of these perfect beings appeared, Junípero's vision would have had a different tenor, a sheen of impenetrability. There would have been no opening, no way for Junípero to insert himself into the dream. But the visitor had been San Francisco Solano, a Spanish Franciscan. A man who had not always been a missionary. He had been a violinist, in fact. And now he was a saint.

"We sail the week after next," Junípero said. "I have been in contact with the missionary college in México; they expect us to land at Veracruz, the principal royal port on the Caribbean coast of New Spain. We shall go over land to México City, thence to our placement in the pagan country."

"Where is the placement to be?" I asked.

"That has not been decided."

"But it will be virgin country?"

"Of course. I have made my intention clear to the authorities."

The night grew cold around us—there would be no fire that night nor on any of the three nights we spent at Junípero's retreat. By moonlight, we discussed the practical details of our journey.

Junípero outlined the special responsibilities we each would hold, over and above stewarding the holy intentions of sixteen hundred Mallorcans. My chores included arranging the logistics of travel and accounting for our small purse of silver. This latter was an unusual task. Members of our Order normally live by alms. In this case, however, His Reverence understood that certain things—for example passage on sailing ships—cannot be expected to fall from the pockets of strangers. Eventually the air began to numb our lips and talk became too difficult. We stretched out on the dirt and drew our cloaks over our bodies. I turned away from His Reverence so he would not hear my stomach growling.

When I woke before dawn, Junípero had already risen and left the site. I heard his voice singing praise to the morning. Seizing the opportunity of his absence, I roused Juan and we ate the cold chicken, throwing the bones as far into the brush as we could. When His Reverence returned I made our morning chocolate, boiling water over a kindling fire and stirring the dark, sweet cocoa powder into three pewter cups. His Reverence raised no objection to this indulgence—there must be some ritual, he often said, to distinguish us from the beasts of the forest—though he drank only half his portion, dividing the rest evenly between his two *condiscípulos*.

"Brothers," he said, "I had a vision last night."

"Describe it to us," Juan said between sips.

"I was in America, on a bluff overlooking the sea. The waves crashed mightily against the rocks, as on the north coast of this island, but the ocean in this new place was infinitely more fierce and menacing. We had planted gardens—flowers and grapes and vegetables—and there was livestock in a pen. Sheep, I believe they were."

"Were there pagans nearby?" I asked. "Had we baptized any souls in the Lord?"

Junípero looked at me suspiciously. "I would hope so, Brother. All I remember is the setting I have described. A sea cliff, and two friars toiling in the fields."

"Only two?" I asked.

His Reverence nodded, but he did not elaborate. Instead he bowed his head and held out his arms to pray.

Two friars. One was certainly His Reverence, but which of us was his companion? I dared not look at Juan, for I was sure he was tortured by the same question. Only one companion—how was that possible? And even if it were true, even if His Reverence had been joined by only one *condiscípulo* on that seaside bluff—why would he reveal such a thing? He must have known how it would torment us.

I closed my eyes tight, hoping that on this windswept rock I would finally be granted the vision I had so long desired. Perhaps there, I thought, in Junípero's secret retreat, the boundary between Heaven and Earth was cracked. Or perhaps it was only the chocolate wending through the caverns of my brain. It hardly seemed fair that I should continue to suffer ignorance. Others were graced with visions in locations as pedestrian as the convent of Sant Francesc. Juan Crespí, for example, had no trouble in this regard. How could I pretend that Junípero's lone companion would be anyone but he? Pious Juan Crespí, who had shared the vision of San Francisco Solano. I had no such qualifications to my name.

My lips mumbled the syllables of our prayers by rote. As ever, I saw no visions that day. It would be years, in fact, until I saw what I could rightly qualify as a vision. By then I would be at the farthest reach of His Majesty's Catholic Empire, more concerned with victuals than visions, and painfully certain whom I would find on that seaside bluff.

THE SUNDAY BEFORE we sailed for America, my mother invited a hundred relatives and acquaintances to a reception at our home in north Palma. For days beforehand, she and my grandmother, who lived in an apartment upstairs, made stews and roasted meats, baked cakes, and rolled out pastries. I took leave from the convent to help with the preparations, but my presence only seemed to amplify their grief.

"Let me be honest with you," I told my mother after supper one night, "there is some chance that I will return to Mallorca, but we should assume that I am leaving forever."

"Is that meant to comfort me?"

She was characteristically calm, her thin shoulders even and steady. The deep set, hooded eyes—my own eyes—snapped back and forth between me and my father. The old man had contributed very little to this conversation. His view was that God would bring me back or not as He saw fit.

"I understand that my words are no comfort now," I said, "but years from now you will find peace in knowing that we said a proper good-bye."

"This reeks of Father Junípero," she snapped. Mother was deeply suspicious of His Reverence; she could not believe that a man so young (or perhaps so short!) could command such unswerving loyalty from his disciples. "This is what he has instructed you to tell your family, no?"

"Actually, it was my decision to tell you."

She sat with this for a moment then said, "So you are the one who wants to kill us off."

"Of course not, Mamá. I only think it is better to acknowledge the likelihood that I will serve out my career in New Spain. Perhaps it would make sense to plan for my return if I were still new at seminary, but I am not so young anymore."

"For a priest you are young."

"He will write us, Miquela," my father added.

"As often as possible," I said. "Though Father Junípero warned us that the post in America is slow and unreliable."

"Better slow than nonexistent," said my father helplessly.

Perhaps because she realized that our relationship was shortly to become only words—or perhaps because she felt that words had suddenly lost their power to express the full extent of her pain—Mother reached out and took me in her arms, pulling me like a child into her rich aura of roses and salt fish. Against her bony chest I was reminded of my vulnerability—a quality Fray Junípero had nearly stamped out with all his talk of glory and conquest and the armor of faith.

"I will never forget you and Papá," I murmured.

"I should hope not! Why must you speak this way, Paquito? Do you really wish us dead? If not, you ought to say that you will miss us and that when your work is finished, you will return."

"Of course I will miss you," I said, but I stopped there. I could not bring myself to promise a return, for I knew that our work in America would never be complete. His Reverence had made that clear.

Our humble stone house stood in the lee of the church of Santa Eulália, where I had learned my first religion. Many of the ancient olivewood pews had been occupied by Palóus for as long as anyone could remember. Once a month, my mother polished the brass nameplate on our bench; others with different names attached contained more distant relations. The distinction between family and neighbor was all but meaningless when it came to our parish. In fact on that Sunday after Mass, the greater portion of the flock of Santa Eulália circulated through our home. It felt like an odd parody of a funeral, with the guests filing past the tables of food and drink while the departed walked among them. Mother led me around the house by the wrist, reminding me of this great-uncle and that great-aunt, this cousin and that nephew and this godson. I recognized very few of the faces, even after Mother whispered their names in my ear.

I grew tired of answering the same questions, tired of feigning candor as I recited for the hundredth time my hopes and fears for the journey ahead. The more I described missionary work, the more abstract it became, the more it felt like someone else's story.

"Tell us, Paco," said a well-groomed elderly gentlemen whom my mother introduced as Uncle Jaime, "is it true about the women in America?"

"Forgive me, sir—what have you heard?"

He looked anxiously to my mother, as though suddenly worried that he may have heard this pearl of wisdom incorrectly. Then he said, "This pertains only to the natives, of course, but I have heard that they eat their mates after coitus."

I searched his face for cracks, for any hints of irony, but his silver mustache did not so much as quiver.

"Well, sir," I ventured, "I confess that I know very little about America, but I shall write you with my observations."

The uncle nodded gratefully. "Best of luck to you, young man. But do not write if it is too much trouble."

"I am sure I will find time to write," I said.

Embarrassed, my mother led me away from this fellow to the next set of well-wishers, a pair of raven-haired girls whom I recognized but could not name. They were sisters, I recalled, one plump and the other slender, between twelve and fourteen years old.

"You remember Esmerelda and Berenice?" my mother said.

"Of course, thank you both for coming. It is a pleasure to see you again."

The girls proceeded to compliment the food and the linens and even the dustlessness of the chandelier—all flatteries which Mother accepted with a graceful nod. She then left to tend to other guests, and I endured a painful interval of silence before the plump sister— was she Esmerelda?—asked if I was hoping for a martyr's death in New Spain.

"I am not hoping for any kind of death," I said truthfully. "Not for a while at least. Not until our work is well undertaken."

"Undertaken," repeated slender Berenice. "That is very funny." Unsmiling, she turned to her sister and explained. "He has made a play on words."

"I know it, silly."

Now the girls giggled—far too childishly, I thought, for young women of their age—and then the plump one said, "Tell another, will you?"

It had been a long afternoon. The query about the native women devouring their lovers had not unsettled me—the old gentleman had only read too many novels—but the idea of martyrdom had. Not because I feared death, but because I feared that I had misunderstood the terms of my commitment. If the blithest girls in Palma could see that a missionary's end was martyrdom, why had I not seen it that way? Had I been naïve? Fray Junípero certainly styled himself after martyrs, but I had never thought that he intended to die a violent death in America. When he spoke to us about his plans, his focus was always on the work—laboring in the vineyard of the Lord, tilling the unworked soil and so forth. Clearly, one could not work after death.

I needed to collect my thoughts. Excusing myself from the company of the sisters, I went up the rear stairs to my grandmother's apartment, where I knew it would be quiet. I took a glass from the cupboard in the hall and went into the bedroom in search of a pitcher.

I was surprised to find a young woman inside, kneeling before my grandmother's statue of Nuestra Señora. Her eyes were closed and a rosary swayed gently from her folded palms. She wore a dark wool frock, blue-black, with a matching knit shawl drawn over her head as a veil. She looked to be about the same age as Esmerelda and Berenice, or maybe a little older. I was of no mind to entertain more giggling girls. I turned for the door, hoping to steal away unnoticed, but my steps caught her attention.

"Oh, Father!" she cried. "Pardon me, I will leave."

"No, continue. I was only looking for the pitcher."

The girl rose and adjusted her shawl. Her face did not meet the conventional standard of beauty, but it held the eye nonetheless, the way a portrait sometimes fails to resemble its subject but captivates the viewer on its own merits. Her large brown eyes were unpainted, widely spaced, and guileless. Below these, a small upturned nose, fair cheeks, and a nervous smile.

She eyed the pitcher on the dresser but made no move to retrieve it.

"Do you remember me?" Her voice was cautious but not shy. Curiously, she addressed me in Spanish instead of *mallorquín*.

"Forgive me," I said. "I have seen so many people today . . . "

"We are cousins. You don't remember? I am Encarnación Mora."

"Do you live in Palma?"

"Of course."

I had no memory of her, so I decided to use a line I had honed with other relatives that afternoon: "You were much younger," I said, "the last time I saw you."

"As were you, Father," she said. Her reply came very quickly, as though she had been prepared for the exchange.

Now I had no recourse but to continue the charade. "So tell me, Encarna—are you married now?" It was a needless question. I would have known if any cousin of mine had been married recently. Even if I had been unable to attend the Mass, Mother would have written me with a detailed account.

Encarna shook her head.

"Are you in convent then?"

"That is a strange question, Father."

"Is it? There is a party downstairs, yet I found you here praying. One might infer from such behavior . . . and from your dress . . . "

"Is there a problem with my dress?"

"Not at all. I only noticed that it is modest." I held out the folds of my coarse gray cassock. "And I should know."

At last, she laughed—a light, exhilarating sound like the fall of water over rocks.

"May I ask you a question, Father?"

"When a priest is family," I heard myself say, "you may call him by his Christian name."

"Very well, Paco. I know that you are wanted downstairs, but I have a dilemma which concerns you directly. You see, I wish to use my life to serve God—"

"A fine ambition."

"I expected you would think so. I plan to seek admittance to the convent of Santa Clara, because I feel that the Franciscan way is the simplest and most direct way to serve the Lord."

"I felt the same way at your age," I began. These were the words I was expected to say. But they were not entirely the truth. My path to friarhood had been anything but certain. Normally I would not have paused to correct such a small misstatement, but I felt that circumstances supported an extra measure of truthfulness. I was leaving for America in the morning. I had nothing to gain by circumspection.

"Listen, Encarna, the truth is that I was not especially inclined to the Franciscans. In fact I was not sure I would join the priesthood at all."

The girl hovered on my words. "What did you expect to do instead?"

"I don't know. I might have worked on the wharves."

"Hauling crates?"

"In the harbor-master's office, I suppose." I thought about this for a moment. My father might have recommended me to his superiors, mentioned my proclivity for books and bookish things, and I would have been installed in his world. It was not difficult to imagine.

"But," I continued, "my mother was devoted to San Francisco. She said that nothing could bring our family greater honor than to have a Little Brother among its number."

"I quite agree," Encarna said. "And of course you almost lost her, so—"

I was startled. "You remember my mother's illness?"

"Of course I remember. I have admired you since I was a little girl."

She was now speaking our mother tongue. I could not recall when she had made the switch.

"Well," I said.

I did not know how to respond. I was flattered, of course, but it seemed that she wanted more from me than I could give.

"You have plenty of time to make your decision," I said. "How old are you?"

"I will be nineteen in October."

"Have you spoken with your mother about your plans?"

"She does not approve. You may recall that my brother, your cousin Marco, is a merchant sailor. Since Father died, Marco and I are her only family. Mother is worried that if I leave for the convent, there will be no one to care for her if she takes ill."

"For me it was much simpler," I said. "My sisters were already married. My parents are welcome to retire to either of their homes."

"That must make it easier for you to go abroad."

"Do you think so? Sometimes I wonder if it was the right decision."

I might have added that "sometimes" meant, in this case, just a few minutes ago, but I doubted that she would care to know the specifics. Thus I was not prepared for the intensity of the interrogation that ensued.

"Do you have doubts, then?"

"Doubts?"

"About missionary work."

"No."

"But you wondered if it was the right decision."

"That is not what I meant. I have no doubt this is God's will for me."

"How do you know?"

"Well, if God did not wish for me to go, He would have put up obstacles. It is no coincidence, you see, that my sisters are able to receive my parents."

I am by nature a careful man. I have always preferred to dwell on my words before giving them voice. But now my thoughts poured out straightaway, without the filter of contemplation. It felt reckless.

"Are you frightened of the voyage, then?" Encarna asked.

"The sea is the least of my concerns."

"Sailing to America is not the same as a cruise to Menorca, Paco. It is hardly a step to be taken casually. You might perish in any number of ways."

"That is what I have been telling my mother . . . "

Encarna smiled. I could see that although she was concerned for my well-being, she was not the kind of solicitous, mothering hen who would make a man feel guilty about serving the Lord.

"And once you reach New Spain," she said, "you will hardly be secure. The frontier is filled with savages."

"That may be true . . . "

"And you are a scholar! What business do you have teaching tribesmen to grow corn? What do you know about farming?"

"They say we will learn these things at the missionary college in México. Naturally, I have much to learn before I can perform any useful service . . . " I held out my palms in a kind of surrender.

"Yes, but Paco . . . "

Beads of sweat had formed on her delicate nose. Several times she parted her lips to continue speaking but then closed them again.

"I feel as though you are trying to convince me to stay," I said.

"If you have these doubts, Paco—why did you volunteer to go?"

"I am following my master," I said. "He plans to create a new Jerusalem in America."

"And do you trust this man?"

"With all my heart."

This was true: just as sailors place their trust in the north star, I had placed mine in Fray Junípero Serra. This did not seem unreasonable. What was a sea voyage if not an exercise in faith?

This, finally, seemed to assuage Encarna's fears. She nodded vigorously, but once again it seemed that she intended to say more.

Then I surprised even myself: "You are correct about the danger," I said. "But my own belief is that if a storm takes my life at sea, it will be a blessing."

I had no idea what this statement signified. Certainly I did not wish to die senselessly. A martyr's death was one thing, but to die before we reached the missionary field would be a tragedy, not a blessing.

Remarkably, the girl was not alarmed. Instead she took my hand in hers and whispered, "I know how you feel."

"How is that possible?" I countered. "You are not sailing for America."

"It is how I feel about the convent of Saint Clare. If I die before the carriage reaches the gate, it will be just as well."

At the time, I assumed she was only trying to match me convent for convent, vocation for vocation, pitiable death for pitiable death—she wanted to keep up with an older cousin. I would be literally a world away before I understood how wrong I had been.

We stared at each other for a fraught moment, uneasy with the intimacy that had risen between us. I had no intention of dying at sea. I wanted to explain this to her. But our silence was broken by footsteps in the hall. Mother appeared with half a dozen strangers in colorful peasants' dress. The group smelled strongly of hay and cattle dung. Mother gave Encarna a polite smile before turning to me: "Paquito! You remember your cousins from Manacor? Come along and say hello . . . "

BERTHS ACROSS THE Atlantic were scarce in those days, even for humble travelers like us, who required no more than a space on the floor to spread out a blanket. "Let there be no tarrying," His Reverence had instructed me, for it was my duty to arrange our transport, "if you can find a ship from Mallorca straight to New Spain, that is my preference." Of course there was no such ship, but I managed to secure passage on an English packet boat sailing from Mallorca to Málaga and thence to Cádiz, where we would join another party of friars for the ocean crossing.

The English ship was to sail from Palma at dawn on Tuesday, and the captain, a small and stiff-necked mariner named Hawkins, informed me that we were not to be late. Even with many advance warnings, I had trouble gathering His Reverence the morning of our departure. After Matins, he insisted on lining up the entire convent community in the chapel and kissing each in turn. Finally, after washing many dozens of feet in his own tears, Junípero let me take him to the harbor. He carried nothing but the crucifix around his neck. Fray Juan and I each brought a small purse with a few personal objects. Mine contained paper, pens, ink, and a worn New Testament. Fray Juan brought his prayer journal and a small sack of provisions.

The captain was surprised when we arrived with so little. He made a display of counting our fare, dropping each coin deliberately into a little pig's-bladder purse. "I suppose you wish to see your accommodations," he said. He spoke in a sort of adulterated Portuguese, which was the only way I could communicate with him, English being his only facile language.

"Sim, capitão," I replied.

We followed him belowdecks, where the crew was busy stacking freight. The markings on the crates indicated a cargo of olives.

"You'll bunk here," said Captain Hawkins, pointing to a small clearing between the walls of crates. The space couldn't have been more than a fathom square, and I wondered how three men might stretch out comfortably. The floorboards were slick underfoot with stinking black mildew. I was about to express my displeasure when Fray Junípero stepped forward.

"Obrigado, capitão," he said in crisp Portuguese.

The captain said, in English, "It don't leave much room for your hocus pocus." He pulled back his chapped lips and grinned. His teeth were flat, stubby things, irregularly placed along the gum and stained brown and gray.

Fray Junípero did not respond.

"I said, it don't leave room for you to set up altars for your sorcery."

I could see from the vein pulsing at Fray Junípero's temple that it took all of his resolve to remain mute.

"Are you dumb, Padre, or just hard of hearing? I said that you and your mates will have to find some other place to worship your God. Because this is a secular vessel. I don't tolerate idol-worshipping anywhere onboard—do you understand? Do you speak English?" He paused, waiting to see if the Father Lector would take the bait. Then he said, under his breath, "Swarthy types are all the same, robe or no."

Then he raised his nose as if he were going to sneeze. But the soiled rag he pulled from his trouser pocket went not to his nose but his lips. He hacked desperately, as though he were trying to expel a demon from his lungs. Several minutes he carried on like this, and every time he seemed to be done, he doubled over and began anew. Finally, he wiped his mouth and stuffed the rag back into his pocket. It was at this point that Fray Junípero said, in perfect English, "Please sir, when do we arrive in Málaga?"

"So, you heard what I said after all."

Of course, neither of us was surprised that Fray Junípero knew English. He also spoke Castilian Spanish, Portuguese, Italian, and French, and had published theological papers in Latin and Greek— all besides the *mallorquín* that was his mother tongue. We joked sometimes that a second Pentecost would be of little use to him.

His Reverence repeated, "Please, when shall we expect to be in Málaga? There is another ship waiting for us."

"I won't keep you long, you little devil. But I'll be damned if I'm going to let you go without getting some answers first." The captain scurried astern, weaving around crates until he disappeared from view. A moment later he returned with a tattered copy of the English Bible.

"Now, I've been puzzling over this book for some time. See, I was brought up in the church. Not a Papist church, but all the same."

The captain began to flip through his Bible. Fray Junípero stood silent, fists clenched at his sides. If I may offer an analogy, it was like the moment before a great footrace where the practiced athlete finds himself seized with anxiety, even though he knows the race better than anyone on Earth. Fray Junípero was such an athlete—in the sport of evangelism.

"Bloody hell!" the Englishman exclaimed. "Take this portion here. The Book of Matthew . . . "

Junípero's fingers tapped his haunches as the sea captain marched his filthy digits through the Gospel.

"Says here that your man Jesus Christ preached to a multitude—no, a *great multitude,* and he healed their sick, and so forth. Then night fell, and the people were hungry. But all they had was five loaves and two fishes. Now I'm wondering how many people there are in this multitude. Could be that the word "multitude" had a separate meaning back then. But then here, just down a trot, it says, "They that had eaten were about five thousand men, beside women and children." What does that leave us with, supposing every bloke brought along a bride and a couple of brats? Twenty thousand people? Eating five loaves of bread and two fishes? We have a word for that kind of miracle, Padre: horseshit."

His Reverence made no reply.

That night, as I lay on the hard deck, unable to sleep, I thought about the surprising restraint Junípero had shown with the captain. If a student had displayed such pigheadedness in a matter of Scripture, His Reverence would have wasted no time in making a stern and forceful correction. I wondered if this was a hint of the new Junípero, not the professor but the missionary.

Eventually I fell into a fitful sleep, and next I knew it was morning. Juan Crespí was shaking my shoulders with both hands. "Brother, wake up," he urged. "His Reverence is on deck with the captain." Juan's skin, I noticed, was even more pallid than usual.

It was an excellent morning, with azure seas stretching in all directions. The wind was strong, and the sails held full overhead. The sailor on watch, apparently content with the rigging, had dozed off at his station. I failed to see the urgency of the situation until I noticed, just behind the rear mast, two diminutive figures engaged in what appeared to be a boxing-match. The captain, who was not much taller than Fray Junípero, poked the little priest in the chest belligerently. I saw that they were exchanging words as well, but I could not yet hear their voices on account of the wind.

Juan and I raced over the deck, dodging coils of rope and chain. But when we reached the spot, Fray Junípero waved us off.

"I see you called in the army of God!" yelled the captain.

"On the contrary," said Fray Junípero, "Go, brothers—this does not concern you."

"Sure it does," countered the captain. "They are agents of the same cult as you." He reached down into his trouser pocket and produced a clasp knife.

Fray Junípero stared unflinchingly into the sour Englishman's eyes. I noticed for the first time that his wrists were tied behind his back.

Keeping one hand on Junípero's chest, the captain turned to Juan and me. "Do you know what your master did this morning? He knocked on the door of my cabin and asked, so politely now, if he might *have a word.*"

The Englishman was having some difficulty opening the knife with one hand, so he grabbed it in his mouth. He clenched the blade between his wretched teeth and used his free hand to crank back the stock. Brandishing the knife casually at us, he spat on the ground.

"Turns out this *word* was actually ten minutes of tripe about your man Saint Francis, and about the other Francis too, the one who went to Peru with your royal looters. And then there was the fellow who justified all this carnage, Dumb Scrotus or some such. He told me this Scrotus was my countryman. I said he was probably smart as the rest of us, which is to say dumb as frozen shite."

With these last words—which I repeat here only in the service of completeness and accuracy—the hideous little man slapped His

Reverence twice across the face with the stock of the knife. At each blow, there was the pop of wood on bone—loud enough to be heard clearly on the windswept deck. But Fray Junípero did not cry. He clenched one eye shut—the more injured of the two—and began to pray loudly: *"Te Deum laudamus: te Dominum confitemur. Te aeternum Patrem omnis terra veneratur."*

"I told him I had made up my mind. There is no God. And I told him to get lost. But this demon would not quit. Rather than speaking good English, he started into this mumbo jumbo . . . "

The captain touched the blade to the soft skin under Fray Junípero's chin. His Reverence sang louder: *"Sanctus, Sanctus, Sanctus!"*

Then, oddly, the captain turned to Fray Juan and me. "I will still take you to Málaga, gents. It's just this one—" Here he pumped his knee into Fray Junípero's flank, causing the little friar's chanting voice to waver. "This one pushed me too far."

This was the moment God chose to make Himself known. The wretched captain was seized by a fit of coughing, this worse than the last, his whole corpus appearing to shudder in sympathy with his lungs. He fell to the ground, landing softly on his rump, where he doubled over and began hacking in earnest into one of his filthy sleeves. The knife skidded across the deck.

I grabbed the weapon, Fray Juan went quickly to untie His Reverence, and the three of us rushed belowdecks. We remained together that entire day, singing a novena in praise of Santa Barbara, to whom Fray Junípero had appealed in his moment of distress.

"Herewith," announced His Reverence in a thin and shaky voice, "Santa Barbara shall be our patroness. Among my own personal intercessors, I grant this virgin martyr her rightful place." His tone of voice made clear that we were to do the same. We continued to pray, relying for food on the dry staples provided by our thoughtful cook—how we praised him now! We were thirsty as well, but there was no water to be had, the ship's supplies being under control of the captain. Fray Junípero instructed us to save our saliva as we sang the Mass. "There are three of us," he reasoned, "so each will sing every third line."

During the third of the nine Masses for Santa Barbara—it must have been midafternoon—we were interrupted by a member of the crew, a man of stocky build whose bristle-stiff hair had gone white before its time.

"Which one of you speaks English?" he said.

Fray Junípero stood up.

"Captain passed an hour ago," he said. "I'm in charge now."

"Please accept our condolences," said Fray Junípero. In his eyes I saw that he was sincere.

The sailor ran a calloused hand through his hair. "I appreciate your concern, Father," he said, "but it makes no difference to me. The sea floor is littered with men like him."

AT CADIZ, WE joined with another group of Franciscans bound for the College of San Fernando in México City. Together we made a party of twelve. The other friars came from the province of Valencia, on the east coast of Spain. When we arrived at Cádiz, we sung Mass with our Valencian brothers and shared a generous supper, for which we gave thanks and praise to the Almighty. Our conversations carried a hint of anxiety, of course, for none of us had ever crossed the Atlantic, but we took comfort in the size of our contingent and the continued strength of our ancient fraternity.

The good feelings were threatened only once. The night before we left port, we gathered in the dingy parlor of our hostel to unseal a letter from Rome. Among other instructions, the letter named a Valencian friar as Father President of our mission. The Padre Presidente was an elderly man, well into his seventh decade, with a slight stoop and a low, almost growling singing voice. He and Fray Junípero had met once before, during His Reverence's academic peregrinations. When the appointment was announced, the elderly friar bowed his bald head and shook away the congratulations of his companions. "I am unworthy of this honor," he insisted. We all shook his hand and assured him that it was God's will.

At the letter-reading, Junípero gave no visible reaction when the Father President was announced, but in our cell that night, he confided his disappointment. "It is not that I desired the post myself, Paco," he said. "I merely think we should have been consulted on the matter."

"I agree. We should have been involved. But you will remember, Your Reverence, that we decided rather hastily to join this mission."

"Was it haste or zeal?" Lying down on his pallet, which was just the thinnest rag on the stone floor, he went on, "He is a good friar. A scholar of San Bernardino."

"We are kin, then," I said.

"Are we?"

"In theology."

"But in theology only."

"Of course, Father. In theology only."

As it turned out, we rarely discussed theology during the long, wet days of the crossing. The joy and fear of the journey—long anticipated and now finally underway—precluded any serious study. Mostly we dissected recent intrigues from Rome. Because we were headed for the American colonies, the recent events in Paraguay involving the Jesuit fathers were a major topic of discussion. The King of Portugal had accused the Jesuits of conspiring to form an independent state—a theocratic empire—around their missions in that landlocked American territory. As punishment, he had barred Jesuit advisers from his court in Lisbon and banished Jesuit missionaries from his colonies. We Franciscans were of two minds about Portugal's sentence: on one hand, we were appalled that a sovereign would act against an order of peaceful monks. We doubted that the Jesuit fathers were guilty of the conspiracy alleged by the Portuguese, but if it were true, it confirmed our most deeply held suspicions about the hidden ambitions of the Jesuit order.

We passed the hours like anxious bees, locked in our seabound hive. The sailing ship was the largest and most advanced I had seen, with three masts and a crew of several dozen, but for the first few days it felt like any of the hundreds of sea excursions I had undertaken in my life. When one is raised on an island, there are many opportunities to sail, and many modes of doing so. Soon, however, the voyage grew longer than any in my personal history, and I understood that I had moved (in all senses) into new waters. We left sight of land before noon the first day, taking with us a detachment of shore birds—gulls, pelicans, and the like—but these curious guests soon fell away and we had no signs of avian life until we passed the Azores two weeks later. Two weeks! In two weeks one can sail from Mallorca to Rome and back—or, I learned, into the midst of a vast blue desert, infinite and inscrutable, like the imagination of God.

FOUR

OUR FINAL DESTINATION WAS to be the royal port of Veracruz on the mainland of New Spain, but sixty days into our journey—
the sight even of the Azores a distant memory by that point—we
learned that we would be stopping at San Juan, Puerto Rico, to take
on water. In fact the ship had been desperately low on water for two
weeks; we had not even enough to make chocolate in the mornings.
But as we sailed into the San Juan harbor, I understood that there were
other reasons besides water for this port o' call.

As our ship approached the wharf, a line of curious ladies sauntered
out from a small house. They had dark skin and thick, tight hair, like
Africans, and their garments, dyed in garish colors, covered only the
most necessary regions of their undulating bodies. From a distance,
one might have mistaken them for a group of girls playing in their
mothers' wardrobes. But these were no girls—they howled at the ship
like a pack of coyotes, wasting no time in making their appeal. They
spoke a kind of clipped, informal Spanish I had not heard before but
would soon come to know as the patois of the Empire—a sort of
frontier dialect that branded the speaker a pioneer, or at least someone comfortable living outside the comfort of European society.

Fray Junípero installed himself at the bow of the ship, so to get the very first view possible of the New World. When we arrived, he was standing amidst a group of soldiers, who had come to get their own first look. The tiny friar was dwarfed by the other men, but by sheer force of will he slipped all the way to the rail.

From the wharf, the women called up to the deck: "*¡Qui-qui-qui, mis soldaditos! ¡Qui-qui-qui!*" A few of them removed their breasts from their gowns and rolled the wide, dark nipples between their thumbs and forefingers.

"*¡Espérame, mami!*" yelled one soldier. "Save it for me!"

And the women replied: "*¡Qui-qui-qui! ¡Qui-qui-qui!*"

And the soldiers: "*¡Ay, ay! ¿Hace calor aquí, verdad?*"

And then, the high-pitched, shrill voice of Fray Junípero: "*Amar a Dios, hijas! Gracias a Jesucristo!* The Good News has arrived! Come hear!"

One of the leatherjackets mocked His Reverence: "No, come *here*," he cried, pointing to his groin.

"God is great! The end of your ignorance is nigh! Prepare to welcome the everlasting inviolable love of El Señor into your hearts!"

"Forget your heart—welcome *this* into your slits!"

"God is goodness, my daughters. Come to the Lord!"

The women jostled one another for position at the bottom of the gangplank. I did not understand their haste: there were at least twice as many soldiers and crew as prostitutes; surely there was work for all.

"Be not ashamed, *magdalenas* of Puerto Rico," continued His Reverence, swept along with the tide of soldiers. "Christ loves the sinner more than the saint! Our Lord says, 'They that are whole need not a physician; but they that are sick!'"

"You say these women are sick?"

"Yea, though I walk through the valley of the shadow of death, I will fear no evil, for Thou art with me . . . "

The soldier knew the Psalm and continued, "My rod and staff shall give plenty of comfort today, Father. Plenty of comfort indeed . . . "

Down the gangplank they poured—soldiers, sailors, and one diminutive friar. The women availed themselves of the nearest arms and escorted their clients into to the little house on the wharf. The men not lucky enough to be served right away went instead to a little bodega beside the brothel, where a dark-skinned man in a tattered linen blouse sold rum by the bottle. A few of the soldiers simply stood underneath their upended bottles, draining the golden liquor into their bellies until it was gone.

Vendors swarmed the disembarking Spaniards like rooks on a kill, hawking *tamales* and watermelons, candles and cigars. Negro women in bleached white pinafores offered baths to families with children. A man held two mules on the end of a rope. Tropical birds squawked in cages. Cheery music poured from the guitar of a minstrel, whose son rapped time on an empty bottle with a stick. In the commotion I lost sight of Fray Junípero.

I returned belowdecks to find Juan Crespí loading his rucksack.

"His Reverence went onshore," I reported.

Fray Juan looked up from his work and said without affect, "I know."

I explained how he had been preaching to the prostitutes when he had been swept down the gangplank with the soldiers.

"And then I lost him," I admitted.

Juan was unconcerned. "He has only gone to find a suitable location for the mission. We are to find him onshore in an hour."

"What mission? He never mentioned this to me."

"It was only today when he gave me the news. 'Let us waste no time,' he said, 'in spreading the News of the Lord.' A fine sentiment, I think. Where were you this morning?"

"I was—" I thought back. I must have been on deck gathering the candles from Mass.

Juan's sea-blue eyes met mine for an instant, then dropped to the floor. "We should go, Brother."

We walked along the wharf, past the brothel and the bodega, where those same over-thirsty soldiers were now splayed unconscious on the planks. We found Fray Junípero a stone's throw from the docks, in a sort of crude square surrounded by market stalls and lodging-houses. No grass grew in this vacant lot, and the earth was unnaturally black, as though it had been the site of a recent fire. His Reverence stood atop a small wooden crate, speaking to a congregation of two young girls—not fifteen years between them—of the same dark complexion as the prostitutes on the wharf. Their dress was similar to their mothers' but more modestly draped. They stood directly before His Reverence, listening as politely as children can at that age. Every so often one of them whispered something in the other's ear, bringing a smile or an innocent laugh in reply. Fray Junípero did not acknowledge me. All his energy, all his attention, was directed onto these first two American souls, as if he meant to move them by sheer will. He preached the story of the flood: "And Noah sent forth a dove! And the dove plucked an olive leaf and brought it to Noah, so that he knew the waters were abated . . . "

The girls found something funny in this. One whispered to the other and they laughed. It occurred to me that they might never have seen an olive leaf, nor even a dove. I had no knowledge of the flora or fauna of this place.

"And when they reached the land, the Lord told them to go forth of the ark, and to be fruitful and multiply."

This the girls understood, and they shared a whisper and a smile.

When Junípero was finished with the story, he called me over. "Two *reales,* please, Paco."

I went into my purse and gave him the coins.

Before I knew what he was doing, he had pressed one *real* into each of the girls' palms. "Love God, my daughters," he said. "Always love God."

Our ship laid in port at San Juan only one week, but during that short time Fray Junípero managed to grow his flock from those first two prostitutes' daughters to a congregation of nearly two hundred. The town's wayfarers and vagabonds pitched their tents in the fire-scarred lot, attracted by the promise of redemption. Though I was suspicious of these men—they reeked of rum even at midmorning—Fray Junípero did not cast them out. He called them "a sign of hope." He instructed Juan to count heads at each of the three daily services—morning, noon, and night. Even at that early stage of his missionary life, His Reverence realized that work was never real until it was proven out in figures.

We slept on pallets amongst our flock. Our co-missionaries from Valencia had taken accommodations at a Franciscan hermitage in another part of San Juan, and the Father President had entreated us to do the same. He saw no purpose to our little outdoor mission. "One should never serve a meal on the ground when a dining room is nigh," he told Fray Junípero. "If you feel the urge to preach, then by all means do so in the cathedral."

But Junípero's methods were not suited for the hushed nave of a cathedral. Earlier that week, for example, a wild pig had disrupted morning Mass in the sandlot. Rather than becoming irritated at the interruption, as many preachers might have, Fray Junípero simply waited until the end of the service and then ordered the animal shot. It was butchered, roasted on a spit, and served for luncheon. Needless to say, this would not have happened on the grounds of the cathedral.

I should note that the people of Puerto Rico were not heathens, but rather baptized Catholics who had been ill served by their shepherds. The island had been part of Christendom for three hundred years, but the wizened old friars of the hermitage had never uttered a word to their congregation outside of the Latin Missal. Fray Junípero aimed to change this—to awaken the spirit of God amongst the *puertorriqueños*. He wanted to bring the Lord out of the cathedral and onto the streets where the people could see Him. With his myna-bird's ear, Junípero imitated the dialect and given homilies in the vernacular. Amazingly, the congregation continued to assemble on the sandlot even after our purse was empty of handouts.

The night before we were to leave San Juan, His Reverence held a special midnight service. "Let us join together one last time," he told the crowd of several hundred, "to celebrate the glory of Christ's passion." The yard was ablaze with two dozen torches, wrapped and lit by Junípero's new devotees. Juan and I wore albs and tunics. "And fill the censers," he instructed. "We are going to have a procession."

Just before the appointed hour, His Reverence disappeared into one of the tents. When he emerged, he was naked but for a cloth around his waist and a crown of rope atop his head. Some small men are compensated for their deficiency of stature with heavy musculature, but this was not the case with Fray Junípero. He had been sickly as a child, and his physique had never fully matured. His chest was concave, his back slumped. His legs bowed outward. Though his hair was dark, it grew only sparsely on his legs and trunk. His pale skin reflected the torchlight.

He said nothing to us but exchanged a few words with one of the vagabonds. The man rushed off down an alley, returning a moment later with something like a cannon carriage, upon which was mounted an enormous wooden cross. The cross—which neither Juan nor I had seen previously—had been fashioned from old wharf pilings. Despite the aid of the carriage wheels, the man strained under its weight.

"My friend!" cried Fray Junípero. "The carpenter of Nazareth smiles on you this evening."

The man bowed his head.

By this time, the yard was full of townspeople, the air filled with the stench of burning turpentine. Near me, a couple of boys held strips of coconut meat over the flames of their torch. When the white meat was burnt black on the outside, they popped the strips into their mouths and laughed. A small group of girls began to sing. The songs were unfamiliar to me—probably local airs. They had a strange lilting rhythm that put one in mind of a horse at dressage.

"Paco," Junípero said to me, "it is time to go."

Without further explanation, he walked to the cross-cart, where he motioned for the young vagabond to step aside. The cross fell on Junípero's tiny back.

"Father, let me help," begged Juan.

The little friar groaned. His body shook with exertion.

"Please, Your Reverence."

"You—" grunted Junípero. He nodded his head to indicate Juan and me. "Lead them to the hermitage."

We did as we were told. Marching at the front of the procession, we swung our censers over the length of San Juan town, from the mission yard to the hermitage, a distance of perhaps half a league. The townspeople followed happily behind, singing and chanting all manner of songs, sacred and profane. It occurred to me that His Reverence did not care if they understood the significance of his "special service" (in a week's lectures, he had not yet covered the Passion). He needed hands to hold the torches, and he had them. What did it matter if the girls sang dancing songs or monkish chants?

The hermitage was an old adobe arranged like a horseshoe around a courtyard. Fan palms and lemon trees grew along the borders. In the center of the courtyard was a well, and beside it a stone bench and a humble weathered cross. The grounds were silent when we arrived, as one would expect at that hour. Slowly, the bodies of our procession filled the courtyard like honey dripping into a bowl. The voices of the singers echoed off the walls of the old building. The torchlight danced. Stepping away from the crowd, I peered back down the long cobbled way but saw no trace of Fray Junípero. I grew worried and went back to confer with Fray Juan. But Juan had already put his censer down, climbed atop the bench, and spread his arms wide. In the spirit of the moment, he began to pray: *"Te igitur, clementissime Pater, per Jesum Christum Filium tuum Dominum nostrum, supplices rogamus ac petimus . . . "* Some of the congregation stopped to listen. Others kept at their own songs. Juan continued, unperturbed, as if he were singing the Mass for himself alone.

It did not take long for this cacophony to wake the sleepers in the hermitage. A candle was lit in a cell on the upper floor, and two robed figures appeared at the balcony. The taller of the men pointed to Fray Juan and said something in the other's ear. Still waving my censer, I moved closer to the balcony to get a better view. I recognized the pointing man as the Father President. The other man was quite elderly, likely the hermit himself. He wrung his hands like a widow.

At that moment a cry went up from the rear of the crowd: "*¡Aquí viene el padre!* Look!"

The townspeople, ever curious, nearly trampled one another trying to squeeze through the narrow portal in the courtyard wall. I stood with Fray Juan atop his bench and peered out. Twenty fathoms down the road emerged the figure of Fray Junípero straining beneath his terrible burden. He was naked now, having lost the cloth somewhere along the way. The rope crown, too, had fallen away.

The people began to holler and cheer. A few rushed into the road toward Junípero, but he turned them back, just as he had Fray Juan. Sweat poured from his brow. He walked deliberately, pounding the earth with each step like the world's smallest dray horse. He stared straight ahead, as though entranced.

At the wall, the crowd parted. The carriage upon which the cross rested was too wide for the portal, so Fray Junípero let it drop. The congregation fell silent. Our humble *penitente* wiped his brow with the back of his arm and limped into the courtyard. His hair was wet, matted against his scalp. His arms shook at his sides. But his instinct remained sharp: he took Juan's place on the stone bench and measured the onlookers in the hermitage windows. Several more Valencian friars, as well as some others I assumed to be residents of the hermitage, had joined the Father President and the hermit on the balcony.

Now Fray Junípero turned his attention to the crowd. Naked

before them, like San Francisco in the plaza of Asís, he cried, *"Amar a Dios!"* His voice was rough and he cleared his throat several times. "Love God, my brothers! You must always love God!"

The crowd held silent. They too were aware of the observers in the windows.

Now the hermit called out, "Father Fray Junípero, is it?"

Unaccountably, this utterance caused the crowd to cheer wildly. They only calmed down again when Fray Junípero raised his right hand.

"I have trained this flock from lambs," he announced to the hermit. "And I shall trust you to see that they do not stray. God will hold you accountable."

"Come inside, my friend," said the hermit. "Put some clothes on."

"These dozens keep me warm," Junípero said.

"As you wish, but I must ask you to leave us now. We are tired and need to rest."

"Only the foolish shepherd sleeps while the flock is awake," said the shivering Junípero. "That is when sheep stray."

The hermit shook his head. He turned away from us, annoyed, as though arguing with this naked, sanctimonious friar required a level of patience undignified for his rank.

Junípero turned to the other man on the balcony, our own hoary Father President, and said, "Your Reverence, I will meet you on our ship in the morning?"

The Father President nodded. I could see that he was mortified.

"Very well," Junípero said. "Good night to you."

With that, the congregation (who could wait no longer) descended on Fray Junípero and lifted him up onto their backs. All night he was carried like a regent through the streets of San Juan, the people trailing with their songs and joyful noise. At dawn they left him in the mission yard, where he paused just long enough to don his tired gray cassock. Then, thinking better of it, he removed the garment, rolled it up, and gave it to the nearest vagabond.

•   •   •

TORMENTED WITHIN AND without was the voyage from San Juan to Veracruz. Though less than a third the distance of the Atlantic crossing, it was still seven hundred leagues through warm and tempestuous waters. That stretch of sea is thick with islands, and from the frequent visits of birds and porpoises, we inferred that we were near land most the time. Visibility was poor on account of low clouds and rain, but we preserved our practice of singing Mass on deck every morning.

It was during one of these Masses, on the second day out of San Juan, that we came upon a patch of particularly rough seas. I had been chosen to assist the Father President in singing the Mass, which was attended by the dozen religious and a comparable number of laypersons. At the beginning of the service, the sea had been so calm, the breeze so gentle, that I had held the Scripture before the Father President with one hand. Now the onionskin pages of the Holy Book spread out, and I struggled to hold my place. The ship pitched between the towering swells, and dramatic sprays of seawater blew over the deck like bird shot, stinging our faces.

The crew emerged from the cabin and scrambled up the rigging to tie the sails. The Father President looked at me nervously, unsure how to proceed. Then the mate came on deck and hollered, "Everyone below right away! Anything not tied down is going over!"

The congregation rose and secured with rope the barrels they had been using as pews. With surprising efficiency, the pious souls made their way belowdecks, until there remained besides the crewmen only the Father President and me. As I have explained, the Father President was rather old, and he did not move well. We divided the vessels between us; he took the chalice, I the paten. We had already consecrated the bread and wine, which were now verily the body and blood of Our Lord. I ate the broken bread and pantomimed to the Father President that he should drink the wine. But it was difficult to communicate with the wind howling in our ears. The Father President squinted in confusion. Finally, he gave a nod of recognition and lifted the chalice to his lips.

At that moment, the ship encountered a terrible swell. The hull pitched as we descended from crest to trough. I clutched the mast-rigging with both hands and wedged my sandal into a coil of stiff rope. For a moment, the deck stood nearly perpendicular to the sea. The brass paten fell into the rush of seawater sweeping past my feet. A second later the deck pitched in the other direction. Monstrous walls of water faced the ship on all sides. I looked left and right but could not find another soul on deck. Another swell crashed over the bow. Another rush of water at my feet. I felt a knock against my ankle and saw the brass chalice just before a tongue of water licked it under the rail and out to sea.

I closed my eyes and prayed to Santa Barbara, begging for deliverance. Belowdecks, I knew that my *condiscípulos* were making the same appeals. Eventually the swells slackened, and the fist in my throat unclenched. But I could not find the Father President. I opened my mouth to shout for help, but already there were hands on my shoulders. The mate and another member of the crew rushed forth with new ropes, tying the ends to cleats and sending the rest overboard. Now I heard cries for the first time—from beyond the rails, cries of men fighting the sea. I followed the mate to the bow and watched him toss out a line with a wooden buoy tied to the end. When he raced back amidships to fetch another rope, I pressed myself against the bowsprit and peered down. A sailor swam for the buoy, slashing at the sea with angry strokes. Soon he reached the rope and pulled himself out of the water.

I scanned the sea, asking God to send a sign. At last I spotted a head and two flailing arms a few fathoms off the starboard side. It was the Father President.

"Help," I cried, "there is a man overboard! A priest!"

The deck was alive with sailors, the air filled with shouted invective. Some of the sailors working to save their brethren had themselves only just been pulled from the sea. The mate was nowhere in sight. Instead I caught a sailor with a coil of rope on his shoulder. I implored him for help. "My brother has been washed overboard," I explained. I pointed off the starboard bow, to the spot where I had seen the Father President. "Do you see there?"

The man was preoccupied by some other urgent task. He looked past me disinterestedly.

I said in my sternest tone, "My son, are you Catholic?"

Suddenly the sailor looked me square in the face. "On days like this we are all Catholic, Father." He dropped the rope at my feet and ran aft.

Sodden from the storm, the coil felt like the corpse of a serpent. With all my might I cast one end of it overboard, toward the flailing Father President, but it hit well short. I fought the urge to cry. Of what value was the preservation of my own life, I lamented, if I could not use the blessing to save my brother? I pitied the poor old Valencian, who by all accounts had led an exemplary life serving the Church and our Order. Was this his reward, to be drowned at sea within sight of salvation? I hauled up the rope, hand over hand, and tossed it again. This time, it came down within reach of its target. I watched the old man use his last ounce of strength to pull the rope to his body. His hands clamped around the end.

"The Lord has blessed you, Fray Francisco," came a familiar voice behind me. "We feared you had washed away when you did not come below."

I took Fray Junípero by the shoulder and pointed out to sea. The Father President, God bless his soul, had disappeared for the moment, hidden behind a swell. When he reappeared, Junípero's eyes turned cold. "He is too far, Paco. May his heart rest in the perfect name of Jesus, but he is too far out."

I was not in the habit of contradicting His Reverence, but I knew more than he about the sea, having spent much of my life among the mariners and longshoremen of my father's acquaintance.

"He is far," I said, "but we can recover him. Help me. Wrap this end around your waist . . . "

Instead Fray Junípero held the rail. He bent his head and began to pray.

"Your Reverence, please!"

He refused to acknowledge me. Frantically, I lifted the end of the rope and tried to haul it up alone. I managed to pull an arm's length of slack. I reached for a cleat, but my hands were cold, and I could not feel what I was doing. After a minute of struggle, I had to let it go. The rope went taut.

Again I implored Junípero, but His Reverence only shook his head and continued his prayer. His voice was so loud I could hear snatches of it even over the howl of the wind: *"Per istam sanctam unctionem . . . "*

It was not an appeal to Our Lady, nor a prayer to Santa Barbara, but these words were just as familiar. In fact I had heard this very friar speak them dozens of times over the sick and dying of Mallorca. But here would be no oil to sprinkle on the dying man. We would send him to God with only the anointment of the sea.

FRAY JUNIPERO TOOK the role of lead mourner, singing the first three requiem Masses himself. The Valencian friars, devastated by the loss of their brother, found comfort in Junípero's diligence, and they came to regard him as the new leader of our party. Indeed, when we arrived in New Spain several weeks later, there was a consensus to make Fray Junípero Serra of Mallorca the new Father President, pending orders to the contrary.

I told no one what I had seen.

A week later we were camped along the road leading inland from Veracruz to México, the capital of New Spain. This "highway" was really no more than a dusty mule-trail, fifty leagues in length. In the blistering heat we managed only a few leagues a day and eventually our soldier escorts decided that we would travel only at night. By day we rested in makeshift *ramadas,* or shade huts, sleeping when we could, but otherwise worrying over what awaited us in this new land.

"El Señor has been generous with us, Paco," remarked His Reverence during one afternoon's rest. "We are not yet to our destination, and He has already allowed us to work in the vineyard."

"You are referring to the mission in San Juan?"

"It is remarkable what we accomplished in just a few days. And don't you agree that the brothers from Valencia have come closer into the fold since we arrived in America?"

"I cannot say, Your Reverence. I did not know them well before."

"Ah. Well, I detected a certain reticence in them from the moment we met in Cádiz."

"Forgive me, but are you speaking of the friars generally, or only of the Father President?"

"That is a curious question, Paco."

"You and he had differences."

"Not at all! How can you say that two men have differences who share the common goal of delivering mankind from sin?"

"The Father President did not approve of our ministry in San Juan—that is one difference."

I had learned from the Valencians that before the storm, the Father President had been building a case against Fray Junípero. The charge was disobedience: Junípero had not asked permission to preach to the townspeople of San Juan. The yield of souls from just a week of ministry was impressive, but why had the people been allowed to sing secular music in a solemn procession? And what about this rumor that Junípero had been paying the townspeople for their attendance at Mass? All of these accusations were only whispered, but there can be no secrets on a ship at sea.

"Paco my son, God himself works in many styles. How else to

outwit Satan? I see no harm in adapting our methods to the circumstances we encounter. In fact, I see only good in it. No matter how the ignorants are led to receive the Word, they are better for it. Surely you agree."

"I did not mean to accuse you, Your Reverence."

We sat silent for a while, stirring only to chase flies from our faces. I wiped my brow with the sleeve of my cassock.

"You want to ask me about the storm," Fray Junípero said.

"If you want to discuss it, I suppose . . . "

"Paco, when will you excise these words from your speech, this *supposing* and *guessing*? When did you stop believing and start supposing? I will tell you about the storm if you ask me plainly."

"Tell me about the storm, Your Reverence."

"Much better." He wiped his forehead with the back of his hand. "What happened on the ship is quite simple: God's will is done."

"But we could have saved him."

"Could we? Ask yourself, Francisco: could we have saved that man? Remember that God saves, not His servants. And that is doubly true for a man like the Father President, who lived his entire life in God's perfect grace." He paused, then said, "You are upset."

"Yes, I am upset. You let that man die!"

"I did no such thing."

"I was there, Your Reverence. You saw an opportunity to seize the presidency of this mission, and you took it—at the expense of a righteous man's life!"

"Was he a righteous man? You said a moment ago that you did not know him well."

"With all due respect, you are evading me."

He opened his mouth to speak, then closed it without saying a word. His eyes searched the shadows in the dust. I could see that my accusation had taken him by surprise. To me, the surprise was his deliberation: Junípero seldom hesitated, even in moments of great consequence.

At last he said, "I will tell you the truth. I am frightened. I have confessed this to no one, not even to God. But with you, Paco . . . Well, you know how I came to this vocation, how I was trusted by the Almighty with a vision, and how he called you and Fray Juan to join me."

"Yes, of course."

"The Lord singled me out, and His confidence has been like a wind at my back. I have flown all the way here on that confidence. Do you know what I was thinking when that Englishman had his knife to my throat? I was not afraid to die. Rather, I was sure the Lord would deliver me from danger. I told myself that the Almighty would not sacrifice his most loyal disciple, his chosen messenger, in favor of a nonbeliever . . . But what arrogance! What heresy! Remember that the Lord let his only son die on the cross. Without question he would let me die as well."

"The Lord does not wish you to die, Father, if that is your fear."

"I am not concerned with the death of my body, nor of hundreds of bodies, nor of thousands of bodies. God did not send me here to save lives. If any number of men must die in the course of our mission, it will not matter as long as we claim their souls for God. But you see, if God had allowed me to die, he would have lost more than my life. He would have lost many millions of souls, for I feel within me the potential to reap more for the glory of God than any man ever has."

"God knows that you have this potential," I said. "That is why he gave you the vision. That is why you are here."

"Precisely. And that is why I am so frightened, Paco. I am afraid I will fail the Lord."

I saw it now. In Junípero's way of thinking, the loss of the Father President was regrettable to be sure, but in the larger context of our mission, it was insignificant. I was persuaded somewhat by his argument, for I too believed that there was more at stake here than the preservation of our earthly lives. What I failed to grasp was that this whole exchange—from the moment we sat down in the *ramada*—was merely a prelude to a much larger conversation, one controlled entirely by Fray Junípero. Even when I thought I had been driving, my master still held the reins.

"Paco, may I ask you a favor? It is a solemn matter."

"Of course."

"As you know, the Father Guardian heard my confessions in Mallorca."

"Yes, Father."

"Here, in our new life, I would like you to take his place."

"Father, are you sure?"

"It has been on my mind since we left home. In fact I knew it as soon as you announced your intention to come to America. You too have been chosen by God, Paco. You are meant to be my conduit to the Lord. The deliverer of His grace and glory."

I would never know him completely, but I would understand Junípero Serra as well as any man might. Over the next forty years, I would listen to the convolutions of a mind both brilliant and singularly possessed. And I would learn, in the end, that there were secrets even a confessor could not know.

"Paco, I will fail without the favor of your assistance. I must reconcile myself with the Lord."

"Yes, Your Reverence. I know. If God will have me, I accept."

TWO DAYS INTO our overland journey, I overheard one of the soldiers in our party reminding his men to finish their correspondence before we reached México, for the muleteers returning to Veracruz would take a bag of post with them. I decided to take advantage of the next siesta to compose an overdue update to my mother. In Puerto Rico I had been too occupied—and besides, that island was not our destination. Now I had no excuse not to write.

I took out paper, ink, and pen. *Dear Mother,* I began.

Nothing followed. All of the incidents I wished to relate—our profane welcome at the port in San Juan, the death of the Father President at sea—were either too lewd or too disturbing to relate to an old woman.

My pen hovered idly over the page for several minutes. Then all at once I began scrawling lines. But the addressee had changed:

Dear Encarnación,

I write to you from the rolling hills of New Spain. I thought I would never see this place after the horrors of the crossing. The Atlantic is every bit as capricious as they say. The crew assured me that we experienced nothing out of the ordinary. They did not react strongly when a man fell from the deck during a cyclone and perished in the churning sea. He was a friar—not one of ours, but a fellow from the Valencia province who had been chosen as Father President of the mission. All the religious on board were affected by the loss, but none more than I, because I witnessed the accident.

Perhaps accident is not the best word. While it is true that no one could have prevented the crashing of the wave across the deck of the ship, the Father President was very much alive after he fell into the sea. I made an effort to rescue him with ropes, but I was too weak to haul him out. Fray Junípero was with me, and he might have lent a hand, but he was . . . busy. And now he is busier still, for he has been elected the new Father President.

I felt the perjury in that word: "busy." In time I would learn to speak tactfully around the truths learned in confession. But I was still new at my trade.

Forgive me if this letter comes as a surprise. I am surprised to be writing it. On the crossing, during the interminable nights in our cramped berth, I occupied myself in recalling our conversation at my parents' home. I fear that my advice regarding convent life may have been confusing to you, and for that I offer my sincerest apologies. I do not know why I felt compelled to express so much doubt about my vocation. In fact I am glad I joined the Friars Minor. I cannot imagine what my life might have been without the perfect model of San Francisco.

That is to say, I could not have imagined it before our conversation. If I may be candid, Encarna, since that day I have indulged in a series of meditations which I am sure were informed by our discussion. Specifically I have imagined myself in an alternate form—an avatar, as they say in the East. In this form I never joined the Franciscan Order. Instead I led a normal life among the laity of Palma, working as a clerk in the office of the harbor master—just as we discussed. Every morning I walk to the wharves with my father, and then return in the evening to my home in the parish of Santa Eulália, where in a stone-block house identical to the one where I was born, I find you.

Yes, in this meditation, you are my wife—or, I should say, my avatar's wife. I hope this notion does not disturb you. I feel that because our last conversation was based on fact and truth-telling, our correspondence ought to be similarly forthright. Forgive me if I have assumed too much.

In a frenzied quarter hour I had filled one leaf *recto verso* and was well into a second. I paused to read the lines. I was horrified by what I saw: what would the girl think I meant by it? In our Order, meditation is understood to be a regular practice, an activity of the healthy mind. We are trained, in fact, from our first days in seminary to seek such avenues to God. But to a layperson—even one inclined to the cloister—my letter would almost certainly be alarming.

Beside me, Fray Juan lay slumbering. A fly circled and landed on his temple. He shuddered.

There was a chance, I knew, that even if I posted the letter, it might never reach its destination. Every ship crossing the Atlantic faces hazards similar to the ones we had survived. Had our ship gone down in the storm that took the Father President's life, many sacks of letters would have been lost along with our lives.

That should have been my signal: I should have known that when one begins to hope for the sinking of a ship—just as when one hopes to die before the carriage reaches the convent gate—it is the sign of a gulf between one's stated intentions and one's true desires. It is laughable to think that I posted that first letter to Encarna in the hopes that it would be lost. But that is what I told myself.

Moving surreptitiously to the edge of our camp, I found a dozing muleteer and passed him the letter, along with a coin for his silence.

The update for my mother would have to wait another day.

THE HILL COUNTRY west of Veracruz entranced us with its subtle charms—the hint of wild roses in the air, white and golden butterflies in the breeze, streams trickling gently through the valleys. Our party was conducted by a pair of native guides who dressed in European clothes and spoke the Castilian tongue with remarkable precision. They had Christian names—Juan Carlos and Cristóbal—and attended our Masses faithfully. In private, we reasoned that if these were the heathens we had to convert, our work would be fruitful beyond our greatest hopes.

Unfortunately, the combination of idyllic scenery and ideal companions ill prepared us to receive the horrors of the capital. The city of México lies at the floor of a basin set high in the mountains, and coming in from the west, we passed through a canyon filled with hastily constructed shanties scarcely fit for human habitation. Figures moved in and out of these hovels like insects. The air was thick with smoke from cooking fires, and clothing hung out to dry in the hazy sun. Naked, filthy children ranged beside our mule train like dogs, barking questions in an accent I could not comprehend.

The city itself was no less appalling. Although the *calles* were laid

out in a grid, there were no paving stones, nor any wooden side-
walks. Pedestrians had to contend with the constant nuisance of mud
and animal waste. Sewage ran freely in the street. In better neighbor-
hoods, such as the central ward where the colonial government had
its offices, the sewage was confined in trenches along the sides of the
roads. I wondered how a man like the viceroy—His Majesty's own
surrogate in America—could exist in such a place, when he controlled
the means to improve it. I learned later that His Excellency was chauf-
feured about in carriages and never experienced this view of the city
first hand. It was said that the sun never kissed His Excellency's skin,
nor the bare earth the bottoms of his shoes.

This is not to say that life languished in México. On the contrary:
we passed a thriving marketplace with stalls selling meat, fish, fruits,
vegetables, and all manner of basketry and textiles. Other vendors
sold cured tobacco in rolls the size of a man's leg. Though I had no
intention of purchasing needless goods, the sight of familiar com-
modities was a strange comfort to me. After so many weeks on the
bland and limitless ocean, I relished the bounty of God's diverse
creation. I wished to stop, even for just a moment, but the guides
pressed us onward.

Winding through a maze of narrow alleys, we finally arrived
at the College of San Fernando, a spacious modern edifice in the
southern part of the city. As the point of departure for all Franciscan missionaries in New Spain, the College would be our home
during missionary training. His Most Catholic Highness had built
the College thirty years before with capacity for a hundred men. I
doubt it ever housed half that number, so great was the thirst for
missionaries in the Empire. When we arrived, there were scarcely
a dozen brothers in residence, mostly administrators and retirees.
I wondered how much training we would be expected to absorb
before we were sent into the field.

Fray Junípero was uncharacteristically silent most of the first
night, quietly appraising the Father Rector of the College, the man

who would be responsible for designating our field assignments. This was the beginning and the end of his usefulness to Junípero, who was determined that the assignments occur as soon as possible. He had not, he told me, come all the way to New Spain to sit in a convent and pray.

I shared a cell that night with an elderly friar named Eugenio, who had just returned from a mission in the Sierra Gorda, a district northeast of the capital. Fray Eugenio's hair was gray only at the temples, but he moved like a much older man. When he reached for the glass of water next to his bed, his hand shook as though palsied.

"I cannot tell you, my friend, how good it is to see a light complexion."

I was not sure how to respond to this comment.

"Have you noticed the air?" he asked.

"The sun seems to shine more brightly here than in Spain," I offered.

"Oh, it is not the air that makes the sun shine that way. It is the Devil."

"Pardon me?"

"The Devil is everywhere. And his vehicle is the sun."

He said this matter-of-factly, as though it were a matter of dogma. I wondered where this friar had learned his theology.

"The Devil has ridden the sun into every heart in New Spain. We make progress, yes, but as soon as we leave, the Devil returns. It is not for lack of trying, Brother. Lord knows I have tried. Eight years I lived in those mountains. Six by myself."

"By yourself?"

"Yes, six years alone, with only the Indians for company. The occasional letter from this place. I thought I was going to lose my mind."

I did not say so, but I suspected he had lost it already. As I have explained, friars never live alone. I said, "What did you do in the Sierra Gorda, Brother?"

"What did I do? Heavens—what did I *not* do? I built a church. I built a school. I built a house for every family in the village—and when they burned those, I built them again. I taught the children how to sing, and I heard the confessions of their parents. But the Mexicans are a sad people, Brother. And superstitious. No matter how many children I taught to read and write—and I estimate that in eight years I must have taught many hundreds—no matter how many times I showed the parents that the way of God was the true and righteous path—no matter how I tempted them with eternal life and threatened them with eternal fire—no matter what, they always returned to their idolatry. How I felt like Moses coming down from the Mount! Several times a year I would return from a day in the fields to find the church deserted and the people gone to worship their old gods. Clay figurines, these gods are, but they revere them so. It is maddening, Brother. Rather, I should say it *was* maddening. I am done with all that now."

"You are going home?"

"To Spain? No, even if my old body could make the trip, I would not recognize the place. I am changed, Brother. This city is enough civilization for me now."

It saddened me to see this old friar so defeated. Had San Pablo been so discouraged, we might never have had a lasting Church. It is our *privilege* to spread the Good News, I believed—not only our duty, but also our delight.

"But what of the pagans who learned the faith and embraced it? On the road from Veracruz, there was a guide, a man named Juan Carlos—"

Fray Eugenio grinned. "They did not tell you? He is no pagan. He one of us. He has taken his vows. So has the other—Cristóbal, I believe is his name. They are Franciscans."

He paused to let my perceptions realign. Then he said, "There are exceptions, friend. There are always exceptions."

Sensing that I did not wish to continue the conversation, Fray Eugenio turned on his side and closed his eyes. A moment later he was snoring.

Exceptions. I was no fool—we would not build a mission from exceptions. But I believed that even under the circumstances he described, we would fare better than this shadow of a man, who had reverted to infancy, sleeping and raving in equal measures.

Had old Eugenio seen what Fray Junípero had done in Puerto Rico, it might have restored his faith in ministry. And that in only a week's time. Imagine what His Reverence could accomplish in eight years!

I leaned back on my cot. It had been months since I had slept on a proper bed, and it felt uncomfortable to lie so still. I rolled onto my back, then my side, begging God to take pity and send the sleep I so desperately needed.

Exceptions. If there were exceptions among them, then there must be exceptions among us. This thought seemed so perfect, so logical, that I considered waking Fray Eugenio just to refute him with it.

WE REMAINED AT the College of San Fernando for the better part of a year. The experience was not unlike seminary, with lectures and regular examinations, but there were a few important differences. Here our subjects were practical rather than theological, and unlike in seminary, where we had scarcely been allowed to leave the premises, in México we spent considerable time practicing our new skills— planting, weaving, sewing, etc.—in the native villages bordering the city. Not all of us, however, were equally diligent in these studies. Fray Junípero especially had little patience for what he called time-wasting activities: "Better that we should swing the censer than the machete, eh?" he complained one afternoon to the young friar instructing us in the proper technique for harvesting cane. I was able to see at the College that there exists no intrinsic difference between pupil and instructor. In fact the difference appeared to be mainly one of attitude. Case in point: here was my master, who had once been my revered instructor, acting like the most incorrigible first-year seminarian.

To the chagrin of Fray Junípero, the administrators of the College of San Fernando proved quite astute. The Father Rector realized quickly that Fray Junípero had a plan that went far beyond—or perhaps circumvented entirely—the normal missionary protocols. They also came to learn that he had secretly written the bishop of México—posted the letter at our landing in Veracruz—to ask for dispensation to perform confirmations. This was a highly unusual request. In Europe, no one but bishops ever performed confirmations. In far-flung regions such as the Pyrenees, young people and converts had to wait months, if not years, for a bishop to travel near enough to confirm them. In New Spain, where the modes of transportation were far worse than in even the most rural parts of Europe, the newly baptized might wait forever. Baptized but unconfirmed, they would be like fish caught in nets that we could not gather. This was unacceptable to Fray Junípero.

One day, the Father Rector called Fray Junípero to task. They had a long, heated discussion behind closed doors. I was waiting for him in the passage when he emerged.

"Walk with me, Paco," he said.

We went to the yard behind the College, where a previous resident had installed some of the native plants of Spain, with varying degrees of success. A stone's throw from the dormitory were three spindly olive trees—I recognized these only by the leaves, for they bore no fruit. Fray Junípero led me to a bench. He did not prefer to sit unless he was praying, but he wished to speak privately.

"It seems that God is testing us," he began. "At every stage there is another gate, and another gatekeeper. I confess I did not expect it."

I was by this point his confessor, but this was to be no confession. This was simply friendship, one of those occasions when Fray Junípero called upon me to guide his thoughts. "What is your news?" I inquired.

"Ah, Paco, it is only this—we have received an assignment."

I was startled. It was not what I had expected to hear.

"You must be overjoyed," I said.

His Reverence's brow creased deeply between his eyes. "I'm afraid I set my hopes too high."

"Oh?"

"You know my preference for virgin lands."

Several times he had emphasized to me his desire to minister in areas where no missionary work had been done before, to work "untilled soil." He said he relished the hardship of such a task, but there was no question he also wanted the glory that would accrue with success in unproven quarters.

"I know your preference," I said. "But it is only a preference. Is the desire so strong that you would reject another mission? Tell me, what is the place they have offered?"

"California," he muttered.

At once I understood. California was the westernmost province of New Spain, a rocky, desolate peninsula dangling from the mainland like a paralyzed finger. No plant life grew there but cactus, and the natives were rumored to be fierce and incorrigible. Through hard work and sacrifice, the Jesuit fathers had established a chain of missions in California, but the territory was otherwise ignored by Europeans.

"Is that not Jesuit land?"

Fray Junípero raised an eyebrow. "It was. The King has banished the Jesuits from Spain. Effective one month from now, all Jesuit fathers must be gone from the kingdom or face execution."

The caprice of royals had always appalled me. I wondered sometimes how many of their senseless edicts were for show, and how many for real political gain. I failed to understand how kings and queens could believe that any Catholic monks—however learned and well organized—posed a serious threat to their power. But of course, once Portugal had taken this step, it was only a matter of time before our regent followed suit.

"The Father Rector has been in discussion with the viceroy and the Jesuit provincials. The missions in California will be turned over to us. The other Jesuit missions, in Sonora and elsewhere, will be occupied by the Dominican fathers."

"All of this in a month's time?"

"Yes, one month."

We sat silent for a moment. Finally I asked His Reverence what he planned to do.

He clutched his robe at the knees. "I have done it already," he said. "I accepted the assignment, and with the proper gratitude."

I nodded. "But what was all the shouting during your discussion with the Father Rector?"

"Oh." He waved a hand through the air. "The bishop refused my petition."

"For confirmations?"

Fray Junípero shrugged. "There will be another bishop."

WE LEFT MEXICO CITY with a train of thirty-six burros, two mounted soldiers, and a band of guides and grooms. Thirty-nine days out, we arrived in the western town of Tepic. On the hill-sides around us, peasants worked fields of tobacco and maize, their straw hats like mushrooms in the grass. In the center of town, we found the Franciscan convent of Cruz de Zacate. Junípero and the Father Guardian of this convent were acquainted from their days as Franciscan academics, and they embraced heartily, exchanging many kisses on the cheeks. Members of our Order are generally slender, on account of the discipline we apply to all aspects of our lives, including the appetite. But the Father Guardian of Cruz de Zacate was rather the opposite. To compensate for his corpulence, he cinched his waist-cord tight, but that only made his belly bulge above and below it like a round of smoked cheese tied with string. He struck me right away as an affable fellow. More to the point, he deferred to Fray Junípero, which guaranteed a harmonious visit.

"I would be honored," the Father Guardian said to His Reverence shortly after our arrival, "if you would lead the Mass for Our Seraphic Father this evening." It was October 4, the feast of San Francisco—the holiest day in the Franciscan calendar.

Out of respect for his friend, Fray Junípero refused, but after the Father Guardian made a second entreaty, citing their long years of friendship and the divine coincidence of our party's arrival on the feast of San Francisco, His Reverence finally agreed. It made me uncomfortable to see the Father Guardian toss aside his rightful place as celebrant—surely he had earned the honor himself through years of hard work and devotion—but I knew all would be served best this way.

The High Mass sung that evening by Fray Junípero was deeply affecting for everyone, none more than the celebrant himself. His Reverence had a habit of renewing his vows every year on the feast of San Francisco ("The mind does not forget, Paco," he explained to me, "but the body must be reminded"). We all sat silent as the little Mallorcan pledged his life to Christ through poverty, chastity, and obedience. After Mass, we ate a humble repast of tortillas, beans, and steamed tomatoes. All together we were a dozen, and we squeezed into the benches around the convent's sole dining table.

After eating his tiny portion—only a fraction, as I have described previously, of what he was served—Fray Junípero wiped his mouth with a towel and turned to his old friend. "Many thanks for your hospitality, Brother. I wish that we could linger, but unfortunately we must continue to the port of San Blas in the morning."

The Father Guardian smiled. "The port of San Blas, you say?"

"There is a ship waiting there to take us to California."

"Yes, I know. Your letter explained it."

"Why are you smiling?"

The Father Guardian wiped his mouth. "It is only that I have never heard San Blas called a *port* before."

"Have I got the location wrong? Where is Father Palóu? Check the calendar, Paco—make sure it is San Blas whence we depart."

"Oh, it is San Blas," the Father Guardian said, "That is the point of embarkation for California. Before they built the pier at San Blas, you had to go north through Sonora, and cross over by land."

"How long ago did they build the pier?"

"It's been only a few months. The poor Jesuit fathers had no time to benefit."

"His Majesty dislikes the Jesuits," said Fray Junípero.

"He does—but the Crown did not build the pier to punish the Jesuits."

"What was the purpose, then?"

Between bites the Father Guardian said, "The Russians."

"Are there Russians on the peninsula?"

"Not to my knowledge. In fact, I queried the retreating Jesuit fathers about it, and none of them have seen Russians either. As far as I know, the Russians have never been south of forty-eight degrees. They trap furs, you know."

For all his strengths, Fray Junípero was never very good at concealing his excitement. His fingers tapped the tabletop, and his eyes darted left and right. "Are there furs in California?"

The Father Guardian took a fresh tortilla from the basket in the center of the table and scooped up more beans. "Honestly there is not much of anything in California. Indians and rattlesnakes. And cactus. Many, many varieties of cactus. Do you enjoy mescal brandy? The Jesuit fathers were able to distill a fine mescal. I have a bottle of it somewhere—"

"How far is San Blas?"

"Ten leagues, give or take. But brother, there is nothing in San Blas but the pier—"

All of a sudden, Fray Junípero pushed his bench back from the table, startling the friars sitting next to him. "Paco!" he cried. "Prepare the group to depart first thing in the morning."

The Father Guardian scrambled to his feet, his paunch jiggling above the waist-rope. "Brother, please. Stay a few more days. Rest your animals—and your men."

"The animals will be rested by dawn. The men need no rest."

"But brother, California is not going to expire! A week here, a week there . . . nothing changes. Stay a while longer, I implore you."

"Had I known His Majesty had rivals in this country, I would not have stopped at all."

"Rivals, Brother?"

"Russians! Why, it may be too late already. I hesitate to imagine what has happened since the Jesuit fathers left their posts. Think of the souls they left behind! With a ruthless and barbaric predator closing in. A heathen, Eastern menace. Paco!"

"Your Reverence. I am going . . . "

I excused myself from the table and hurried out to the stable. Our guides were playing cards with the convent's grooms. They were seated in a circle on the floor, and despite the presence of dried hay all around, they were smoking cigars and tapping the ashes wherever they pleased. There was an unlabeled bottle of brown liquor going around the circle. This disappeared behind someone's back as soon as I made myself known.

"*Buenas tardes, padre,*" said the lead guide.

"*Buenas. Amar a Dios.*"

I explained the situation, making sure to mention the Russians in the hope that a little fear would inspire them to speedy action.

The guide only laughed. "As you wish, Father. *Pero yo no sé nada de los rusos . . .* "

"Fray Junípero expects you to be ready by dawn."

"*Claro, padre.*"

As I walked back across the plaza, I heard the men in the stable erupt in laughter. There was a pop as a fresh bottle was uncorked. "*¡Ay, peligro!*" someone cried. "*¡Ay-ay! ¡Los rusos vienen!*" More laughter, then silence as they drank. Finally, the voice of the lead guide: "*Pues. Muévense, pendejos.*"

FIVE

THE BARK CROSSED THE Sea of Cortés to Loreto, on the east coast of the California peninsula, under the widest, clearest sky I had ever seen. The crossing from San Blas was an uneventful two days, marked only by flocks of strange and wonderful birds overhead. I had never seen such diversity of feathered creatures: families of long, slender fowl flew in precise alignment, beak to foot, slicing the sky. They were animate clouds, these flocks, chattering and dodging, diving and pecking. I thought I recognized some of the species from their markings, but when they passed close above the ship, I always noticed my mistake—a stripe where I expected a spot, a flat beak instead of a hook. I was left to marvel, ignorant.

In the sea as well we found marvels. A navy of porpoises made our acquaintance early in the voyage and did not leave the side of our vessel until we were nearly at the opposite port. In the evening, as we lay in our hammocks belowdecks, we heard the songs of these fish, their squeals and hollers like children at play. In the morning, they greeted us with spray from their glistening skulls, and we threw them the scraps of meat and fish heads from the previous night's supper.

But as rich was the sea, so poor was the land in that benighted corner of the world. And how strong the reek of Satan! We had been on terra firma not even an hour before our party found its first snake. It was Juan Crespí who saw the beast coiled on a flat rock by the side of the road. Though we had been warned about rattlesnakes and even given special walking sticks with notched ends so that we might pin serpents behind the head, Fray Juan wasted no time in resorting to the ultimate defense. Dropping his pack, he knelt in the middle of the road and began to pray, asking God to cast out the beast, and to deliver this forsaken land from the clutches of Darkness.

"Get up!" Fray Junípero cried when he discovered why the procession had stopped. "Shoulder your pack, Juan, and move along. There will be time enough to pray when we reach the *convento.*"

"But Father, behold—" Juan rose and pointed to the flat rock. It was empty now, the snake having slithered away at the sight and sound of our mules.

"Your pack, my son," commanded Fray Junípero. "Lift it."

Juan obeyed. But no sooner had we shouldered our loads than did Beató's high-pitched wail pierce the air once again: "Your Paternity!" he cried. "He is behind you!"

I turned just in time to see the snake strike once, twice beneath Fray Junípero's cassock. Clutching my fork-ended walking stick, I lunged after the beast and struck it across the head until it ceased to move.

When Fray Juan saw the remains of the serpent at my feet, he crossed himself. "It is a sign," he declared. The other friars in our party murmured their agreement. One hand still clutching the instrument of death, I considered whether he was correct.

"It is a beast," Junípero said, "and that is all." He was in pain from the bites, his brow wet with perspiration, but he had not lost his focus. He bent down and began kneading the wound between his thumbs. The twin punctures, two fingers' width apart, gave up beads of dark blood, which he blotted with the hem of his cassock. When he was satisfied with his work, he stood up and turned to me.

"It was only a beast, and now it is meat. Francisco, take the creature up in a sack. You will serve it to us for supper."

We reached the mission of Nuestra Señora de Loreto just before dusk. Leaving our packs in the courtyard, we walked around to admire the Jesuit fathers' striking church. Constructed from blocks of quarried stone, Loreto deserved its reputation as the jewel of the California missions. It was perched on the highest bluff overlooking the harbor, in exactly the spot where I would have expected the soldiers to site the presidio. But such is the strange power of the Jesuits: only by their guidance would the King's house be relegated below their own.

To compensate for the poor soil, the Jesuits had engineered a rudimentary system of irrigation—open ditches tracing the hillsides from a hidden reservoir. But these canals were thick with silt, as if they had not been dredged recently. The cornstalks in the *milpas* were so short that upon first inspection I assumed the plants were tobacco or a variety of bean. Hungry crows prowled the fields like farm workers, moving up and down the rows, methodically defoliating every living thing. No humans interrupted their progress—indeed, no humans could be seen in the fields at all. It was a disturbing preview of the discovery I would make years later when Fray Juan led me through the desolate fields at Carmel. There of course the crime would be worse, for we would have no one to blame but ourselves.

The neophytes had taken care of the church: votive candles burned in all the niches on the exterior walls. We followed around to the ornate double doors and went inside. Immediately I knew why I had seen no people in the fields: all were here, in the pews, fast at prayer. A choir of children sang psalms, their voices like tiny bells in the rafters. A native man stood before the altar dressed in the robe and stole of a deacon. He held a gold chalice in his hands and bowed his head as we entered.

"Love God!" exclaimed Fray Junípero. His voice reverberated through the arching nave.

The entire congregation rose from the pews and answered, "God is great," pronouncing the words in perfect Castilian Spanish.

The emboldened Junípero moved quickly to the altar. He spoke to the deacon, and the man rushed off, returning from the sacristy a moment later with an alb and tunic, neatly folded. He also held a small canvas sack, which he placed unopened on the pew at the side of the altar.

His Reverence donned the sacred vestments and crossed himself. The choir hushed, and the congregation knelt. Fray Juan and I remained at the rear of the nave with our mule-drivers, who bowed their heads respectfully in prayer.

"My children," began Junípero, "let us begin fresh today. May the peace of God be with you."

The neophytes replied, "And also with you."

Juan and I exchanged glances, so amazed were we at the training the Jesuit fathers had given these humble brown-skinned people.

"Let us pray," said Junípero. After the standard rites—the responses to which the natives knew in Latin—he shifted to the vernacular, narrating Saint Mark's parable of the sower:

> Behold, there went out a sower to sow: And it came to pass, as he sowed, some fell by the way side, and the fowls of the air came and devoured it up. And some fell on stony ground, where it had not much earth; and immediately it sprang up, because it had no depth of earth: But when the sun was up, it was scorched; and because it had no root, it withered away. And some fell among thorns, the thorns grew up, and choked it, and it yielded no fruit.

It was an inspired choice of Scripture. Had we not that day witnessed the fowls of the air? Was the soil here not rocky and thin? As for thorn trees, the Father Guardian at Tepic had been perfectly correct when he said that cacti outnumbered all other plants. In fact, I saw no other plants, save the haggard cornstalks planted by the Jesuits.

And other fell on good ground, and did yield fruit that sprang up and increased; and brought forth, some thirty, and some sixty, some an hundred. And He said unto them, He that has ears to hear, let him hear!

The natives nodded solemnly at Junípero's words. A few, however, appeared to doze off, their eyelids fluttering and finally dropping shut. The children of the choir, God bless their innocent souls, began to poke one another in the sides, playing a game to see who might falter first and interrupt the priest with laughter.

Junípero came to the end of the parable and paused. With a whisper, he summoned the deacon to his side, and then, with the man's help, he lifted his alb, tunic, and finally his ordinary robe over his head so that he stood before the congregation completely naked. His hard black eyes remained fixed on the rear wall of the church, never once looking down to observe the mix of horror and strange delight on the faces before him.

From the altarside pew, His Reverence took up the canvas sack and removed a short length of iron chain, as might be used to hang a candelabrum from the ceiling. He stepped deliberately to the front of the sanctuary and turned to face the crucifix of Our Savior. He knelt before the altar. In the rear of the church, a baby's innocent yelp was silenced quickly by its mother.

I had studied the same *Lives* as Junípero. I knew that his patron, San Francisco Solano, was famous for injuring himself with chains, or else burning his skin with a four-wicked candle to show the Indians of Perú the depth of his devotion to Christ. Before him, San Gerónimo had done the same. And San Juan of Capistrano. There were dozens of examples, so I should not have been surprised—nor fearful.

In spite of myself, I was both.

In a loud, shrill voice, His Reverence began to pray: *"Agnus Dei qui tollis peccata mundi, miserere nobis . . . "* Then, with a terrible cry, he raised his arm straight in the air above his head, fist clenching the chain, and brought it down. There was a hollow *thump*, like a melon hacked by a knife, as the metal struck his flesh, then an oddly pleasing jingle as the links slackened down his back.

The flesh tore just above his left shoulder blade. For a moment, the stunned blood vessels held their flow. Then all at once, blood began to pour from the wound. It came in dark rivulets, spreading like oil into the black bristles on His Reverence's narrow back. Before we had time to react, he raised the chain and struck again, this time opening a wound on the opposite shoulder.

Women began to cry, followed by their children. The wailing of one girl was so loud, and so near my ears, that I turned at once to see who she was. To my surprise, I discovered it was no woman at all, but my *condiscípulo*, Juan Crespí.

Juan seized my arm. His face was wet with tears. "You must stop him, Paco."

I ran, passing pews where men and women were now clutching each other in fear and confusion. Babies wailed. The warm, bready smell of fresh urine began to rise in the air. Junípero struck himself a third time. The blow knocked him sideways, and he balanced on one knee for a moment before falling over. When I reached him he was unconscious. Thick blood oozed like molasses across his back. The horrified deacon thrust Junípero's sackcloth robe upon me. I swaddled His Reverence as best I could. His breathing was faint, but his heart beat vigorously in his chest.

I stood up and faced the congregation. Though of course I pitied my damaged brother, I also resented him for leaving me a mess. If he had told me ahead of time that he intended to enact this drama, I might have invented a role for myself—a role which, while preserving the *effect* of the charade, might have prevented irreparable bodily injury.

I cleared my throat. I considered the sower, and cursed Junípero under my breath.

"The meaning of the parable," I said, "is obscure for those who do not yet believe. Christ said to his followers, 'Unto you it is given to know the mystery of the Kingdom of God, but unto them that are without, all these things are done in parables.' These stories are a kind of code. Do you understand?"

How ridiculous I must have appeared, preaching theology while my master lay bleeding like a joint of meat. None of the congregation listened to my words, and when I paused to take a breath, a man in the second pew, whose woman and children sat beside him covering their eyes and shivering, asked me, "Is this man—" He meant Junípero. "Is he the Son of God?"

This brought a rumble from the assembly, spoken in an Indian tongue I could not understand.

Another man rose. "If he lives, he is the Son!"

"He lives," I said, "but he is only my master, Father Junípero Serra. He is a brother of Saint Francis. Do you know San Francisco?"

The congregation, baptized and schooled by Jesuits, did not respond.

"Look—he is moving!" a woman cried.

Junípero struggled to his knees. The cassock I had draped over him clung to his back, attached by coagulating blood. His eyes were unfocused, and his head swayed from side to side as he crawled up the steps to the altar.

The first man in the congregation called out, "He lives! ¡Viva San Junípero!"

All at once, the congregation descended upon the sanctuary, hoping to get closer to the wounded friar. I was pushed to the ground. When I regained myself, I saw that the crowd had lifted Junípero onto the altar itself—a vulgarity I was sure His Reverence would not tolerate. But he only raised his hands weakly to embrace the Indians' faces. And when the chant rose up all around him suggesting that he were no longer merely the humble Franciscan brother José Miguel Junípero Serra, late of Petra de Mallorca, but rather some higher figure in the Roman Catholic universe—San Junípero—he did not correct them, but only closed his eyes to bask in the adoration of his new disciples.

A MONTH INTO our residence at Loreto, Fray Junípero asked me to a private audience in the sacristy after morning Mass. "I have something important to tell you," he said. "And *por favor*, Paco— bring a bottle of brandy."

He instructed me to dampen a cloth with the liquor and to swab his back. He had not repeated the display of self-flagellation, but his wounds from that first demonstration were not yet healed—mainly because he refused any kind of rest and could be seen most days shouldering a long wicker basket in the *milpas*, showing the neophytes the proper way to harvest maize.

I weighed the bottle in my free hand. "Would Your Reverence like a drink to dull the pain?"

Junípero shook his head. "If the Lord did not want me to feel pain, he would not have given me these wounds."

He changed the subject before I could remind him that his injuries were self-inflicted.

"How do you find California, Paco?"

We had settled easily into the former Jesuit missions. The missionary college had sent another dozen friars from México City, and Junípero assigned them to stations with names like San Ignacio and San Francisco Xavier—places named for Jesuit saints. In each instance our brothers found a settlement in some stage of physical disrepair; but as at Loreto, the flock left to us by the Jesuit fathers always proved docile, respectful, and well versed in the Gospel of Christ. Those first months in Old California did much to improve my opinion of the Jesuit fathers. I saw no evidence of the crimes alleged by our monarch—no treason against Spain and certainly none against God. I came to appreciate their good work in what was truly an unforgiving environment. In general, I came to view the Jesuit fathers as valuable partners, not as adversaries or rivals. We were divisions in the same army—the army of the Lord. Indeed, I would defend this position many times in the ensuing years, even when it made me unpopular.

"The Jesuit fathers left us fine stock," I said.

"Yes, the neophytes do seem well disposed to learning," Junípero replied. "It is a shame; I know that the teachings of the Seraphic Father would have taken quick root here."

I paused my work. "Are we leaving? I thought that California was to be our vineyard."

His Reverence took a deep breath. His back expanded under my touch and then contracted as he exhaled. The beads of brandy ran down his skin like tears. "Do you remember in Tepic," he said, "when we learned about the Russians?"

"I have seen no Russians here. Have you?"

"None."

"So it was an unfounded rumor. Not the first, I would imagine."

Once more, Fray Junípero's back rose with breath. "It seems there are two Californias, Paco. I had a letter from México yesterday. The Czarina is threatening to settle the coast of Alta California."

"Alta California?" I had never heard the name. It called to mind snow-capped mountains, elevated Alpine meadows—nothing like the terrain of this place.

"This is the name the court is giving to the territories beyond thirty-two degrees north latitude—although the boundaries are approximate. This is the first time His Majesty has cared to define them."

"How far north do His Majesty's claims extend?"

"That remains to be seen. Assuming His Majesty cedes Russia the land she has claimed, we are left with eight degrees currently uncontested." Fray Junípero closed his eyes. "At twenty-three leagues per degree, that would make Alta California a territory of approximately . . . one hundred eighty-four leagues."

The figure startled me; it was a distance almost greater than the east coast of Spain.

"Has the King sent soldiers?" I asked.

"None so far," Junípero said.

"Then how does he mean to enforce his claims?"

Junípero lifted his arms, and I slipped his cassock over his head. When our eyes met, I saw that he had already explored this question.

"So we are to move north," I said.

"Had you any idea this country was so vast, Paco? What fortune for us—and for God!"

"What about the missions here?"

"That is what I must discuss with you. As we speak, an expedition is being prepared at La Paz, near Cape San Lucas. I am told the fullest resources of Spain are being readied there. An adjutant of His Majesty, Don José de Gálvez, has been appointed Visitor General, with dispensation to establish three missions in Alta California. My letter was from this man."

"Is he a soldier?"

"He is more of a statesman, known apparently in all the courts of Europe as the regular emissary of His Majesty's ill will."

"You say Señor Gálvez is on this peninsula?"

"As of last week. I am going to La Paz tomorrow to meet him."

"You must be terrified."

"Not at all. I have come to understand from Don José's letter that he is a man of faith. For a layman, he demonstrates remarkable zeal. Take for example that nearly half of his letter to me —and it was a long one, three sheets—was given to a list of liturgical vestments and vessels he has procured for the three new missions. A variety of linen albs, two embroidered chasubles, six bronze candlesticks a yard high, and so on. As I say, he filled three leaves."

"We are blessed to have him as our champion."

"Indeed. His Majesty's emissary could as easily have been one of those gents who dreams only of gold and precious stones and cares not a whit for spreading God's immortal Word. But here, to find that His Majesty has sent such a pious man as Don José . . . "

"Forgive me for saying so, Your Reverence, but it sounds as if you know him already."

"Perhaps I am more nervous than I thought."

We shared a laugh, and after a brief moment of reflection, I said, "You will get your wish after all."

"What is that?"

"Untilled soil."

"Yes." I thought Junípero would go on, as was his fashion, to sketch his dreams for the expedition in the boldest colors, to tell of the thousands of souls we would capture, the glory we would win for the Savior. But he was silent. He seemed preoccupied.

"Is something wrong, Your Reverence?"

"Not at all," he began, and then he stopped abruptly. "Brother, what I have to tell you is not easy for me to say, and I fear it is catching in my throat. So I will simply tell it plain, as our friend Fray Rafael was so fond of saying. My son, you will not be coming with us to Alta California. You will remain here on the peninsula."

He paused to let the words sink in.

"You will live here in Loreto, where you will serve as Father President of these missions."

"What about Fray Juan," I asked. "Will he remain as well?"

Junípero's eyes shifted sideways, avoiding my gaze. "Juan will accompany me north," he said. "Forgive me, Paco. It is only because of your superior skill in administration that I am asking you to stay."

Junípero dropped his voice to a whisper. "With respect to our pious friend, I do not believe these missions would last six months under his direction. I have always seen great promise in you. Now you will prove me right."

"I hear the language of praise," I said, "but I feel as though I am being punished."

"This is not punishment, Paco. This is the opposite of punishment."

"You say that I am your favorite, but—"

"Listen to yourself! Do you think that when San Francisco gathered his brothers to divide the towns and villages of Italy, they argued over who would go to Genoa, who to Florence, who to Venice?"

"No, but I wish to be near you."

His Reverence waved this off. "We must not be distracted by wishes, my son."

FRAY JUNIPERO WAS in La Paz all the winter and spring of that year. He wrote me often to recount the rapid progress of preparations for the Alta California expedition, and to sing the praises of the Visitor General, Señor Gálvez, whose commitment to our mission continued to surprise His Reverence: "All my past experience with courtiers suggests that while they do honor their Lord—that is, their sovereign King—they leave much to be desired in their devotion to the King of Heaven." By contrast he described Don José packing crates himself, making sure that each of the three proposed missions had its proper allotment of liturgical supplies: "This is no ordinary courtier, Paco, but a true laborer in Christ."

Junípero used page after page to list the bounty being packed away—the riches of the Spanish Empire polished up for the purpose of impressing whatever natives existed north of thirty-two degrees. An entire altarpiece—which included, among other adornments, hand-painted *reredos* of San Buenaventura and our Seraphic Father San Francisco—was delivered from México, dismantled, and loaded on board the ship. "It gives me great courage, Paco," His Reverence wrote, "to know that we will never be alone among the heathens— indeed, that San Pablo will be there, and San Pedro, watching over us from the walls."

The same saints watched over me in the old Jesuit church at

Loreto, but they brought me no succor. I would have traded them all for the attention of Fray Junípero.

One afternoon in the middle of May a neophyte reported that a visitor was approaching. He had seen a pack-ass raising dust on the south road and a man walking beside the animal. I gathered that it was one of the friars under my direction. Perhaps there had been trouble. A few of the younger men could not seem to grasp the temporal aspects of running a frontier mission. And who could blame them? They had been trained as monks and theologians, not as overseers of large estates.

I went out to greet the visitor, as was our custom. The road was unusually dusty, and the traveler was almost within earshot before I recognized that he was our Junípero, limping along beside a stubby little donkey. He grasped a tall walking stick, taller than his person, which he occasionally leaned against with both hands. The ass was quite content to participate in this start-and-stop promenade, and he chewed his bit with relish whenever Junípero took a rest.

I sent two men ahead with a litter, so that they might spare His Reverence the last half-league or so. Not surprisingly, he sent them back, with a message to me: "My dear Paco, Christ was not carried to Golgotha."

Finally he reached the bluff, and we embraced with the fervor of a long separation. His cassock was drenched with sweat; nevertheless, he refused my offer of a drink. Later, the neophytes who unloaded his belongings would tell me that both of his canteens were full.

I did convince him to sit down. We reclined in the shade of the arcade beside the mission's dormitories. A pair of blackbirds scattered from a nest overhead. Junípero clucked to them under his breath.

"You are not well, Your Reverence," I said.

"How so, Paco? I am here with you. This mission prospers. I am very well indeed."

"But your leg . . . " I reached to lift the hem of his cassock. The lower half of his limb was swollen to twice its normal girth. The skin was wine-colored, and nearly purple in places, centered around the site of the serpent-bite suffered our first morning on these shores. Not one of us had thought the injury very serious, least of all Junípero, who refused all assistance. Now I saw we had been mistaken; the wound was serious indeed. I should have known better than to trust the assurances of a stoic.

Junípero pushed my hand away. "I am well," he snapped. "So long as God spurs my heart to beat, I am well."

"Will you stay here?" I asked.

"Only briefly. I must go to Velicatá to meet Fray Juan and the land party."

Velicatá was the northernmost bead on the necklace of California missions. Few Spaniards had traveled beyond it, and none for more than a week or two.

"Fray Juan is in Velicatá already?" I said, trying to keep my voice level, emotionless, even at the mention of Juan Crespí.

"Perhaps. He and Captain Portolá have taken a different route." He paused and broke his stare, turning to face me at last. "I came this way so I could see you."

"It is a relief to see your face," I said.

"You are lonesome, I think. You should know that I regret leaving you here without a companion. But Fray Luis Jayme arrives next week from San Blas."

He gave a smile—or what passed for a smile with Fray Junípero. His eyes narrowed slightly and the edges of his thin lips turned up at the corners. Mirth came to him with great difficulty. False mirth even more so.

"I will persevere," I said.

"God does not want your perseverance, Francisco. We are not here only to hold a place for the next man. We must do more, or else we discredit God's wisdom in keeping us alive."

"That is precisely my point. I too hope to work untilled soil."

"And you will."

"But when?"

Junípero ignored my plea. Instead he called for his purse and produced a bundle of letters. "The Visitor General brought more than candlesticks, Paco. I had a letter from my mother—my sister is with child."

"That is wonderful news! Congratulations."

"You will distribute these to the others?"

"Naturally."

Later, alone in my chamber, I sorted the letters. I made stacks to dispatch to each of the missions under my supervision. In my own pile of three letters, I recognized the minuscule, painstaking hand of my mother and the addled script of my elder sister. But the third author was a mystery. My name—*Father Fray Francisco Palóu, OFM*—had been etched efficiently, without blot or smudge, along with the address of the College of San Fernando in México. I told myself I could not imagine who she was, this third correspondent, but the fact that I had settled on her sex even before reading her name belied a much deeper understanding than I was willing to admit.

Unable to wait any longer, I broke the seal with my thumb:

My dear Paco,

Do you see? I have not called you "Father." I see no reason to strip you of an honorific so well deserved, but I strive to honor your wishes. Therefore Paco you are.

You were concerned that your letter would surprise me. In fact it did. I was forcefully surprised—but only as a girl is surprised to find a bowl of chocolate pudding in place of her morning gruel. I never expected to hear from you again. I was delighted.

You were concerned, also, that your advice to me was poor. How wrong you were! After our conversation, I dwelt for days upon the story of your entry into the Franciscan Order. Your testimony set my mind at ease, for I too have doubted that the cloister—for all its attractions—was meant to be my home. With your guidance I have learned that such doubts are common; or if not common certainly not antithetical to a meaningful vocation. That is why, scarcely a month after your ship left our harbor, I announced my intentions before the prioress. I am now a sister of Santa Clara—a "poor Clare" if you like, but I maintain that I am rich on account of your friendship.

But! You may wonder what became of my concern for my mother's welfare. Well, Paco, a wonderful thing has happened. It turns out that I was not the only one concerned for Mother. My uncle, a tailor in Sóller (and also a widower) has agreed to take her in. Mother was at first too proud to accept the invitation, for she never imagined taking alms from her little brother. However she eventually succumbed to his entreaties, and now they live quite happily together. She had been accepted into his community, and she runs his house with the same rigor she employed in running ours. By all accounts they exist quite like man and wife.

On that subject—appearing as man and wife—let me say that I was not disturbed in the least by the "meditation" described in your letter. On the contrary, I was flattered (though not too much, as I am an obedient nun). Like you, I was affected in a profound way by our conversation, by the frankness of our talk, and I agree that we ought to be truthful with each other. Therefore I shall reveal that I miss you. Any "meditation" or "scenario" which makes up that distance is a blessing and not a source of shame.

You will notice there are no corrections in my letters. I am a firm believer in the sanctity of expression; that is to say the privilege of words to be read precisely as they were written, before they were tinkered with and appended to. The hazard of this policy is that when I am writing a letter, I often remember points I wished to make on topics already addressed and abandoned. Here is one such item, which I shall place here even though it concerns the topic of a previous paragraph.

When I joined the Poor Clares, the prioress suggested that I take another name. She felt that the word "encarnación," in its common meaning, was too vulgar, too fleshly. At first I took offense: what if we were to judge words such as "cross," "wound," or even "virgin" by their common meanings instead of their sacred ones? I was given my name because Christ was made flesh for our salvation, not because my parents indulged unchastities. But my outrage subsided, and in time, I realized that Mother Superior had given me an opportunity. That is why I chose the name Guadalupe—after the patroness of your new continent. You see, Paco, you are not the only one with the ability to transcend place. Think of me whenever you wish, and know that I am closer than ever to you.

In Christ, I am,

Your faithful,

Sor Guadalupe (Encarnación) Mora

I read the letter thrice before I put it down. Right away I took out paper and pen and, inspired by Encarna's "sanctity of expression," scrawled out three leaves without any corrections.

I am in California, soon to be rechristened "Old" California, because we are sending a party north into the unexplored regions of the territory. No one knows what we will find there—beasts or savages or acts of God. Did you know California was named for the island of the Amazon queen in *Las Sergas de Esplandián* by Montalvo? Have you read that book? I had not, but the Jesuit father whose place I have taken here left a well-weathered copy behind. It is a lively tale, but I assure you that Señor Montalvo is no Cervantes . . .

I told her about the Russians, the Visitor General, and the preparations for the voyage. I shared that I would not be going north, but instead remaining on the peninsula to administer the Jesuit missions. Strangely, I felt my disappointment lift as I related it to Encarna. With each line I wrung anger and frustration from my heart like water from a rag. I wondered if Encarna came by the same relief from her own writing.

When at last I paused, I discovered that an hour had passed. Fray Junípero was asleep in the adjacent cell, snoring loudly. Perhaps it was this reminder of my master's presence, but as I looked back over the leaves I had written, I worried that they might be construed as trespass. To be sure, there was nothing vulgar in the lines, but I had never written letters like these before—letters filled with frank admissions of longing, of admiration, of wild speculation. I wondered, had two religious ever shared such a correspondence? I had heard of the odd instance of priest and nun leaving the cloister to marry. But that could not happen for us—thousands of leagues of roiling sea made sure of that. And even if it could happen, I had a duty to perform here, a solemn duty under God. To be swayed by—was it the heart? Had Encarna colonized my heart? We were yet strangers, were we not? Except for one chance encounter and a few earnest letters, we had no history together. Was that the genesis of love? I was appalled by my ignorance of such things.

I gathered the three leaves of paper and held them above the candle. The edges wavered in the rising soot, flirting with the flame.

But then, what harm could a letter cause? Why should I deny my cloistered Encarna the joy of news from the farthest reach of Christendom? Nothing improper would come of our correspondence, I reasoned, because nothing could.

I took up the candle just before the pages caught. Tipping it sideways, I dripped wax on the crease and sealed the letter with my ring.

HIS PATERNITY STAYED only one night in Loreto. When I woke he was already limping around the plaza, loading his burro's saddlebags with jugs of wine from our sacristy.

"What about food?" I asked.

He waved his hand. "Portolá will bring food."

"But you will meet him six days from now. What will you eat until then?"

Eventually I convinced him to take two small meal-sacks—one each of maize and biscuit—even though I knew he would not use them.

"And a soldier," I said.

"Paco . . . "

"You cannot get to New California without first reaching Velicatá."

"Fine. One soldier."

When the dust settled behind the northbound party—friar, soldier, and burro—I gave word to the Indian woman who kept my home that I was not to be interrupted for the rest of the day. I went to my writing-desk and took up quill and ink to compose the monthly updates for the College: the count of baptisms at each of the peninsula missions, the agricultural produce, the size of the herds. But my thoughts drifted northward, imagining the reunion of Fray Junípero with Juan Crespí. Gone was the relief I had found while writing Encarna. Once again I felt the burn of envy in my chest as I saw my master and my rival embrace and shake off the dust of the journey. With each passing day, their bond would grow stronger. And I would still be in this place, alone with my figures and letters.

Putting aside my reports, I took a fresh sheet of paper and dipped the pen. There was only one man in California with the power to do what was required.

My Dear Don José de Gálvez,

I write you this letter after much hesitation, for I do not wish to worry Your Illustrious Lordship. However I felt that I could not in good conscience keep my concerns to myself. Our mutual friend, Brother Junípero Serra, has just been to see me here in Loreto, on his way to meet the expedition party at Velicatá. Though His Reverence's spirits seemed very much in order, I could not help noticing the alarming state of his physical person. In particular I am referring to the swelling of his foot and leg, the vestiges of a serpent-bite sustained several months ago—indeed on the very day we arrived in California.

My dear sir, I will be brief: I am certain that my brother will not survive a land expedition such as the one you have planned for him. Bear in mind that I know the contents of his heart as I do my own, for we have been intimates since I was but a novice and Fray Junípero was my master. I also know, by sense, that he has assured you he is fit. However we can both see that he is a small man (in stature) and that injuries of this sort are not to be dismissed when they affect such a fragile corporation.

You are the only person whose authority my brother is likely to accept. I urge you to forbid him from continuing on the expedition. Surely it is within your power to send a messenger to intercept him, or at least to send word to Velicatá before the scheduled date of departure.

Because I know how you value this expedition, and I do not wish to see it tarried in any way, let me recommend my brother Fray Luis Jayme to serve in Fray Junípero's stead. Fray Luis is due in Loreto any day now, and he is healthy and eager to serve. Fray Junípero would thus remain here on the peninsula, his convalescence supervised by me personally. Perhaps at a future date we might join our brothers in the northern frontier, but I am sure you agree that the first priority should be Fray Junípero's health and well-being.

Thank you, Your Excellency, for your consideration of this matter. I will await your reply.

Yours in Christ,
Fray Francisco Palóu, OFM

Sealing the letter with double the normal wax, I dispatched it at once to La Paz. For several days I felt the wind at my back as I moved through my daily chores, knowing that in short order the Visitor General would receive my news, and that, being a sensible man in addition to a pious one, he would dispatch a runner right away to intercept Fray Junípero. And, if he were inclined to accept the substitution of Fray Luis, he might also send word to me.

On the eighth day, I received a letter from Don Gálvez on another topic—a matter of administration unrelated to Fray Junípero or the northward expedition. The letter was dated just two days before. I concluded that my letter had never reached him. This was not unusual, unfortunately, and although I was annoyed at the poor quality of our post, I was also relieved because it meant my request had not been refused. The Lord's message was clear: writing was not the proper medium for my request. If I wanted to be heard by the Visitor General, I would have to go to La Paz myself.

TO MANAGE AFFAIRS in this farthest reach of Christendom, His Majesty could not have found a more impressive gentleman than Don José de Gálvez. Over two yards tall, with a voice so deep and sonorous that even his most brusque commands pleased the ear, Don Gálvez was the embodiment of everything the Spanish nobility believed itself to be but mostly failed to achieve. That is to say he was intelligent, generous, and not the least bit paranoid. It occurred to me that Don José might have had less noble Spanish blood in his veins than any Spanish noble I had ever met—owing, I suspect, to his mother's Swiss heritage.

I was shown into the rough-hewn shack which passed for his field office near the port of La Paz. "Padre," he said, kneeling before me and making a cross on his forehead, "it is a great honor to receive you. It would be my pleasure to receive any man named for the Most Seraphic San Francisco, but I must say that I feel especially privileged to make the acquaintance of one so highly esteemed by Fray Junípero."

Even in the stifling heat, Gálvez wore a black velvet cape over his waistcoat and trousers. Strangely, he did not sweat: his starched white collar looked as though it had been fixed to his neck only moments before. Rising from his knees, the courtier maintained his bow from the waist, so that his eyes remained below mine until he stood fully erect.

A servant brought a kettle of boiling water. Don José and I took seats at a small round table, and there we made chocolate.

My intention had been to ease gently into the subject of Fray Junípero's infirmity after a bit of light conversation. The problem I found, however, was that all of the commonest subjects men discussed on the frontier—the scarcity of foodstuffs and proper beverages, for example, or the senselessness of His Majesty emptying his purse to reach such a dry and desolate corner of the Earth—either would not concern a gentleman like Don José, with his extraordinary means and his iron-clad mandate, or else were wholly inappropriate, given his position as the eyes and ears of the King. Fortunately I recalled Junípero's mention of the man's piety.

"It is the feast of San Gregorio . . ." I murmured between sips. The chocolate was rich and dark, vastly superior to the bitter dust which passed for cocoa in Loreto. "He is a favorite devotion of mine." I raised my eyes to Don Gálvez. "And of Fray Junípero's."

"Is he? I confess that I know little about San Gregorio, other than the most basic facts."

"It is a fine story," I explained. "You see, the *vida* of San Gregorio is actually a parable on the subject of desire—"

There was a sharp crack as Don José set his mug down on the table. "You mention Fray Junípero," he said, "in nearly every breath."

"I only meant to say that His Reverence has a special devotion—"

"I received your letter last week, Fray Francisco. Pardon me for not sending my reply at once, but I have been occupied at all hours with preparation of the packet ships." He paused, holding my eyes as if by leash. "More to the point, I did not feel that your request warranted the quick reply you were seeking."

"Sir—"

"As you know I hold my faith most dear, but I cannot claim to know the nuances of decorum in your world. In my own milieu, which is to say the courts of Europe, what you have done would be considered not only rude but also treasonous, for any challenge to

authority within the hierarchy—at any level, do you understand?—
serves to weaken the throne it supports. In other words, Father, if
I were to write His Majesty with the suggestion that the viceroy
be replaced—and I am not at all suggesting this, but only using it
to illustrate my meaning—I should expect that His Majesty would
not act to fulfill the request without first considering how the move
would appear to France, and to England. And Russia . . . "

As he paused on this last word—Russia—he searched my eyes.

"So you see, Fray Francisco, your request bears on more than you
know. In my world, the penalties are swift for insubordination. At
best, a man would be removed from his delegation, perhaps reas-
signed to a post office in the Philippines." He raised his brow as if
surprised by the direction of his thoughts. "More likely, he would
be hanged."

I said nothing. For what argument could I make? I had stumbled
into a trap of my own devising.

"But I am a Catholic," the Visitor General continued, "and I do
not wish ill upon the clergy for missteps in protocol."

"Please, Don José," I said, my eyes filling quickly with tears. "I
was only concerned for his health—"

"Surely a man as learned as Fray Junípero can mind his own
health."

"He is easily distracted."

"But that is not your actual view of him, is it? You would not
patronize your superior."

"Don José, I beg your mercy. In the name of the Sinner who gave
His life so that we might all be saved from sin—"

The Visitor General allowed a smile under half of his mustache.
"This is quite a reversal, Padre. I have never before heard a priest's
confession."

"Your Excellency, please do not relate this meeting to Fray
Junípero. As you can see, I have been corrected—"

"By me alone. What if Fray Junípero wishes to add his own

admonishments? As you know, my authority extends only to temporal matters."

"And Fray Junípero's authority is similarly circumscribed! My confession, and subsequent reconciliation, will be to God, not to Fray Junípero. That is the nature of the Sacrament."

The Visitor General gave this idea several long moments of consideration, during which his handsome brow settled over his eyes like a Capuchin hood. Finally, he spoke the words I hoped to hear: "As you wish. I shall not tell Junípero."

It was as though a great stone had been lifted from my chest. Blood filled my corpse the way a vase of fresh water irrigates a wilted flower. I had never experienced such relief at confession—and this to a layman!

"The Lord be with you, Your Excellency." I made the sign of the cross on the nobleman's wide, dry forehead.

"And also with you, Padre."

As I readied my mule for the trail, I heard from the office—did I not?—the faintest hint of a laugh.

•　　　•　　　•

Port of San Diego de Alcalá, New California
July 12, 1769
LIVE JESUS, MARY, AND JOSEPH!
Most Reverend Father Lector Francisco Palóu, Beloved in Christ:
My friend, I greet you from Our Lord's most fragile beachhead. This harbor is magnificent and scenic, and every bit deserving of its fame. The hills rising up from the shore abound with nut trees and fragrant underbrush, including several species of our familiar rose of Castile. Many times already I have knelt and kissed the ground, so glad am I to be finally here in virgin territory.

The natives ply the seas in canoes made of tule reeds, which they use also to sheathe their domed houses. Unlike the pagans of Old California, these go about clothed modestly, women and children included. They subsist chiefly on seeds and acorns, which their women mash with giant stone pestles. This masa they use in cakes and gruel. The men supplement the staple with fish and game, which they appear to catch with relative ease, despite their ignorance of firearms and metal hooks.

I am anxious to establish the mission, but as of this writing, the civil authority has not granted me permission to do so. All our activity has been focused on the Monterey expeditionary party, which will depart tomorrow morning in search of the other great bay on this pagan coast. Fray Juan has been selected as diarist of the party, which is to be led by our estimable Royal Governor, Don Gaspar de Portolá. By the time you read this, they will be gone well north— God willing even to the welcoming arms of Monterey harbor.

My beloved Paco, I am conscious of the strong emotions this news will inspire in your heart. I urge you to resist the claws of envy. Your Reverence can aid this work here more by staying where you are. Note well that I do not ask after the affairs of the peninsula missions—for I know they are infinitely more secure in your hands than they would have been in mine. The better part of wisdom lies in knowing one's limitations. Our patron San Francisco Solano might have continued forever as a violinist and composer, happily ensconced in his friary outside Madrid, but God gave him the wisdom to see he was no Vivaldi. Thus he embarked across the sea to this land and filled the purpose that was meant for him all along. So must we serve, Paco, even when that service causes pain. Know that you, and your service, are always in my thoughts and prayers.

> I kiss the hand of your Reverence,
> From among the pagans of New California,
> Fray Junípero Serra

Your Reverence can aid this work here more by staying where you are. The great Catholic poet Dante, bless his soul, could not have conjured such a phrase, which in one stroke instills hope and then sucks it away! It is a type of sorrow to go about one's normal tasks knowing that absent friends are embroiled in similar drudgery elsewhere. It is quite another to hear news of one's brothers making progress toward glory.

Shivering, I realized that His Illustrious Lordship Don Gálvez had been correct in his assessment of me: I was insubordinate. Were I a soldier, indeed I should have been shot. But in a sense my fate was worse than a soldier's, for a soldier can hide his disloyalty as long as he never disobeys orders. His thoughts remain private to him; he cannot be punished for his thoughts. But my commander knew my thoughts. God Almighty knew my sins, my desires, my fears, and my misgivings. And through his earthly lieutenant, Fray Junípero Serra, He continued to punish me as I deserved to be punished, heaping indignity upon indignity, sorrow upon sorrow, letter upon breathless letter.

A week later my companion Fray Luis Jayme arrived by packet boat from San Blas. Fray Luis was fond of snuff, and he brought in his belongings a tin of excellent Oaxacan weed, which I did my best to enjoy with him. But the lightness I felt was artificial. Even in the company of a countryman I felt abandoned. We three *condiscípulos*—Junípero, Juan, and I—had been like the strands of a braid. Missing any one of its three strands, the rope falls apart. Is that not the case? Even the laws of the physical world seemed upended.

But where was my faith? My charity? Why could I not be glad for my brother's successes? Juan's glory felt like my humiliation. Every time Juan was chosen instead of me; every time Don Portolá called his name instead of mine; every time Fray Junípero sent him instructions instead of sending those instructions to me, I felt the sting of injustice. If my brother Juan were to succeed in finding Monterey—and he would succeed, or else the entire mission in New California would have to be abandoned—I would not be glad. I could not wish my brother failure. But neither could I welcome his success with an open heart.

SIX

THE MORNING OF AUGUST 26, 1770, I woke in my cell at Loreto to the cacophony of church bells. Peal after peal rang into the steamy morning, as though all the Heavenly Hosts, all the innumerable Seraphim and Cherubim, had been mustered to our town to pull the ropes of our humble carillon.

I could not imagine what occasion would precipitate such a noise. Rubbing my eyes, I left the cell and went outdoors. Normally at that hour the plaza was paved with indolent gulls; today the birds had been scattered by the noise of the bells. A scant few carved circles in the sky, but the rest had disappeared in search of their usual morning calm.

I went to the church, where I found arrayed in the pews a crowd of neophytes, with others arriving every moment in pairs and trios. My companion, Fray Luis, was nowhere in sight. Finding one of the boys who served at Mass, I asked if he had seen my companion.

"He is in the belfry, Father. Can't you hear the bells?"

I found Fray Luis directing a squad of three boys at the bell ropes. On his face was a look of such bliss, such unbridled pleasure, that I worried he had been intemperate with the altar wine.

Upon seeing me, he cried, "Brother Paco! His Excellency the

viceroy has issued a decree: all the bells in New Spain are to be rung this morning to commemorate the founding of the mission at Monterey. Let us rejoice! God's will is done!"

Of course, Monterey. Fray Junípero had written me with a full account of the proceedings: the raising of the cross on the beach where the mariner Vizcaino and Padre Asunción had done the same in 1603; the siren-cry of Fray Junípero: "Come, come you pagans, come, come to the Holy Church of Jesus Christ!"; the presence, by the end of the inaugural Mass, of a handful of curious heathen children. I knew about the hardship, the privation, the near-starvation they experienced on the journey from San Diego. And all of this came about only after Fray Juan returned from the first Monterey expedition—the one Fray Junípero had warned me of the previous July—without a clear sense of whether or not the Portolá party had found the Bay of Monterey. *At the specified latitude, all they found were great berms of sand,* His Reverence wrote me from San Diego that winter. *The governor believes the harbor described by Señor Vizcaino has been filled in.* He had chastised Fray Juan, "You have been to Rome and not seen the Pope!" But no sooner had I learned of Juan's failure than I learned of his incipient success: *Good news!* read the next letter. *There will be another expedition to Monterey . . .*

By the bells of every church in New Spain, the world now knew that this second expedition had found its mark.

From his cassock, Fray Luis produced a letter bearing the seal of the royal printers in México. "What joy, my brother! Read!"

The pamphlet contained a dramatic account of the expedition from San Diego to Velicatá, and the subsequent forays north. The author made certain that his audience understood the political significance of the Monterey settlement:

The dominion of His Most Catholic Majesty Carlos III of Spain has thus been extended over three hundred leagues northward, into hitherto claimed but unsettled territory.

I expected that a copy of the circular would be delivered to St. Petersburg as well as to Madrid.

Fray Luis was impatient for me to finish. "Have you read the mention of our brethren?"

Letting my eyes skip down the page, I found the passage:

> The Reverend Father President of those missions notes especially the contribution of Friar Juan Crespí, son of Palma de Mallorca, who served as diarist and chaplain of the two Monterey expeditions . . .

Nearly twenty years my junior, Luis Jayme had come to New Spain in a second wave of Mallorcan friars—inspired, he said, by the letters I had written home to the convent. While I was cheered by this fact (for it was proof that our rock in the sea, that wellspring of the faithful, had not yet run dry of evangelists), I also bore in mind that these men came with expectations in their hearts, visions of glory that our humble endeavors might never fulfill.

"Imagine our mothers and fathers, Paco," Fray Luis gushed, "imagine them reading this with pride in their hearts! The whole rock of Mallorca will cry for joy."

I recalled those nights at Junípero's hill retreat just before we left home, looking down on the glittering lights of Palma. How many of our countrymen had each of us adopted? Sixteen hundred? Juan Crespí had done right by his share. But what about me? What had I done?

"My mother will know," said Fray Luis, "that although it is Fray Juan whose name is published, her own son follows close behind."

"Wouldn't your mother wish it were your name instead?"

Fray Luis shook his head. "She would never. She is far too modest."

I folded the letter and handed it back to my companion.

"Do you worry about Fray Juan, Brother?" Luis asked.

"Why should I worry? He is famous now. The empire of God is so much larger for his efforts."

"But he will be embarrassed by the attention, don't you think?"

I raised my brow. "Perhaps Juan would have preferred martyrdom."

Fray Luis looked aghast. "Surely," he said slowly, "you are not suggesting that our brother wished to die . . . "

Calmly—for I did not wish to admit I had spoken out of turn—I said, "I only meant that Juan might have preferred to enjoy the glory of his accomplishments without the scrutiny of public attention."

This further confused Fray Luis. "Does he fear scrutiny? I thought he was only humble."

"He is humble," I said. "But we must not confuse humility with virtue."

Now I had confused even myself, for what was humility if not a virtue? Envy had twisted my tongue so that I could hardly control my own utterances. Fray Luis, ever generous, never again mentioned this conversation, and I myself did not recall it until years later, when Fray Luis was himself martyred, murdered at the mission of San Diego de Alcalá by a heathen whose soul the Devil refused to cede. Only then did I understand the full extent of my misstatement. For then, deprived of one of our most capable missionaries—not to mention a loyal friend—I saw that martyrdom may be a glorious end, but it is an unspeakable loss when the martyr is cut down in the prime of his usefulness to God.

At their bell-ropes, the boys were anxious to resume the celebration. "Carry on," I told them in a voice stripped of emotion. "We must praise the Lord this morning. The realm of God is greater than ever."

Fray Luis, guessing that I needed extra encouragement to feel the joy of the occasion, exhorted the boys to ring the bells with special force "for Brother Francisco, whose example we heed today!"

The boys pulled. Above our heads the hinges squealed as wood and iron conspired to produce that joyful noise, the earthly voice of God. Never has a bell so strained my heart.

.   .   .

THE VICEROY OF New Spain, Don Antonio Bucareli, was a stern-faced gentleman with a sharp nose and thin lips. On his head was the customary white powdered wig, which gave his face, by contrast, a rather ruddy character. His clothing was typical of the Andalusian nobility from which he was bred: a black velvet waistcoat, embroidered with gold thread in an oscillating, Moorish pattern. Though he was free, one must assume, to wear whatever jewelry he wished, his only adornment was a plain iron cross affixed like a brooch to his lapel.

Fray Rafael Verger—the same burly Mallorcan who had once been my master at the convent in Palma, and who related this scene to me—was shown into the viceroy's apartment by a factotum in tasseled epaulets. The windows in the apartment had been thrown open to El Zócalo, the central square of México, bringing in both a refreshing breeze and the noise of the rabble below. When the boy announced Fray Rafael and his companion, the nobleman stood and made the sign of the cross. He bid the friars to sit, referring to them as "Your Reverences," and offered them a drink of water, which they refused.

Like Fray Luis Jayme and dozens of other *mallorquíns,* Fray Rafael had followed us to New Spain, drawn by our letters and the promise of glory in God's needful vineyard. Rafael had been detained in México City, where he was appointed Father Guardian of the College of San Fernando when the old Father Guardian succumbed unexpectedly to a killing fever. In six months as Guardian Fray Rafael had never met face to face with the viceroy; Don Antonio normally preferred to correspond with the missionary officials. Thus when His Excellency summoned him to the palace, Fray Rafael was both worried and confused. Worried because the viceroy was known as a grim, humorless man; confused because work in the New California mission field had been proceeding well: Monterey had been found, the mission and royal presidio had been established and staffed. By all accounts the King—whose avatar the viceroy was, in name and in function—should have been pleased. Nevertheless, Fray Rafael prepared himself for bad news as he and his companion, Fray Emilio Rodriguez, took seats in the two elegant Philippine-mahogany chairs facing the viceroy's desk.

Bucareli did not sit. Instead, he began to pace back and forth before the windows, making two or three circuits before beginning his presentation. "We have summoned Your Reverences here today to hear a proposition which we hope will prove satisfactory to you and to your counterparts in the Dominican order. We shall speak with their Father Superior as well, though we thought it wise not to bring you here together."

After the expulsion of the Jesuits from His Majesty's realms, there remained only two missionary orders at work in the northwest frontier of New Spain. Although we had hoped for increased cooperation in the face of such insecurity, what resulted was much more like two dogs fighting under the table for a bone. The Dominican superiors in México resented the previous viceroy's decision to award the Old California missions to us, and though they had busied themselves with missionary work elsewhere, they had not forgotten the slight.

Fray Rafael knew this history, and he chose his words carefully. "We appreciate your consideration, Your Excellency," he said.

"It is well," said the viceroy, "to be judicious in such matters. The division between your orders, it seems to me, is like the one between Aragon and Castile before Fernando and Isabel. Unfortunately here we lack the tool of marriage to unite you."

He continued to pace the floor, pausing only to take a pinch of snuff from a silver box on the desk. "Nevertheless, I shall try to make peace."

"God bless Your Excellency," said Fray Rafael.

"As you know, my esteemed colleague Don José de Gálvez, His

Majesty's Visitor General, has been called back to Madrid. We feel his loss acutely, for his knowledge of the California campaign, and of the proper course of action therein, is rivaled by none except perhaps your Father Junípero, whom Don José commends above all other religious in his acquaintance. I can report to you that His Majesty is encouraged by the news from Monterey, as well as from San Diego de Alcalá, and he has authorized a considerable sum for the establishment of five new missions in the territory between these two."

"Five missions, Your Excellency?"

"Yes, five: San Buenaventura, Santa Clara de Asís, San Gabriel Arcángel, San Antonio de Padua, and San Luis Obispo de Tolosa—these are the names chosen by the Visitor General, in keeping with Father Junípero's preference for the patronage of Franciscan saints. Administratively, the process will remain the same as in San Diego de Alcalá and Monterey. However, in addition to the usual allotment of two thousand pesos per mission, His Majesty has also authorized the importation, at royal expense, of thirty additional friars from Europe to the College of San Fernando. These are meant to provide labor for the new missions and to replenish the population here at the College, which His Majesty understands has been somewhat depleted of late."

"Somewhat depleted," it should be said, was a gross understatement. In fact the College of San Fernando lacked the priests to field a choir for High Mass, let alone to staff five additional missions.

"Forgive me, Your Excellency," said my brother when the viceroy had finished explaining the finances. "You said that this proposition would benefit the Dominican fathers as well. Please, sir, how is that to happen? Are we to split the new missions among us?"

A hint of smile warmed the corner of the viceroy's dry mouth. "That is an interesting idea. But I would sooner bed my hounds with hens. No, the new missions are yours alone. Or rather, if one is to believe Don José's characterization of Father Junípero, they are *his.*"

"Quite so, Your Excellency," said Fray Rafael. "This news will please Fray Junípero more than you know."

The viceroy went on, "We do not intend for the Dominicans to work in Alta California at all. Instead they shall take over the missions formerly held by the Jesuits on the California peninsula."

Fray Rafael sat up in his chair. "But there are eighteen missions in that field!"

"Nineteen, counting the one that your zealous Father Junípero established while waiting for his supplies to reach Velicatá."

"And in return we shall be given only two?"

"Plus funds for another five. And thirty new friars from Spain. I understand that you do not allow yourselves to live alone, but even in pairs, you shall have more than enough labor. The thirty fresh men might relieve the ones who have toiled on the peninsula these many years. But that is for Your Reverences to decide."

Before Fray Rafael had occasion to speak another word, the gold-tasseled factotum was at his elbow. The two friars were led out to the passage by a side door. All the while, His Excellency never stopped pacing, his mind already on the next vexation in the anteroom.

MY JOY AT the news that we were to move north was offset in perfect proportion by the dourness of the Dominican priest who arrived to take my place. Padre Tomás Jimenez de Cuellar arrived at Loreto on the appointed day precisely, which I took as proof both of the legendary punctuality of the Dominicans and the improved efficiency of the barks in the California service. The vessel which brought Padre Jimenez would also be my passage to San Diego. She was christened *El Salvador,* and it was an apt name indeed, for I could not leave that desiccated, cactic peninsula soon enough.

Like most Dominicans, Padre Jimenez had no use for banter. In our first interview he cut straight to the heart of the matter: "You say the pagans are docile?" I recalled that I had asked nearly the same question of the ancient Fray Eugenio when I was new at the College of San Fernando. I recalled how jaded he had seemed, how hardened to the possibilities of missionary work. Now I considered if he hadn't only been eager to end the conversation, as I was with this ill-mannered Dominican.

"Docile? How do you mean?"

Padre Jimenez sneered. "Is the word not in your vocabulary? I have heard, Father Palóu, that you are famous for your skill at correspondence, but I hear no eloquence in your speech."

He had the grating voice of a jaybird, and he poked his beak around my quarters without discretion, asking after every ledger and account-book, and even the placement of the inkwell on my desk. His was the order of the Inquisition, to be sure: it was not difficult to imagine Padre Jimenez as a younger man, turning the screws on a poor sinner's thumbs. To be fair, his was also the order of the great theologians Thomas Aquinas and Catherine of Siena. Let us say that Padre Jimenez's inability to reconcile reputation with example was shared by me.

"Will you be returning to México, Padre Palóu?"

"Our Guardian extended that offer, but I have decided to go north to join my master, Father Junípero Serra."

"Ah yes, Father Junípero . . . "

"Do you know Fray Junípero?"

"Only by reputation." He paused to brush dust from a bookshelf with the meaty edge of his palm. "But that is quite enough. I have no interest in making the personal acquaintance of a missionary whose only goal is his own greater glory."

"Is that his goal?"

"Don't be naïve, Padre Palóu. Any schoolboy with a *Lives of the Saints* can see the target your humble archer Junípero aims to strike."

"Is it wrong to aspire to greatness in the name of God?"

"You and I both know that great crimes have been committed in the name of God."

With more than a little trepidation I asked, "What exactly are the crimes of Fray Junípero?"

Again the preacher smiled wanly from one side of his mouth. "I would criticize not a single act but the general pattern. Your Junípero is like a racing pony, quick from the starting line but unable to sustain his pace over greater distances. As we speak he is sprinting through pagan country, eager to raise the cross, to hang the bell from a low-hanging bough—above all, to claim the establishment for his *curriculum vitae*—but he is uninterested in the hard work of helping these missions take root. Take as an example the little congregation he gathered in Puerto Rico—"

"You have been to Puerto Rico?"

"My dear Padre Palóu, there are no secrets in America! You are an intelligent man; some part of you must have understood that your master's work in Puerto Rico was only theatre."

"By whose account?"

"I can see that you are upset. You have every right to feel as you do, for it is upon your back that Fray Junípero transfers his burden when he tires of carrying a load. Is that not correct? In these peninsular missions, for example—where is your Junípero? If you go north, Padre Palóu, let me offer a prediction: within a short period of time, perhaps a year or a little more, this pattern will repeat, and you will be left with responsibility for a new field of missions. Your Junípero will have gone on to some new place, seeking glory there, because the glory of Alta California will have been mined out like a vein of gold."

"You are rude and presumptuous."

"I have only heard the rumors about your master."

"I pity the men who serve under you, that they should be indicted by hearsay!"

My skin was hot to the touch. The Dominican's words had pierced my armor. Men of the cloth often make bold statements about the nature of this and that, but this repulsive Salamancan had touched a sore place in my heart, a wound I had thought was well hidden. I wondered who else might have glimpsed my bitterness. More to the point, I worried that when we were reunited in Alta California, Fray Junípero would know instantly the content of my heart, no matter how I tried to conceal it.

"One more question, Padre, before you go. I have read the names of the five new missions that have been authorized by His Excellency the viceroy, and I could not help but notice that there remains no mission named for your patron, San Francisco. Forgive me if this is, as you say, *rude and presumptuous,* but I should say that if it were a Dominican campaign and not a Franciscan one, the very first mission would have been named for Santo Domingo."

I had expected that the mission at Monterey, as it was to be the headquarters of the northern field, would be named for San Francisco. When it came back that the mission had been dedicated to San Carlos Borromeo, namesake of His Majesty King Carlos III, I understood the political necessity but decried the spiritual injustice. When the names of the five new missions were announced—and no Francis among them—I was simply confused.

"I hoped you would have an explanation for the omission, Padre Palóu, because it has been the subject of much discussion among my brethren."

I had searched my correspondence, as well as the travel diaries Fray Junípero had sent from Monterey, but had found no explanation for the names in the new list. Finally I remembered a conversation Junípero recalled having with the Visitor General, which His Reverence had related to me at some remove. The two had been packing crates full of vestments and liturgical vessels, each destined for a proposed mission in the north. Typically blunt, Fray Junípero had demanded of Don José when a mission would be named for Our Seraphic Father. The Visitor General had not missed a beat, but had replied right away that "San Francisco shall have a mission when he shows us his bay."

Fray Junípero had not known what to make of the statement. "He speaks like the Sphinx, Paco," he had said.

Later we learned that there was a marking on Vizcaino's old chart of the California coast, an inlet north of thirty-eight degrees which he had named for San Francisco. Despite the best efforts of more recent survey expeditions, that bay had not been found. But just as Monterey had at first eluded Don Gaspar de Portolá—and his diarist, Fray Juan Crespí—it was believed that the Bay of San Francisco would eventually be found. Until then we would abide.

"It is an oversight," I said to Padre Jimenez. "It will be rectified soon enough."

"I would not stand for such an insult if I were you."

"What luck, Father," I declared. "For today, you are me!" I heaved another ledger into the Dominican's unsuspecting arms. "Congratulations, Father President, and best of luck with your missions."

I TOOK MY berth aboard El Salvador with my head held high, having logged over a thousand leagues across the unpredictable Atlantic, followed by another seven hundred through the stormy Caribbean. During my tenure as Father President of the Old California missions, I had skipped from port to port along the rocky coast of the peninsula, sailing in vessels no sturdier than the launches used by the Indians in their pearl-fishing expeditions. Thus I had no reason to be afraid of the passage to Monterey. But God has a way of chastening those who go to sea with their hearts full of pride.

We left Loreto under calm skies, the kind of weather that the Indians say "lures fish to the air." Indeed our ship passed more than a few fishing boats on its leisurely cruise down the Gulf of Cortés, the fishermen and their boys always waving and making the sign of the cross to bid us good fortune. We were a formidable regiment of God—fifteen friars including myself, all of us drawn from the peninsular missions and thus well acquainted with the harshness of this geography. Those first few graceful days on the Gulf, we sang Mass with a full choir of five priests—rotating the duties every three days—and there was great joy among us. Most were glad just to have escaped the dry toil of Old California, which while fruitful in terms of herds and harvests had not yielded the quantity of souls we had hoped for. I myself was grateful for a happy reunion with Fray Junípero.

Onward we sailed, around the rocky capes at the southern end of California. On several occasions, the crewmen spotted the fearsome razorback fish, or marlin, as well as his cousin the swordfish. Our captain, Don Juan Pérez, a *mallorquín* and veteran of the Manila run, forbade any type of recreational fishing, despite the ardent protests of the crew. We religious too hoped that Don Juan might permit a harpoon or two to be cast out, so zealously did we relish the prospect of Satan's finned demons being hung, tail-up, for our inspection.

But no sooner had we turned the cape than was Don Juan vindicated. Just as the American continent is akin to Europe only in the most superficial sense—its earth brown, its rivers wet—so is the vast and inscrutable South Sea, into which I sailed now for the first time, dissimilar from the Atlantic. Just past the last cape, a great northwesterly wind rose up, causing the main sails to luff like the wings of a pelican. Without much alarm in his voice, Don Juan instructed the pilot to turn to lee and the crew to trim the sails. Then, in a similarly steady but firm tone of voice, he ordered everyone else belowdecks. "And take care please not to light your candles, Your Reverences," he added with typical Mallorcan grace, "for the hull may roll, and I would not want to see your wax go to waste." Though the warning was undoubtedly kind, I suspected Don Juan of concealing the seriousness of our situation. Why should he order us away from the wind? And further, what did it portend for our journey if so much caution should be exercised on a day which was, to all observation, so calm and clear?

I had my answers soon enough. By dusk the breeze had

strengthened to a gale. The captain ordered the sails tied up and all crew but the pilot sequestered below. It was close and uncomfortable belowdecks, the normal heat and odor of the livestock augmented now by the animal scent of several dozen frightened men. The vessel was, as I have mentioned, all but new, and her beams creaked with the grating timbre of Moorish wailing. The night passed sleeplessly, with the sailors playing dice and cards until one man, or just a few, had taken all the money at stake.

At daybreak, the captain announced that the worst of the storm had passed, but we had drifted further south than he had expected. We were below eighteen degrees north latitude, or approximately even with the port of Manzanillo on the west coast of the New Spanish mainland. I asked the captain if he was worried about our position. "We are above water," he replied promptly. "That is the only measure that merits my concern."

With each passing day, the atmosphere through which we traveled became thicker and more tropical—a progression confirmed by Don Juan on the twenty-fourth day, when he announced that we had drifted still farther south, crossing seventeen degrees. "This puts us at the same latitude as Acapulco," he said. It was not clear to me whether Don Juan provided these points of reference for his own sake or ours. It meant nothing to me that this stretch of endless sea was akin in some way to a seaport five hundred leagues east. Perhaps it comforted Don Juan, or gave the unflappable mariner the context that the featureless ocean withheld.

Lest one conclude that in perseverance my heart grew steely, know that throughout the ocean journey I continued to write Encarna, painting the often harrowing occurrences with a light touch.

We are now twenty-five days at sea, and our coterie is getting restless. Yesterday I rose for Mass to find my companion Fray Felipe Fuster already on deck. He had in his hand our entire morning biscuit—meant to feed ten men—which he was crumbling at his feet as though feeding birds. Note well that we are so far from land that we have seen no birds in over a fortnight, so even aside from the wastefulness, his action struck me as odd.

Well, I approached Fray Felipe and asked what he was doing. "Look, Paco!" he cried. "It is Our Lord, Christ Jesus!" He pointed up into the rigging, where on a yardarm sat perched the most grotesque and ill-mannered albatross one has ever seen. I guessed it weighed two stones.

"Is that what you mean?" I asked Fray Felipe. "That bird there?" He looked at me, uncomprehending. "What bird?"

He resumed crumbling the biscuit, stopping occasionally to pray in the direction of the bird. The albatross, you can imagine, was unimpressed. I gathered Fray Felipe in my arms and led him belowdecks, where he was given a cup of chocolate. By evening he was conversing normally again, and we all concluded that he was mended. However at supper, when the conversation lulled, Felipe quite calmly stated, "I saw the Lord today, and He refused my biscuit."

The only man who is not at his wits' end is our captain, Don Juan Pérez, a *mallorquín* who spent time in the merchant marine before entering His Majesty's expeditionary service. By chance he and I were talking about common acquaintances in Palma and he mentioned that he knows your brother. Typical for sailors, they met not in their native place but on the other side of the Earth, in Manila. He sends Marco his best. I myself wish Don Juan good fortune, because he has promised to carry my letters to post. If a storm were to sink this ship, I would mourn of course the loss of a good man's life, but more so the loss of our correspondence.

My meditations continue apace, Encarna. I have invented a pair of children for us—Enrique and Ysabel, ages ten and twelve. Our son excels at figures and wants to follow his father into the harbormaster's office. The girl is the image of you: tall and fluid, with eyes that catch the evening light. She is pious for her age, interested in the virgin martyrs, Jeanne d'Arc, and so forth. We have encouraged her not to confine herself to sacred studies before her time. Needless to say, both children love us dearly.

I am a little ashamed at how much time I spent imagining these details, but in my defense, there was little to do on the ship but meditate. At times I felt like a child playing with dolls. Other times I felt like a man lost at sea. Often I was both.

In the letters I received from Encarna before I left Loreto, she said that she enjoyed my game, that it brought her lightness in the close and humorless convent. She said it gave her joy to know that in another life, we might have been man and wife—though she did not regret her choices, nor should I regret mine. Perhaps if I had been a better reader, I might have heard the sadness behind Encarna's words. If I had paid attention, I might have known that what I had created was impossible. Two souls cannot share a world casually, as two strangers share a carriage. These "meditations" (only I continued to use this word; Encarna called the fantasy simply "our life") had become much more profound and inescapable than I ever intended. It was folly to think that when I opened my eyes and rejoined the world of the packet ship *El Salvador* I could set aside the life in my minutely detailed dreams. Nor could Encarna simply leave her reign as Queen of the Americas, Nuestra Señora de Guadalupe, to attend morning Mass in Mallorca—not when her image, surrounded by roses, was hung on a hundred thousand walls in New Spain.

AFTER A HUNDRED days at sea, we finally came even with Monterey. Shore birds lighted on our sails, and in the water bobbed the giant sea onions that grow so thickly along the California coasts. When we spotted the Point of Pines, upon whose precipice sits the Royal Presidio of Monterey, the captain ordered all the guns discharged. The battery onshore replied immediately with a salvo of its own. Thus began our celebration, with the guns embracing until our launch slid into the sandy beach and we could exchange human words and kisses.

Fray Junípero stood on the beach with a dozen neophytes in plain wool ponchos. He had taught these boys and girls to sing hymns, and their melodies came as sweetly to the ears as a draught to parched lips. With raised arms at his sides, His Reverence echoed the form of the enormous wooden cross erected behind him atop the dune. This structure, weathered from several years of seaside watch, was adorned with feathers and strings of beads, linked mussels and animal hides. The sand before the cross bristled with arrows sunk tip-down into the earth.

"*Amar a Dios!*" cried our master. "Love God, my brothers! Love God!" Then he turned to the Indian children: "See what God brings, my children? Witness the great providence of God!"

The neophytes regarded us with the most curious expressions of wonder. I would learn that for many of them, we fifteen were like a heavenly host of angels. Never had they seen so many priests together.

There were loud clunks as the rowboats lodged themselves into the sand. A soldier came to help us down from our launch, and we friars lined up to greet our kin. There is special weight to reunions among missionaries. The work is so perilous that each good-bye must be presumed to be the last, and each hello an unexpected gift. When my turn came to kiss His Reverence's hands, I could not control my tears. His sharp black eyes now wrinkled more than I recalled—weathered like the cross by time and deprivation. His palms were dry and cracked, evidence of labor he refused to delegate. I knew from his letters that he had recently moved the mission from the site of the presidio to a place two leagues south, on the banks of the Río Carmelo. *This is where the heathen have their villages,* he had written, *and thus it is where we must be.* I glanced up at the royal fort—little more than a stockade with holes bored out for the guns—and wondered how much more spartan the mission at

Carmelo might be. Junípero had described log cabins, dormitories for boys and girls, hastily constructed with what labor the governor could spare from the presidio. When I thought of relating the danger of the seas, how we had drifted south for two months, how the swells had been like the backs of leviathans, I returned to the thought of His Reverence living in this place, hundreds of leagues from the nearest civilization. He was sixty years old and in less than optimal health—my exaggerations to Don Gálvez notwithstanding. By comparison my toil at sea seemed insignificant.

"You are well, Paco?"

"More so now, Your Reverence, since we are together."

I waited for him to return the affection, but he was too impatient for news. "What of the peninsular missions? Have the Dominican fathers taken charge of them all?"

"They have. The transition went as well as could be expected."

His Reverence raised an eyebrow.

"They are glad for the challenge," I said. "And I am glad for their gladness."

Junípero chuckled. "Very well. And I am glad that you have come. So many of our brothers chose to return to México."

Thinking of Fray Felipe and his albatross, I said, "The work is demanding on the back and the heart."

"I'm afraid you have no idea, Paco. Satan's reach is strong here. The pagans cling to their ignorance."

"Not these?" I said, indicating the singing neophytes.

"No, but they are few. Even in our dormitories, the Evil One curses them with fever. We buried another yesterday, God save his innocent soul. And as we speak, Fray Juan attends the sickbed of another."

I had wondered, of course, why Juan Crespí was not among the welcome party.

Junípero shook his head. "And there are other problems, for which I have less patience, if you can imagine, than the ruses of Satan." He turned his head quickly toward the knot of soldiers farther down the beach. They passed a flagon of some dark liquor back and forth, spraying mouthfuls over the sand whenever one slapped another on the back. "Do you see the fellow with the side-whiskers? That is our governor, Don Pedro Fages."

I knew Don Pedro only by reputation. He had served as scout on the original northward expedition. According to Fray Juan's journal—a copy of which I had received in Loreto and forwarded to the College in México—Don Pedro had reconnoitered the southern and eastern coasts of an estuary believed to have its outflow at Point Reyes, fifty leagues north of Monterey. His work had earned a commendation from the leader of that expedition, Don Gaspar de Portolá.

"See how he raises his arm now and then? Listen to the cannon. He has a man at the battery who is watching for his sign."

Now that His Reverence had alerted me to it, I saw the pattern exactly: once every minute Don Pedro quit his laughing and drinking and raised his right hand in mock solemnity. When he brought it down, a gun fired on the hill. Each shot was answered by one of the guns on *El Salvador,* anchored half a league out in the bay.

His Reverence furrowed his brow in consternation. "He is that way with all our provisions. Coffee, maize, flour, wine—all of these he wastes as though he had only to click his fingers and another crate would be brought off the wharf. As though we were in Cádiz and not the edge of Christendom. Tell me, why must he pepper the bay with lead?"

"It is a celebration," I offered.

"A celebration? There was no cause for celebration last week, and still he and his soldiers drank the last cask of wine in the storehouse. At Mass, we have been using juice pressed from blackberries."

"I'm afraid I do not know Don Pedro well enough to explain his actions."

"But you will, Paco. During my absence, you will certainly make his repugnant acquaintance."

"Your absence?"

Fray Junípero's eyes burned. "The reign of Don Pedro as master of that Gomorrah on the hill can be measured now in steps. Tomorrow I leave for México, where I shall take our indignity before His Excellency!"

"But you do not mean *tomorrow* . . . "

"Yes, tomorrow! I thought your ship would never come, my friend. But now that you are here, I am free to go. I have arranged the route most expeditiously, so that I may plant the seeds of three new missions on my way. With the hands you have brought with you, we shall raise the cross on the missions of San Antonio, San Luis Obispo, and San Gabriel. Imagine the delight on the face of Don Antonio when I announce that already we have five active missions in the north. He will be sure to grant the favor of replacing the governor."

"But Your Reverence—" Was it possible that our reunion, made true after three years' wait, would evaporate so quickly? "I will go as well," I said. "You will need a companion."

"I shall have many companions," he said. "Two for each of the new missions, and when those are left behind, I will travel with Juan Evangelista." Here he indicated one of the singing neophytes, a cherub-faced boy of perhaps thirteen years. His eyes were clear, his voice strong.

Desperate for even another week in my master's company, I made what offers I could: "Let me go to San Antonio. Or San Luis. Just let me go with you."

Fray Junípero smiled knowingly. "You must remain, Paco. There is no one else I trust while I am gone."

And there I was, trapped once more by my competence.

"But I have only just arrived!" I protested.

"Yes, and already you are better suited to take my place than any Spaniard in this country." He turned once more to the soldiers cavorting on the beach. One of the youngest, whose innocuous confessions I had heard all the way from Loreto, rolled himself down the dune like a log. "Look at them," said Fray Junípero. "They are no wiser than the heathens in the bush. Many less so."

I UNDERSTOOD AT once why Fray Junípero had moved his mission to the banks of the Río Carmelo. Whereas the Point of Pines suited perfectly the requirements of a defensible fort, the near-constant wind and mist made the location inappropriate for human habitation. In fact the only living thing on those cliffs was a kind of craggy cypress tree, its foliage facing all in one direction as though turning its back on the wind. The papery gray bark came away from the trunk in sheets, and there were very few cones. It amazed me that such a plant existed—proof of God's desire to give all life a chance to thrive, no matter how ungainly.

Farther uphill, under cover of the ubiquitous pines, the wind decreased to a whisper. Light came irregularly through the canopy, as every interstice between treetops was plugged with a kind of hanging moss or lichen. The forest floor was blanketed with damp pine needles. Our steps made no noise whatsoever. The only sounds came from the birds soaring between their high nests and the seals barking on the beaches. In Monterey one could hear the seals virtually everywhere from field to forest. The soldiers made jokes about *las focas amorosas,* suggesting that the calls were the agonies of copulation, but I had seen the truth with my own eyes: hauling himself onto the rocks like a legless dog, undulating like a snail, the seal barked to confirm his survival. "I am here!" he cried. "I have lived another day! Praise the Lord!" Rising for Matins, Lauds—it did not matter when—I found comfort in their cries. We were not alone, and neither were they.

Beyond the ridge, where the winds blew less severely, the terrain slackened into a meadow of mallows and fragrant herbs. Ryegrass grew abundantly here, along with numerous lupines and prickly leaved flowering bushes I could not name. The slope decreased as we approached the mouth of the Río Carmelo. The earth underfoot, which had been thin and rocky in the higher reaches of the meadow, turned to a rich, brown loam. Here and there one found mouse-holes by the side of the path, and the furry excretions of owls. Beyond a final low hill stood a salt-marsh, full of reeds and cattails and the sharp white heads of egrets.

"Is this the same country?" I asked Fray Junípero.

He was shielding his eyes from the sun—an act unthinkable only half a league distant, on the foggy landing-beach. "Another country? If it were to place us farther away from Don Pedro, I would answer yes. But look—"

With an outstretched arm he indicated a grassy swale above the marsh, dotted here and there by low, domed structures resembling haystacks. A haze of smoke from cooking fires prevented close scrutiny of the hillside, but I could make out children playing in the clearing and women carrying baskets under their arms.

"Is that the heathen village?"

"That is their encampment, yes. But they do not have permanent villages. Those huts are constructed quickly, with bent saplings and thatching. In a way it is an ingenious design because the reeds repel water. Unfortunately the labor is wasted because they refuse to keep house. They make no provision for sewage, nor any for garbage. When the house becomes ridden with vermin, they simply abandon it. Or set it on fire."

"They burn their own homes?"

"My friend, Satan's rule is complete over these tribes. They burn their fields as well. Last autumn the entire valley went up in a general conflagration. All but the sturdiest oaks were burnt to the ground."

"No!"

"Yes—and when I asked Juan Evangelista why one would do such a thing, he told me that the deer command it."

I did not know whether to laugh or cry. "And after that? When the ground is scorched and the people are homeless—do they realize their mistake?"

"The grass grows back, as you can see. In the meantime, the heathen move elsewhere."

"Have they tried to burn the mission?"

"Not yet," Junípero said. By his tone of voice I could tell that he had considered the possibility.

At last we reached the mission site, a group of half a dozen low log buildings arranged around a packed-dirt plaza. The largest of the structures, a chapel dedicated to San Carlos Borromeo, was a square of six yards on each side and perhaps two and half yards tall. Fat gray doves perched on the roof and in the unglazed windows. When we were close enough to be noticed, a dog woke from sleeping in the doorway and ran to greet us. A couple of neophyte boys followed quickly on his heels. They were attired, like their brothers in the choir, in undyed wool. The two girls I had seen—both thin and not yet into their womanhood—wore long skirts of broadcloth and peasant blouses. None of the children wore shoes of any kind.

They came to Junípero and touched the hem of his cassock. He blessed them each in turn.

"This is Padre Francisco," he explained to the children. "He has come from the south to work with us."

A boy not more than fourteen years old, with eyes that shone like pools of ink, bowed before me. "My brother wanted to meet you, Father," he said in confident Spanish, "but God has taken him to Heaven."

The boy's voice betrayed no sadness, and so I assumed that the brother had passed some time back, and perhaps even months ago. But the anguish on Junípero's face suggested that the death had been much more recent—perhaps it was even the burial he had mentioned at the landing.

"Paco," he mumbled, holding back tears, "this is Rigoberto Palóu."

It was common in our missions to give neophytes a Spanish family name in addition to their Christian or baptismal ones, but it had never occurred to me that Fray Junípero would use mine.

"Hello, Father," the boy said. "It is a privilege to meet you at last."

"Rigoberto is a fine boy," Junípero said. "Our most gifted student of Scripture. His brother was a fine student as well."

I watched as Rigoberto—yet a stranger to me then—went to my master and put his arm around the little friar's narrow waist. "It is well, Father," he said in an even and well-composed tone. "Santiago is with Christ."

"Yes, yes," whispered Junípero. "That is true."

I HAD HOPED the next day would bring His Reverence a change of heart, that upon reflection he would no longer see the need to go to México. If the words of his youngest disciple did not move him to stay, then perhaps the sight of so many of his Franciscan brethren in this wild country would do so. There was no need to walk a thousand leagues; he could simply lift a pen. He could post a letter to the viceroy outlining his concerns about Governor Fages—and send the mission parties out on their own. But I should have known better than to doubt his resolve. True to form, he was gone before the sun cleared the ridge.

The night before, when we arrived from the beach with a two-stone sack of dried beans, the cook had slit the burlap even before it was loaded off the mule. All night the smell of simmering *frijoles* filled the mission buildings. In the morning I found Fray Juan in the kitchen, scooping beans with a tortilla. I had promised Junípero that I would be generous with Juan. We were to be the only priests in Monterey until His Reverence returned from México, a period by his estimation of at least six months. The prolongation of our row, I knew, might be fatal to the mission. His Reverence had tolerated our bickering in the past, but he could not abide distractions if they threatened our work. "I have asked Juan to keep me current," he told me. "And I expect you to do the same. You shall send dispatches to the College of San Fernando, under separate seal."

All night I had dwelt on this request. It was on one hand a brilliant tactic, worthy of a Caesar, and one which was sure to provide His Reverence with the true sense of affairs at Monterey. On the other hand, it implied a lack of trust in the two deputies he professed to trust most. Had Christ asked Andrew to keep watch over Peter, and *vice versa?*

"It has been too long," said Juan between mouthfuls.

"Three years," I said.

"I meant since we had beans."

I pulled out a bench and sat down. Juan pushed the plate of tortillas toward me with the heel of his hand. Like Junípero, he had aged considerably. The skin below his jaw had begun to wrinkle and sag, as though pulled by weights. He was more gaunt than I remembered, though his appetite had not waned. As he ate, drops of bean gravy sprinkled the tabletop. These he wiped with the next tortilla before plunging it back into the dish.

"How have you been, Brother?" he asked me.

"I am well. Glad to be done with the peninsula. I wish the Dominican fathers all the best, but I can tell you that I left that place without regrets."

"Your regrets may come yet."

"Why is that?"

Juan did not look up from his meal. "This place," he said, "is a form of torture."

His frankness surprised me, but Fray Junípero had prepared me for his sour attitude. "The heathen are hard won, I know. And the fevers. God save the soul of that poor boy's brother."

"There is that, yes. Also I miss the sun."

"The sun?"

"I feel as though I am living in a tent, a tall, gray, wind-battered tent. It has been weeks since I enjoyed a morning in the open air. Every day, the fog smothers my life a bit more."

"The clouds lift eventually."

"For a few hours. But they always return."

I thought of my experience walking over the hill to Carmel. "You must enjoy this site better than the presidio," I said.

"It is better, but still bad." He tore a strip of tortilla and used it like a rag to clean his teeth. "Brother," he sighed, "I am afraid I will suffocate here."

"Have you brought this concern to Fray Junípero? I have heard it is sunnier in the south. Why didn't you go with the others just now?"

Juan chewed the tortilla. "His Reverence did not ask me to go."

I remembered now why we had called this man Beató: his devotion—to God, yes, but also to his earthly masters—was absolutely unbending.

"Perhaps when His Reverence returns you can broach the subject of a transfer."

"I have discussed it with him already."

"And what did he say? Wait—" I raised my voice an octave, hunched my shoulders in imitation of our beloved master. "'Christ did not ask to carry the cross!'"

Juan allowed the narrowest smile, and raised his watery blue eyes. For a moment they met mine, then retreated.

I ASKED JUAN to show me the rest of the mission grounds. I was especially anxious to see the herds and cornfields, which His Reverence had mentioned only briefly. Fray Junípero had painfully little interest in agriculture (despite all his talk of "working the vineyard") and even less in animal husbandry. Though my own interests were no more earthy, I had begrudgingly acquired in Old California a working knowledge of farming and ranching. I had also studied the care of roses.

One cannot imagine how far roses were from my mind when I saw the tillage up-valley half a league from the mission buildings, close to the heathen hutches I had observed the day before. Juan showed me an overgrown *milpa* of perhaps a quarter-league square. Roughly speaking, it would have been enough to produce ten or twelve fanegas of corn, had it been planted properly. However I saw at a glance that there were as many weeds as cornstalks, and the heavy undergrowth suggested that the previous year's stubble had not been properly turned under. Such basic tasks would have been second nature to any Spanish farmer. In fact, many of the standard texts on farming—including the ones provided to missionaries by the College of San Fernando in México—only glanced at field maintenance before moving on to the more complicated topics of planting, irrigation, harvesting, and storage.

Another dire omen was that aside from the crows, Juan and I were the only living creatures attending the field that morning.

"Where are the workers?" I asked. "Have they gone for water?"

"Water?"

"To drink. If they have been here all morning, they might be thirsty."

"Oh. No, I don't believe any have arrived yet."

I looked at the sky. The sun was hidden behind the thick marine haze, but I guessed it was at least half past nine. "Tell me, Juan," I said. "How many men work this field on a daily basis?"

"Do you mean now, or when they were planting the seed?"

"Either time."

"Well, during the *sembradura,* there were perhaps a dozen. Maybe more; I don't know exactly. Fray Junípero came up here without me."

"And now?"

Juan looked confused. "Am I forgetting something, Brother? My understanding is that once the seed is in the earth, it is God's task to make it grow."

"Yes, of course. But how many came to thin the field, and to pull the weeds? Can you give me an estimate?"

"With due respect, Paco, my estimate is zero."

"Zero."

"I suppose the neophytes may have come to check the progress of the crop from time to time, but Fray Junípero and I have been so busy with the construction of the new dormitories that we did not have time to be sure."

The state of the herd was not much better, despite the excellent pasturage available nearby. A large section of the bluffs, perhaps ten times the area of the cornfield I had just seen, was enclosed with split-rail fencing. But there were no paddocks or divisions to allow for proper rotation of the stock. As a result, the herd had grazed the entire area uniformly, leaving only stubble and the gnawed stems of flowering shrubs. The herd itself numbered only two dozen head. This included the half-dozen cows we had brought in the hold of *El Salvador*, and the two calves birthed at sea. By contrast, the mission at Loreto had between five and six hundred head of cattle at all times—and that was one of the smaller herds in Old California.

In vain hope, I asked Fray Juan where the rest of the herd was kept.

"The rest, brother?"

"The milk cows, I mean. Is there a barn?"

"Oh, these cows do not give milk. They did at first, of course, but once their calves quit the teat . . . " He waved his hand, as if the rest of the story needed no explanation. Oddly, the fact did not seem to bother him much.

"Brother Juan." My voice was stern, but not so severe that it would scare him. "Listen to me. You must gather the neophytes in the chapel right away. And send a runner to the presidio. We need the carpenter."

"Is something wrong, Paco?"

Just then the wind off the ocean picked up. I felt the dampness through my cassock and tasted salt on my tongue. The seals barked on the rocks. The day before they had appeared so playful; now they seemed to be mocking me. And they had every right to laugh: we had no crops, very little stock, and in two days it would be September.

SEVEN

WORKING ALONGSIDE THE NEOPHYTES on a rare morning of sunshine, I recalled Junípero's accounts of Don Gálvez, the Visitor General, laboring like a common man, loading crates for the voyage to San Diego. What a luxury that seemed to me now—to elect labor. That morning, as in every spare hour until the barn was completed, I labored out of necessity. I performed the lowly tasks of a carpenter's apprentice, hacking bark from pine logs, whittling pegs from oak scraps, drilling holes in the beams with an ancient dull drill. The population of neophytes at the Carmel mission was a scant fifteen—most of them only boys. And the number was dwindling. Every week another neophyte fell ill with the fever and went to live in God. Only the very strongest shook Satan's curse. Every Sunday, it seemed, there was another requiem Mass, which replaced physical labor with the exhausting spiritual labor of mourning, forfeiting our only day of rest.

We enjoyed little cooperation from Governor Fages, despite the presence at the presidio of numerous able-bodied men who might have speeded our work. When I explained the dire state of our provisions—namely, that our ill-tended crop of maize would be insufficient to sustain even our mules through the winter—he shook his head dismissively: "Another packet ship is due shortly. Not to worry, Your Reverence, another packet ship is due . . . " He repeated this like a devotion, as though the act of speaking it would make it so.

"Your Excellency, suppose the ship is blown off course. When I was aboard *El Salvador,* for example, we drifted much farther south than anyone anticipated."

"Bah!" Don Pedro drew on his pipe with such force that the bowl threw sparks. He was a stout man, wound tight as a watch spring. His nickname, earned in Sonora, was *El Oso,* and indeed his chest was so wide relative to his height that one might imagine there was a small bear stuffed inside his blouse. "We were not sent here to till the fields," he told me. "This is an outpost of the Crown, and the Crown shall provide for its maintenance. That is simply the order of things."

"I do not doubt the largesse of His Majesty, sir, but only wish to remind Your Excellency that the sea is rough and fickle—"

"I know the sea! I know vastly more than you, I would wager, on that particular subject. I know also that we have flour and lard enough for six months at a minimum. At a minimum, do you understand? And if no packet boat reaches us in that time, then I should think the Spanish Empire will have fallen altogether! We shall be men without country then, and even you can see that would be far worse than the deprivations you are describing. A little hunger we can all abide, Padre. Tighten that cord around your waist."

However much it pained me to see Fray Junípero leave for México, I understood that he had been correct about Don Pedro. Left in this man's care, the colony would almost certainly fail.

In spite of the governor's intransigence, the dairy barn was completed the first week in October. During those weeks of heavy labor, I became close with many of the neophytes, especially Rigoberto, the boy who bore my name. At first I did not know how to approach him, my unexpected foster son, but after a few awkward exchanges, we found a comfortable rapport. He was, as Junípero promised, an avid student of theology, but his curiosity ranged far beyond the sacred. I shared details of my childhood in Mallorca, that tiny speck of soil which must have seemed like the capital of all Europe to these Indians. And Rigoberto reciprocated with stories from his upbringing among the local tribes, whom he called the *oh-loh-neh*. One evening we sat together on a bench outside the chapel, muscles aching from the day's labor. On the hillside behind the mission, smoke rose from the *rancheria*—the semi-permanent village where the pagan people kept their huts.

"Tell me, Rigoberto," I said, "Why do your people celebrate the harvest of the acorns? We have a harvest festival in Spain, but in that case we are celebrating the fruits of our labor. If your people have not labored in cultivating the oaks, nor irrigated them in hopes of greater produce, what is the substance of their celebration?"

Rigoberto puzzled over this for a moment, his dark eyes searching the hills. "I believe it is the Earth, Your Reverence. They thank the Earth."

"But God made the Earth," I reminded him.

Lines of worry stretched across the young brown face. Though he had adapted very quickly to our language and religion, Rigoberto still had not accustomed himself to the idea of useful debate. For him, a disagreement was something to be resolved quickly, rather than chewed like tripe for one's intellectual edification.

"Father, I have insulted you."

"Not at all. I only wondered if their celebration is not like giving thanks for the waves of the sea, which come every minute without pause for ever and ever, no matter how we dance and cry out."

"But the acorns are not like the waves, Your Reverence. They fall either lightly or heavily, and sometimes not at all. There were years in my youth when the oaks gave nothing and the people had to eat only roots and herbs for many months. The same is true for the sweet nuts of the piñons—there are good years and bad."

"Yes, but whom do they thank in the good years, if not God?"

"Do you mean to say that they cannot thank Jesus Christ because they do not know he is Lord?"

"Of course. But who do they believe is responsible for a plentiful crop?"

I saw my son's frustration. Bless his faithful heart, he traveled every day to the edges of his knowledge like a mower in a field of grain, pushing the boundary a yard farther, the next day another yard, then another. A lesser neophyte would have abandoned the effort, laid down in the field, and let the grass grow around him, but not Rigoberto.

"If you are willing, Father," he said brightly, "tomorrow I shall show you how my people think of the spirit world."

THE *RANCHERIA* WAS perched on a shelf overlooking the valley of the Río Carmelo. Rigoberto and I followed a deer path up the side of the valley, threading our way between the hard-leaved sages and manzanitas. Because the hillsides had seen so little rain since spring, the knee-high grass was brittle and golden, the seed heads waving in parody of our failed wheat crop below. Rigoberto, normally so full of questions, spoke very little on our walk, and normally only to warn me of a thorny cane or a patch of poisonous herbs up ahead. I was content to be silent, for the wind made a pleasant noise in the dry grass, and several species of thrushes called from their perches in the oaks.

Just below the *ranchería*, I heard the first human voices, singing in the staccato rhythm characteristic of the tribe. It was a work song. The women of the village sat before the doors of their huts next to wide baskets filled with acorns. Between her legs, each woman held a stone *metate*, or grinding mortar, a trough of smoky gray granite. In her fist was another stone, like a pestle, though larger and more unwieldy. The women had no trouble lifting these heavy pestles over their heads and slamming them down upon the *metates* with tremendous force. The resulting crack was timed to correspond with the chanting, so that it enhanced rather than detracted from the music. When the acorn mash reached the desired granularity, the woman swept her forearm across the surface of her *metate,* whisking the masa into another basket, this one of much finer weave. Amazingly, the woman missed hardly a beat before throwing another handful of acorns upon the mortar between her legs.

Like all the pagans I had seen in Monterey, the women of Rigoberto's village wore loincloths of rabbit skins to cover their nudity. The grown women also wore aprons adorned with beads and shiny black cormorant feathers. The girls had only the rabbit skirts, leaving their breasts bare but for a layer of dark mud-paint. The skin of men and women alike was covered in hideous raised scars—on their arms, legs, and even faces. Rigoberto himself bore these disfigurements as a reminder of his pagan childhood.

Curiously, I saw no men or boys amongst the acorn-grinders, although I knew not to trust my eyes. Like players on stage, boys often masqueraded as women among these tribes. Junípero himself had been fooled on at least one occasion, when he erroneously baptized a young woman "Maria Josefina," only to learn the next day that she was a boy. The mistake was borne out in the baptism register, with the name corrected, in His Reverence's hand, to the masculine "José Maria." I never met the boy. He perished before my arrival and was buried in the chapel yard.

Though I had been warned by Fray Juan and others that the heathens were hostile to members of their tribe who had joined us at the mission, I did not find this to be true. Rigoberto, attired in his ordinary woolen poncho, approached the women peacefully, and they put down their grinding stones and listened. He spoke rapidly in the heathen tongue, which he was teaching me one phrase at a time. I picked out the words for "father" and "acorn," but little else. As he conversed with the elder women, curious young girls emerged from the huts until there were perhaps fifty girls and women gathered all around. I was surprised by the size of the settlement, which appeared so small from a distance. In fact the heathen of New California were much more numerous than those of the peninsula, although they did not confederate themselves like their southern neighbors. According to Rigoberto, the inhabitants of one *rancheria* did not consider themselves kin to those in the next, even if the two villages were only a league apart. As proof, he demonstrated that he could not understand the native tongue of Junípero's servant Juan Evangelista, nor Juan Evangelista his own, although both hailed from villages in the Río Carmelo valley. When pressed, he admitted that the villagers intermarried, but this still did not explain the separate languages. *The curse of Babel,* wrote Fray Junípero in one of his early letters, *descended here with particular force.* By the time I left Mission San Carlos several years later, the population of neophytes would represent eleven tongues, each as dissimilar to the next as Hebrew is to Castilian.

With caution I approached the gathering of women, opening my arms to demonstrate that I meant them no harm. *"Amar a Dios,"* I said gently.

Rigoberto translated and made the sign of the cross in the air. Several of the girls imitated his gesture, drawing crude crosses of their own and trying to reproduce the sound of my voice with their untrained lips. This displeased their mothers, who chastised them with rapid clicks that sounded like the chattering of squirrels. Finally an older woman came forward and said something to Rigoberto.

"She has a gift for you," he explained.

"And I have one for her." I bowed and untied the sack of beads from my waist-cord.

At the sight of the sack, the Indian women snapped to attention and jostled one another for access to me. Rigoberto issued a long string of foreign sounds and tried to hold them back with his arms. He failed, and the sack dropped from my hands, spilling its contents onto the ground. All around me now, women and girls picked at the earth like birds, snapping up whatever glass and ceramic beads they could grasp. The air was thick with dust and the odor of unwashed bodies.

Finally there was a sharp crack like the sound of a gun, though I knew it could not be, for the heathens owned no firearms. When the dust cleared I saw the older woman, the one who had begun our discussion of gifts, standing apart from the group. Above her head she held two pestles. In a torrent of rough words she lambasted the others, and many began to cry.

Rigoberto was mortified. "Had I known this would happen," he said, "I would not have asked you here."

"Tell them to keep the beads. They are a gift from the fathers of the mission. Explain that if they wish to have more, they may join us for Mass."

Rigoberto obeyed. I saw him point several times down the valley. Gradually the aggrieved faces relaxed. Next to the headwoman stood a girl, only recently into her womanhood, to whom Rigoberto addressed himself most often. She interrupted him several times to ask questions, which he answered in his normal style, pausing to consider his words carefully. It was curious how easily I followed their exchange, even ignorant of their tongue. From the way he held himself—shoulders curled inward, head bowed, looking up only to speak—I surmised that he held the girl in high esteem.

"Father, they wish for you to taste the *atole*," he said, returning effortlessly to Spanish. "It is the first of the season, and the honor of the first taste goes normally to the headman of a neighboring village."

"I would be honored."

"They wish also to apologize for their behavior over your gift—"

Here the girl interrupted Rigoberto with a few more words. He nodded and replied.

"The chieftess herself," he explained to me, "wishes to apologize for her behavior. She hopes that as a close neighbor, you will forgive her."

"Jesus Christ forgives all."

Rigoberto conveyed this to the group, making a slow sign of the cross when he invoked, in Spanish, the Holy Name of *Jesucristo.*

Now another woman, this one perhaps even older than the chieftess, emerged from the crowd bearing a small basket, the size of a soup bowl, full of steaming porridge.

In silence, I lifted the basket to my lips and felt the warm, wet meal slide onto my tongue. Surprisingly it was not at all bitter. It tasted instead like unseasoned wheat porridge. According to Fray Junípero, this was the staple of all the heathen he had encountered in New California. I wondered how anyone would care to eat more than a spoonful of something so bland. More to the point, I wondered how a palate raised on acorn stew might adapt to the strongly spiced dishes so popular in the rest of New Spain.

Lowering the basket, I said to the chieftess, "Thank you, *señora,* for this honor. I hope that you will join us soon at the mission so that I may repay the favor."

The chieftess said something to Rigoberto and called for another basket of porridge, which was delivered to his hands by the same wizened cook.

"Come, Father," he said. "There is more to show you."

I followed my son behind the row of thatched huts, where the deer path continued along the valley wall. Not ten fathoms gone from the village, I heard a series of thumps and turned to see the women had gone back to their work, hunched over their *metates* as the chorus of their voices filled the heavy morning air.

THE SWEAT LODGE, or *temescal,* was dug so deeply into the hillside that I did not see it as we approached. My first thought, upon seeing the plume of smoke rising from the earth, was that some of the dry grass had caught fire. I reached for Rigoberto's elbow.

"There is no danger, Father," he assured me. "That is from the men's lodge. Come."

The low walls of the building were fashioned from saplings and pine branches, like the sleeping huts. However the roof was not grass thatching or reeds, but dried mud. In the center of the roof a hole the width of a man's hand belched bright white smoke in a continuous, wavering stream. The entrance, facing the deer path, was a square like the cabin-hatch on a small sailboat, just wide enough for a man to wriggle through on all fours. The hole was covered by a flap of deerskin.

Rigoberto shed his sandals before kneeling and signaled for me to do the same. He put his hand to one side of the flap, as if he meant to lift it open, then paused and called out a string of words in the heathen tongue. The call was answered, verbatim, by a man inside. Now my son lifted the deerskin, and a great cloud of smoke poured out, obscuring my view of the entrance. When the smoke dispersed, he was gone. But he was only negotiating permission for me to enter, and in a moment, a familiar hand emerged to beckon me in.

At first I could see nothing; the smoke stung my eyes and lungs like poison. I began to cough. Each vain inhalation brought nothing but more smoke. My chest felt as though it would collapse. Then a hand gripped the back of my head and shoved me down to the floor, smashing my nose against the earth. I thought for sure this was the end, that I would be martyred this way, and that it would be left to hapless Fray Juan to seek out my bones in this infernal earthen hut. But then I took a breath and found the air much more pleasant than above. Along the floor it was cool. The earth smelled damp.

I heard laughter, surely at my expense. I did not care. I only wanted to regain myself, bid good-bye to Rigoberto, and take my leave. This was the clearest evidence I had encountered that these pagans were in step with the Devil. Who else would spend his time in a replica of hell?

I could not determine how many others were present with us, but from the timbre of the voices, I knew all were men. Amid the tangle of foreign words I recognized my name: Fray Francisco.

"Father," said Rigoberto in Spanish. He was somewhere to my right, but I still could not see him through the smoke and dark. "Are you breathing well now?"

With great difficulty I replied, "Yes, my son." The smoke had scorched my throat so badly that it hurt to speak. From the left, someone handed me an object which felt like a wooden spoon. By the time I realized it was a dipper, I had spilled water all over my cassock. The hidden hand took back the dipper and a few seconds later it was returned to me, refilled. I raised it carefully to my lips. I gave thanks, but my words were drowned by the sudden noise of two sticks rapping against one another in regular time. At last my eyes became accustomed to the haze. I saw a weathered heathen man, very old by Indian standards (though not more than fifty), slashing the air with a wooden switch which had been split down the center line. When the man's stroke changed direction, these parallel tongues slapped together, producing a crack. He was expert at keeping the rhythm of the cracks in time with his chanting—the substance of which I did not comprehend. The old man and I were not five feet apart, but he did not acknowledge my presence in any way. Rather, he appeared to be in a kind of wide-eyed trance as he waved his musical stick.

Gradually the other men began to accompany his song with their own chanting. On my left two men thumped their chests, using the impact of the blows to make their voices rise and fall in pitch like African drums. Curiously, the heat and smoke inside the lodge did not dull my senses, but rather enhanced them in unusual ways. After my eyes became accustomed to the low light, I found that my sight was especially sharp. I was able to see, for example, the gradual disintegration of each stick in the fire. I learned that the old man with the clapping device performed a variety of duties in the lodge, for it was he who stoked the fire and also he who passed around the sharpened deer ribs that the men used to wipe sweat from their limbs. From time to time he also added to the fire handfuls of what appeared to be the small dried leaves of the manzanita bush. This addition gave the smoke a nutty aroma and made it thick and white, like a paper fire. The mixture must also have contained tobacco, for after each addition I smelled the earthiness of pipe-smoke and felt the pleasant lift one feels after taking a pinch of snuff.

I was passed half an abalone shell filled with dark paste. Copying the motion of the previous man, I dipped two fingers into the shell and licked them clean. My mouth filled with a burning sensation that was neither the fruity, acid bite of *chiles* nor the scalding of coffee sipped too hot. I became convinced, in my altered state, that the fire itself had entered my body. I began to sweat profusely. In a minute's time my cassock was drenched. The weight of the wet cloth pushed me back against the wall, and there I crouched, curled upon myself like a frightened dog, as the chanting grew louder. A man who had been picking lice off the scalp of his neighbor now produced an unstrung bow from a long deerskin sheath. He stroked the weapon from end to end, running his rough fingers along the diamonds and curls carved into the wood. Then he threw back his head and howled like a coyote. The other men joined him, so that now the walls of the lodge reverberated with the howling. I reached up to clap my palms against my ringing ears but found my hair soaked, my cheeks slippery and cool. All along my arms and legs, my skin felt as though it were crawling with ants. Like a beast, I began to scratch at myself, rubbing the skin until it broke, until my fingertips were wet with blood.

Then my skin turned cold and I stopped scratching. I began to shiver instead. I looked to Rigoberto for help and saw instead the unmistakable face of Fray Junípero. *Know that I love you,* said the face. The voice was Rigoberto's, but the words were *mallorquín,* a tongue he did not know. *All these years, Paco, I have loved you most.*

"Why, Your Reverence?" I cried. "I am a disgusting sinner! If you knew the contents of my heart, you would hate me even more!"

Why do you think I hate you?

"You favor Juan. It is obvious. I cannot shed my resentment. And what's more, I have been carrying on a correspondence with a cousin, a woman, that I fear is unwise. Forgive me, Father, please."

You shall be tested.

"When, Your Reverence?"

At that moment, the face of Fray Junípero disappeared, and the speaker was once more the neophyte Rigoberto. His eyes were filled with tears, perhaps as a result of his own ill digestion of the paste.

That is the last I remember. When I came to my senses, I was outside, and it was night. Crickets chirruped in the sage. I was splayed out along the deer path, my lips caked with vomit.

RIGOBERTO WOKE BESIDE me, also shaken. For a moment he held his face in his hands. He did not know yet that I was awake. He looked toward the sun, saw that it was in the eastern hills, wiped his mouth with the hem of his poncho.

"Where are the others?" I said.

"Father—" The sound of my voice had startled him.

"Are they still inside?" I nodded in the direction of the sweat lodge, just a few paces down the path. The smoke had ceased to flow from the outlet, but its scent was still on the air.

"They have gone to hunt deer. Do you remember the dance?"

I shook my head, worried what else I did not remember. I had spoken aloud to the image of His Reverence, I was sure of that, but I could not recall my words, nor the tongue I had used. If it were *mallorquín*, I had nothing to fear: I would explain to Rigoberto that it was only an old prayer, that I had felt God nearby and simply wanted to pray. It was very nearly the truth.

"You do not remember my brother dancing with the antelope mask?" Rigoberto folded his shoulders. "You said that he looked like Satan."

"I hope you did not convey my meaning."

"Of course not."

I felt depleted, bone-weary, and gained my feet only with great difficulty. "We should go back. Fray Juan and the others will think we have been killed by coyotes."

There had been howling, I recalled suddenly: had that been from animals or men?

The walk back to the mission took only twenty minutes, and I was reminded once again how near we dwelt to the pagan world. Also how few we were, relative to them, and how isolated. We were two friars and a tiny band of vulnerables. This was our army against the legions of Satan.

There were horses in the paddock when we arrived at the mission. I recognized Governor Fages's filly by the white blaze on her face. My pulse quickened. Could it be that an absence of one night had prompted Fray Juan to call the governor?

A neophyte met us in the road. He implored us to come inside. His face was stricken, as though someone had died.

"Is it the fever?" I asked.

"Don Pedro has come from Monterey, Your Reverence. He has news."

I hurried to the receiving-room, the neat but unadorned chamber we kept for entertaining guests. Like all of the buildings in the mission compound, it had been constructed hastily of rough lumber and was already showing signs of age. In time it would have to be replaced by proper structures of adobe or stone. For now it was ideal: I did not wish Don Pedro to forget our deprivation.

I found the three of them—Don Pedro, his lieutenant, and Fray Juan—seated on benches around the shipping crate we used as a table. Fray Juan had made chocolate, to which the soldiers (by the smell of it) had added spirits.

Don Pedro rose to greet me. "Fray Francisco, we were worried. Are you well?"

"What is your news?" I was in no mood for false concern.

Don Pedro acted as though he were offended by my manner. "Who told you I had news? Is it so unfathomable that I should visit for pleasure? We Spaniards are so few here; we should enjoy one another's company, don't you agree?"

"With respect, Your Excellency, your pleasures and mine are not the same."

"Perhaps. But it remains that in this wilderness, people of reason should stay close."

"Especially now," added Fray Juan. As soon as the words had escaped his lips, he flushed and stared sheepishly at his sandals.

"Why do you say that?" I asked my brother. "Why especially now?"

Don Pedro spoke quickly. "It is nothing, a small inconvenience. Nothing more."

"Sir, I am in charge of this mission until Fray Junípero returns. I have a responsibility to our neophytes, and if there is news which concerns their welfare, you must share it with me. That is your responsibility."

Don Pedro tapped his fingers on the hilt of his sword, as if considering a more expedient end to this conversation.

"There has been a letter from the south," he said. "The packet *San Antonio*, which was to have reached us next month, was damaged in a storm and has returned to San Blas."

"But there will be another—" added Fray Juan. The consistent note of innocence in his voice, which so magnified his perfect faith during Mass, now seemed like naïveté.

"There will be no ship until spring," said Don Pedro. "It would be foolish to send it earlier; the sea is too rough." His face grew long, and he drew out his pipe. He made a great show of packing the bowl from a leather pouch—a gesture that seemed now, under the circumstances he had just revealed, the picture of imprudence.

I anticipated the ultimate purpose of the governor's visit. "You have come to ask for grain," I said. "But we have none to offer."

"Is there wheat remaining from the spring?" asked the lieutenant, his brow poised thickly over his weak eyes. He looked, in his pathos, like a hungry retriever.

"The portion which is not spoiled already we must reserve for the mules."

"For the mules!" scoffed Don Pedro. "You will give our last fanega of grain to your mules?"

"Without them we cannot work."

"When there are two mouths to feed, Fray Francisco, and one belongs to a mule, it is an easy choice."

"Would you eat the mule as well, after he has perished?"

Don Pedro's eyes burned. "I have eaten worse."

It was well known that on the first northward expedition, the party had been reduced to eating bear meat, which the soldiers killed in a valley called Los Osos. Fray Juan, in his diaries, described the flesh as tough and oily but not foul tasting. When the meat ran out, the men ate their saddles, cut into strips and boiled. After that, they simply starved.

"What example do we set for the heathen," I said, "when they see us slaughter our mules? Already they think we are cursed by fevers and evil spirits. To that you suggest we add savagery?"

"They are the savages, not us!" Saliva dripped from the stem of the governor's pipe. "I shall never predicate my decisions on how they will be received by a population of ignorants!"

"Even a savage admits his mistakes," I said. I was not afraid of Don Pedro. This revelation about the packet boat, which all but assured our starvation, made me fear him even less.

"It seems as though you are referring to a particular mistake, Padre."

"I am."

He snorted, "Tell me, what is my great fault?"

"When I asked for your assistance with the construction of the dairy barn, you refused to lend your men. You said the packet would provide for us. And now we learn that the ship has returned to port."

"Are you vindicated, Fray Francisco?"

"I am not measuring my decisions, sir, but yours."

"You argue well. Much better than your brother Junípero. I could not argue with him. Every disagreement became a matter of life and death. Do you get that sense from him as well?"

I heard Juan shift in his seat. I had no intention of answering. Don Pedro had no right to know my private opinions of Fray Junípero— even when they concurred with his own.

Then, without prompting from me, Don Pedro said, "It was wrong to rely on the packet for supplies. I should have sent the assistance you required. It was a mistake." The lines on his face relaxed, and he puffed his pipe with relish. "But I see that you have the barn completed anyway. Very fine work, I should say."

"The cows are glad," I said. This earned smiles from the soldiers, but they would prove to be the last smiles any of us would allow for many months. As the little governor and his sad-dog lieutenant swung onto their ponies for the ride back to the presidio, I began to count in my mind the mouths those glad cows would have to feed. There were twenty-five soldiers at Monterey, outnumbering the milk-cows five to one. When one added myself, Fray Juan, and the neophytes of our mission, the conclusion was grim. The cows' gladness, like our health, could not possibly last the winter.

THE RAINS CAME in November, one furious storm after another. On the bluffs above the sea, where cattle grazed heedless of the chaos around them, the water came from above and below, falling from the sky in great sheets and rising off the rocks in thick clouds of spray. This was weather for seals and other beasts with the good sense to keep themselves hidden beneath the waves.

Indeed, some of God's creations flourished in the wetness, yet the Lord's greatest creature, the one cast in His own image, suffered profoundly. For us, the rains had come too late: the corn crop had yellowed through September until the fields were indistinguishable from the golden hillsides, and when a wildfire swept down the valley in late October, we did not bother to fight the flames. Besides the fact that there was no crop to save, we simply lacked the energy to perform such an arduous task. Each morning we were given a single bran tortilla smeared with a spoonful of beef tallow. By noon, when the small satisfaction of this meal had worn off and the hunger returned, many of us retired to our cots, being too fatigued to do anything else.

Supper was a ration of milk, two standard cups, warmed if the night was cold. One of the neophytes—whoever was least ill that day—walked a mule over the hill every morning, strapped with casks of milk for the soldiers. We waited every noon for his return, watching the ridgeline for his lengthening form and the long pointed ears of the mule. Sometimes the boy returned without the mule, and I knew that on those occasions, there had been no negotiation: a soldier had simply stepped up and commandeered the animal, without explanation or payment. I never asked the boy to explain. I only thanked God the butchery had occurred on that side of the hill, hidden from the impressionable tribes.

I had learned from Rigoberto that the heathen believed all men to be descended from one of several animal lineages. Rigoberto's family was Coyote, for instance, and Juan Evangelista's was Bear. The elders had recently decided that white men came from none of the old families but a new and extremely powerful lineage— Donkey—whose discordant cry and fumbling gait belied his true cunning nature. I could only guess how the pagans would react if they knew we were now cannibals as well as connivers.

Our only salvation, as Don Pedro had been quick to point out, was milk. Sheltered in the barn from the frigid night winds, the cows produced happily as long as they were allowed afternoons in the newly verdant meadows above the beach. Without the daily ration of milk, I am sure that I would have perished. Even with the daily cups, my strength was low and my bowels were loose most days. The problem was much worse for the neophytes, who seemed unable to hold down even the most modest amount of milk. As soon as it was down their throats, their stomachs began to clench and twist, and like babies, they spit the mixture up half-curdled. Those who did manage to hold a day's ration were besieged by intestinal troubles, such as occurs when one drinks from a contaminated well.

Up on the hillsides, the fires continued to burn in the kitchens and sweat-lodges of the heathen, and the smell of boiling acorns, once repulsive to me, danced down the valley like the scent of fresh bread. The temptation was strongest for the neophytes themselves, who had once enjoyed that type of food and surely longed, in some portion of their hearts, to be once more seated around a fire with their fingers in a bowl of mush.

But the Lord could not permit regression. As missionary, it was my solemn duty to prevent any soul baptized in Christ to be wrested back by Satan. Thus if a neophyte endeavored to flee the mission, I was forced to react with swiftness and due force. Only the most trusted neophytes, such as Rigoberto, were allowed to visit the *rancherías,* and then only accompanied by me or Fray Juan. Though it pained me to do so, I had already reprimanded half a dozen boys and girls that winter for attempting to escape.

One cold morning in December, shortly before Matins, I heard a noise outside my cell. I did not wake Fray Juan, but went outside alone to investigate. I found one of the littlest neophytes, a boy called Juan Diego, struggling with the latch on the outside gate. The entire fence around the compound had been recently reinforced by order of Governor Fages, who had also installed two guards outside the dairy barn to protect from theft and predation the colony's only reliable source of food. This evening however the guards were nowhere to be seen, but their brothers' handiwork had foiled the boy, who could not unlatch the gate.

I called out, "Juan Diego, what are you doing?"

The boy regarded me with wet deer eyes. He turned back to the gate, gave it one final, futile attempt, and then said, as calmly as he could, "Hello, Father. I had a dream this gate was open. I came to check it."

"Very well," said I, "now that you have your answer, you may return to your cell."

"Yes, Father," said the boy. He hung his head and walked slowly across the plaza toward the dormitory.

Feeling satisfied, I began walking to my own quarters. But as soon as my back was turned, I heard feet scratching on dirt. The boy had taken off running, this time toward the opposite corner of the compound, where the fence was lowest. I hurried after him, but he reached the fence first. Like a squirrel, he scaled it instantly, but his clothes became entangled at the top. There was the horrible sound of cloth ripping, and then a yelp. I found the boy suspended like a snared rabbit, dangling by the sleeve of his poncho.

"May God forgive you and keep you," I huffed. That quick pursuit was the most I had exerted myself in weeks. Already I felt my muscles ache.

The boy cried, "I love Jesus, Father, but I am so hungry! Why does God ignore our prayers?"

"Satan's curse endures, my son."

"But I do not feel cursed, Fray Francisco, only hungry. If you will permit me to go to my sister's house in the *rancheria,* I will bring enough food for everyone."

By this point others had heard our noise and emerged from the dormitories. Fray Juan, who still had some strength left in his ropy muscles, lifted the boy off the post and set him down at my feet.

"I cannot let you go," I said to the boy. "You have been baptized in the Lord. I must keep your soul for Him."

I thought of something Fray Junípero had said about the soldiers when I arrived at Monterey: "They are no more wise than the heathens. Many less so." I wondered if His Reverence might have condemned us all, for I felt no wiser at that moment than the most ignorant infantryman. Lord forgive me for saying so, but if it were wisdom to let this poor child starve to death, I would have preferred to remain ignorant forever.

The boy's poncho was torn down one side, so that I could see his ribs, plain as finger bones, through the skin. All his stores of extra flesh had been exhausted, and his stomach was now distended like an infant's. I knew that if he did not have food soon, he would perish.

I walked to the gate and lifted the latch. "Go," I said to the boy. He did not move at first. Perhaps he sensed a trap. But when he saw that I was earnest, he took one small step, then another, and then finally dashed through the opening. When he was a hundred yards away, he paused and turned back. "I will return soon, Father," he yelled. "Thanks be to God!"

THE NEW YEAR was a procession of gray days linked by long, black nights. I knew in my head that each time the sun rose it would hang there longer than it had the day before, but in my heart I could not believe this was so. This was probably because we never actually saw the sun, but only a gradual lightening of the gray shell over our heads. The grayness affected some more than others, but none more than my companion, Fray Juan Crespí, who spent most days alone in our cell, emerging only to take those humble rations I have described previously. He received no visitors, not even those neophytes whose principal shepherd he had been since baptism.

One of these was a shy boy named Teófilo, who had taken Fray Juan as his spiritual guide. With his light eyes and broad chest, Teófilo bore a striking resemblance to Fray Juan, so it was no surprise to me that the boy had chosen my brother as his model. Indeed, Teófilo was inseparable from his master, as though held by a tether. All of Juan's Masses were served exclusively by him, with no assistance from the other neophytes. When Juan went to the *ranchería*, it was Teófilo who volunteered to be his interpreter. Teófilo even fetched my brother's chocolate in the mornings after Lauds. But as the winter set in, and our privation grew more dire, Juan began to reject the boy's offers of assistance and companionship. I found this especially odd because I had never known Juan to favor solitude. He took great pride in the completeness of his religion, which among other things meant respecting Our Seraphic Father's sincere wish for community among his followers. To see my brother pull away from Teófilo, therefore, was to see a rare failing in Juan's devotion to the Franciscan Rule.

Of course I did not point this out to him. I had no time for remediation. My own work had been increased in direct proportion to Juan's truancy, so that I had only enough energy to get through each day without collapsing from hunger and fatigue. Juan's negligence was not lost, however, on Teófilo, who came to see me one evening as I knelt in the chapel at silent prayer.

"Forgive the interruption, Father," he said. "May I speak to you about Fray Juan?"

I crossed myself and rose to meet him. "Let us find a bench," I said.

The boy stopped me. "If you do not mind," he whispered, "I would prefer to stay here." His shoulders, once so strong, were still broad but now turned in upon his chest like curled paper. "I am worried," he said. "His Reverence never leaves his cell, much less the mission compound. The elders in the *ranchería* have begun to ask about him."

In the weeks since poor Juan Diego had gone to beg at his sister's door, we had sent several more neophytes to the *rancherías* in search of food. The heathens had not hesitated with their generosity: they sent the boys back with baskets of acorn meal, dried berries, and smoked deer meat. When I finally climbed to the village myself (it was not easy to find the strength), the head woman refused to accept my thanks. "She says this comes from the Earth," Rigoberto explained. "The oaks produced more heavily this year because you were here. Thus the acorns were always yours; she only gathered them up for you." Privately, I wondered if the chieftess would have been so generous towards the mission if we had not been sheltering young people of her race. Had we been composed of only white men, like the presidio encampment, I doubted she would have been so free with her surplus.

I asked Teófilo, "You say they mentioned Fray Juan specifically?"

"Yes, Father. Last I was there, the headman of my village asked if Fray Juan had passed away."

"And what did you tell him?"

Teófilo looked confused. "I told him His Reverence was very much alive, of course, but ill." He paused, looked quickly into my face. "Is that not true?"

"It is a kind of illness, yes. But tell me, what do they say about him?"

"They understand that His Reverence is especially devout, which they appreciate even though they do not yet accept Our Savior."

"And does Fray Juan's devotion make them more inclined to hear the Good News?"

Lately I had begun to fear that Junípero, when he returned, would be furious to find the number of neophytes so greatly reduced. Being powerless to ward off the fever—and only somewhat able to counter starvation—I realized that my only hope for rebuilding the mission population was baptism. Thus I paid close attention to Teófilo's news. The headman's asking about Fray Juan might be a sign that he was warming to our cause.

"I cannot answer you for certain, Father, but I suspect that if Fray Juan were to visit the *ranchería* just once more, the people would be reassured."

"That may be difficult to arrange."

Teófilo's eyes filled with tears. "I know you wish to spare my feelings, Father, but if Fray Juan has the fever, I hope that you will tell me, so that I can prepare myself to mourn."

"Fray Juan is not ill in that way. He is only sad, that is all." It was the most likely explanation, and probably the correct one. When I had been Father President of the Old California missions, several friars had petitioned to be released from service on account of melancholy. Our old friend Fray Rafael Verger, now the superior of the College of San Fernando, had informed me that such afflictions were a known hazard of missionary work. Now of course, hundreds of leagues farther north, a request for dismissal would be out of the question. Who would replace Fray Juan if he returned to México, and how could we assure his safe passage, given his condition?

"Will you talk to him, Father? I have tried, but he brushes me away."

From the pained look in the boy's wet eyes, I gathered that he could stand no more rejection. I was seized by a feeling of great tenderness for young Teófilo, as though I myself were about to shed tears. In the last month I had experienced many such onsets of overwhelming emotion, often with little warning. I wanted desperately to attribute the odd moods to my diet, as I did the nagging dizziness I felt upon rising in the morning, and the tendency of my gums to bleed under the tooth-rag. Anyone's heart would rise and fall under such poor nourishment, I told myself. But another explanation occurred to me as well: perhaps this was the test Fray Junípero had promised in the sweat lodge.

Then I came to my senses. I had not seen Fray Junípero in the lodge any more than the men in masks has been transformed into stags. I knew that if I continued to indulge these notions I would end up alongside Fray Juan, huddled on my cot with the blanket pulled under my chin. Then I would surely hear the voice of Fray Junípero. And God help me, he would not be pleased.

THERE WAS NO proper window in the cell Juan and I shared, only a tiny aperture cut into the back wall at eye level. It offered a view of the small mission plaza, with its well and wooden cross, and beyond that the green hills of the Río Carmelo valley. But on this morning there was no light in the cell at all, for Juan had blocked the window with a woven mat. When I entered, he did not stir, though he must have been awake. It was nearly eight o'clock.

"Your boy came to see me last night," I said.

A grunt. "What did he say?"

"He said the *ranchería* is worried for your health. And he speculated that if you were to make a trip up the hill, we might enjoy a harvest of souls before His Reverence returns from México."

"You would like that to please His Reverence."

"And you would not?"

"I do not care."

"That is clear."

My brother sat up on his cot. Though he must have slept twelve or fifteen hours, dark circles remained under his eyes. "Do not patronize me," he said wearily. "The fog I can abide, but your little words make me tired."

I had promised Teófilo that I would make this appeal, but I had promised myself that I would not become emotional. Now, not two minutes into the encounter, my resolve was slipping.

"Is that the essence of your problem? My words?"

"The fog is only water, Paco. Your words are pure bile."

I stomped to the little window and ripped down the mat. The California sunlight, diffuse from the clouds but still bright, streamed into the room like water kept too long behind a dam. Juan recoiled, scurrying for the cover of his blanket.

"Look at you," I cried. "You have not left this cell in a week! The neophytes are in tears. Even the pagans believe you are dead. Is that what you want, Beató? Do you wish this cot to be your deathbed?"

I had hoped these words—which were, finally, of the bilious sort—would wake him from his catatonia. With luck, they would brace him like a splash of cold water on the face. Instead, my words broke him down. The only water on his face came from his eyes.

"Oh, Paco," he wailed, wiping his cheeks with the cuff of his cassock. "I have tried to persevere. But my heart is weak."

"Your heart is fine," I said. "The Lord wants you to work."

"Then why does He curse me with sadness?"

"There are greater goals than one's own happiness."

"I know." He inhaled deeply, as though what he had to say would take all his strength. "Still, I cannot find the strength to work."

I was exasperated, but that is no excuse for what I did next. I took the mat I had torn from the window, rolled it up, and struck my brother across the face. For a moment he remained dumbfounded, as though refusing to believe what had just happened. Had it been Fray Junípero striking the blow, he might have understood. He might even have delighted in being the object of that legendary rage. But to be struck by Fray Francisco Palóu, that effete and bookish priest? It must have seemed to Juan that nature was upended.

I meant the blow, I realized, to elicit the response my words had failed to produce. Quite unexpectedly, the strategy appeared to succeed. Juan growled like an animal and sprung from the cot. He seized me in his long arms and bent my head. I felt my whole body turn like an hourglass. Some time must have passed. Next thing I knew, I was lying on the cool, damp earth of the cell. My skull ached. I heard whispers.

Juan was kneeling beside me, rosary in hand.

"What happened?" I asked.

His smile was the exact image of the Mallorcan sun, all radiance and undiluted heat. The color was restored to his face, and his eyes burned with life.

"You are revived!" he proclaimed. He heaved himself to his feet. I saw that Teófilo was with him.

"Where are you going?" I asked.

"To the *ranchería*. Haven't you heard? The people think I am dead."

•   •   •

FRAY JUAN AND Teófilo took along the customary sack of beads, which I instructed them to trade for venison, should any be available. The heathen were generous with meat when they had it, but they hunted infrequently; their customs required that they give Deer (a pagan deity) time to lick his wounds before he was chased again.

The neophytes at the mission had begun to cook *atole* with acorn flour acquired from the *rancherías,* and under this regressive diet, many had shown signs of improved health. I emphasized to them that we did not condone the eating of Indian food but only tolerated it as a temporary measure, until the spring planting proved the superiority of proper agriculture.

At breakfast, I insisted that Juan and Teófilo take double rations— extra milk for Juan and acorn gruel for the boy—to brace them for the walk uphill. Juan was reluctant at first, but eventually he agreed it was a good idea. He seemed a new man. "Paco, remind me of their word for hello," he said between gulps of milk. "I cannot remember a thing unless it is written."

I obliged Juan with a short list of common phrases, though I assured him Teófilo would not dare misrepresent his words.

"Why would he do such a thing?" Juan looked devastated by the suggestion, and for a moment I thought I had lost him back to the darkness. Then he calmed himself and said, "The Lord will lead us. The Lord will make us heard."

I spent the morning mending garments, a task I enjoyed because it gave me time to reflect without stealing from prayer. As usual, my thoughts drifted to Fray Junípero. He had been gone six months. His plan had been to make both *ida y vuelta* by land, using the Jesuit fathers' trail through Sonora, bypassing the California peninsula altogether. I allowed myself to imagine our reunion: there would be a High Mass, sung by myself and Fray Juan in addition to whomever Junípero might have brought from México (for he would not countenance making such a trip without bringing back fresh recruits). Afterward we would have brandy, if His Reverence were generous enough to bring some. By then our spring vegetables, the cabbages and hearty roots already sprouted in a cold frame, would be ready for their first harvest, and we would have real food. God willing, His Reverence would have brought seed for more vegetables, and perhaps even some milled corn for proper tortillas.

I also thought about Encarna. I had not written her in months. All the mail that was to go out on the autumn packet boat still sat waiting at the presidio. What was the point of adding another letter to the stack? Still, I had so much to tell her, from my experience in the sweat lodge to the continuing idiocy of the civil authorities to the unexpected rehabilitation of Juan Crespí. I tried, as I sat mending, to drift to the world she and I shared, but lately it had been difficult to reach. Whenever I set my mind on Palma, my thoughts always doubled back to Monterey. When I tried to see my father working the wharves, I saw instead Don Pedro and the stockade on the bluff. Instead of my beloved Encarna, I saw the melancholic Juan. Then I pricked my finger with the needle. Holding up the shirt to the light, I noticed that my stitches had been crooked all along.

I was relieved at this awkward labor by the arrival of Rigoberto. He was out of breath, and his forehead shone with perspiration.

I pinned the needle to my sleeve.

"Teófilo is here," he heaved. "He is back from the *ranchería.*"

"Already? That is fine news, my son. 'Nets full by noon are happily gathered.' Do you know this phrase?"

Rigoberto looked at me bewildered. "Teófilo is alone, Father. Fray Juan left him on the trail."

IN THE CENTER of the mission's plaza, next to the cross, hung a brass bell on a hook, one of the originals packed in La Paz by the Visitor General. Surely he and Fray Junípero had imagined a flock of peasants summoned home by its sound: the great angelus of New California, its knell reverberating over the hills and valleys, calling legions of new Christians home for supper. The reality would have embarrassed him. My ringing brought out six neophytes. Only six. And now perhaps just a single shepherd.

They gathered around me, eager to hear the news. The *atole* had saved their lives, but none of the six was in perfect health. Juan Diego, the boy who had once tried to climb the fence, had been scratched a few weeks later by a raccoon he found rummaging in our kitchen. It was a superficial wound and he had not cried, but the scratch had not healed. Now his entire left side was infected and suppurating. No matter how we tried to cool it with poultices and damp cloths, the wound would not mend. No one wished to say so, but he had begun to smell like death.

We joined hands beside the bell-post. The dogs, whose ribs were no less plain in their sides than their masters', stopped nipping at one another and laid down in the silence.

"Holy Father," I began, "we beseech you to have mercy on the soul of our brother Juan Crespí. If you have taken him to the Kingdom of Heaven, let him rest happily with you. But if he is still on this Earth, give him the fire to keep up his struggle. Give him the strength to persevere—and us the strength to find him before too much of his life has slipped away."

I looked up at my ragged flock. For all their afflictions, they were eager to help. I began to give instructions. "Those of you who can climb," I said, "will go as far as the *ranchería*. Rigoberto will lead you."

Suddenly one of the dogs rose up and barked. Everyone turned to look, but even before I laid my eyes on the intruder, I heard his voice—the familiar countertenor, which stirred within my heart both love and fear: *"Amar a Dios, mis hijos! Amar a Dios!"*

My whole body came alive—fingers, toes, arms, legs, all tingling with nervous energy. But I was paralyzed. I stood impassively as Fray Junípero tied his donkey to the post. He unlatched the gate.

"Fray Francisco!" he cried. "Look who I found on the trail."

There beside him stood a chastened Juan Crespí, eyes cast down, cheeks sagging. His cassock was covered with dust and burrs, but he was not obviously injured.

"Where have you been?" I said.

Both of my *condiscípulos* assumed I meant him. They began to speak at once.

"Please, Your Reverence," said Juan, still not looking up to meet my gaze.

"You speak first," Junípero said to Juan. "I have been to México, of course, and to many other destinations in between, which I shall recount in due time. But what about you? Am I to infer that Fray Francisco did not know your whereabouts? Tell me, Juan, how long have you been away from this mission?"

"He went this morning with a neophyte to the *ranchería*," I said, making sure that my voice betrayed no hint of annoyance. I remembered well how Junípero despised our quarreling. "But it is not a crisis; we were just now expecting him back."

"And what happened at the *ranchería*, Brother Juan?"

"Nothing," Juan mumbled. "We never arrived."

"And why is that? I assume you are speaking of the little village just anon?" Junípero glanced at me to confirm.

"The heathen have been asking after him," I explained. "They were worried for his health."

"Are you ill, Juan?"

"Not especially."

"But you must be ill, or else the pagans would not have spread such a rumor. They are nothing if not observant."

As Juan toed the dirt with his sandal, I waited for the inevitable breakdown, for him to weep and claim he was a worthless creature, God's humblest speck of dust, et cetera. His Reverence would hesitate to accept the plea, but when he saw that Juan meant it truly, he would console him. Fray Junípero had heard Juan's confessions since our convent days; the pattern was well established between them.

But this time Junípero stood firm, even as tears began to well in

Juan's guileless blue eyes. "Do you wish to die, Brother?" His Reverence asked. His skin was dark from the sun, his lips chapped and flecked with saliva. He bore down on poor Juan with vituperation reserved normally for soldiers and despised civil authorities. "I hope you understand that your foolishness would have harmed many more than yourself. Look around: there are no friars waiting to take your place. It might have been half a year before you were replaced. Or more, if the governor were allowed to choose what is included in the next packet ship. And who could blame him, Brother? Why accept another friar when the last one set such a poor example? I accept your brooding; even the Lord Jesus Christ required more time alone than his friends would have liked. What I cannot abide is the wanton destruction of our mission."

"That was never my intention, Father—"

"Your intention is immaterial."

An uncomfortable silence ensued. His Reverence let it gather like dew on a blade of grass.

Finally Juan spoke: "It is not the body that ails me, Father, but the mind. All the time I lay on my bed I worried that I might never again see the sun."

"You want sun? Go to San Diego de Alcalá."

Juan was silent, clearly surprised by the suggestion.

"You may direct the second friar at Mission San Diego that his presence is required here. It is Fray Alfonso Higuera whom I mean. Send him back in your stead."

"I shall think on it," said Juan.

"No," said Fray Junípero calmly, "you will decide now."

EIGHT

THE DAYS FOLLOWING JUAN'S departure were some of the happiest of my life. With Fray Junípero in command once more, the coterie of six neophytes felt like three times that many, finishing tasks they had left lingering and taking on new responsibilities without so much as a cross look. Fray Junípero had this effect—but so did the tortillas we made from the maize he had brought from México. Together with the vegetables now sprouting in the garden, our diet was nearly as improved as our spirits. In two weeks, we had baptized another twenty-five neophytes—including fifteen girls, whom we intended to house in a new convent behind the chapel.

"I have an order from the viceroy to relieve Don Pedro of his duties," said His Reverence casually one afternoon.

"Do you?" I had forgotten to ask about this. I saw Don Pedro so infrequently—and had grappled with so many real hardships besides—that I could not believe the removal of that ungracious boor had been the whole reason for Fray Junípero's trip to México. I wondered if His Reverence had come to the same conclusion, for already he had been back in Carmel two weeks, and this was the first I heard of an official order.

"Yes, I thought I would see to our affairs first, before I turned the presidio on its head."

I imagined my master walking through the deserts of Sonora, Juan Evangelista leading their mule, plotting the most advantageous way to deliver the governor his termination.

"Tell me about México," I said.

"The viceroy is a learned man. A bit of a prig, but one must be in his position. Actually we spent most of our time together discussing Ignatius of Loyola. He was rather proud of himself for having discovered a connection between Jesuit spirituality and our own, the debt owed by Ignatius to San Francisco and so forth. Apparently Bucareli studied under the Jesuits when he was a boy, and had believed Ignatius to be *sui generis*. He even went to Manresa and saw the cave where Ignatius convalesced—all of which I was delighted to hear of course. In fact I was so captivated by his story that I lost track of time. But the mention of Manresa reminded me of our friend Señor Fages."

"Because he is *catalán*."

"Precisely. By that point I had only a moment to make my case. Luckily the poor gentleman was by that point so frothed up by our theological discussion that he would have signed anything I put before him." Junípero paused, then added, "Strange how God can be a liquor to some men."

"So you are going to deliver the news soon?"

"I have not decided. What do you think?"

Lord, let me die at such a moment—with my master begging my advice!

"It would be folly to waste the order," I offered, "after you made such a long trip. Also, Don Pedro would be disappointed if you avoided him. You know how he loves to argue."

Junípero looked around the dinner table. When he could be sure none of the neophytes were watching, he allowed himself to smile. "Paco," he said, "you are a man after my own heart."

•   •   •

THERE WAS MORE to Fray Junípero's audience with Bucareli, which he related to me later that evening. Like Fray Rafael before him, Junípero had been shown into the gilded viceroyal apartment by a servant in velvet attire. He too was offered water and refused. But Junípero refused to sit, which put him even with Bucareli, who paced as usual behind his desk.

"I have reviewed the reports from the northward expeditions," Bucareli said, "and the diaries of your colleague Father Crespí."

"I hope you found them clear and helpful, Your Excellency," said Junípero.

"Actually, I have a question about geography. It appears that when Governor Portolá's men reached a certain ridge—"

Bucareli bent over his desk, where he ran his finger down a sheet of paper filled with handwritten notes. The notes surprised Junípero; he had assumed the viceroy was only being polite when he said he had read the reports.

"Yes, here it is: a ridge along the creek of San Gregorio."

"Sir, you are referring to the first expedition of Governor Portolá?"

The viceroy looked up from his notes. "Yes, the failed one."

"Sir, we did eventually find Monterey . . . "

"I understand—and thank you for your diligence. The search for Monterey is proof of Spanish resolve et cetera. My question, however, involves what your colleague Father Crespí saw from that ridge." The graceful *andaluz* bent over his notes again. "He called this body of water an 'arm of the sea, which might accommodate all the navies of Europe.' These are his words, Your Reverence. You understand how such a claim might attract the attention of the Crown."

"Certainly, sir. But we have not yet found the egress of that estuary. At first we believed that it emptied into the sea near the peninsula called Point Reyes, but further exploration by sea suggests there is no such connection."

"Ah, but what if this 'arm of the sea,' this estuary, were not an open-ended sound, as we have hitherto supposed, but instead a protected harbor?"

In an instant, Fray Junípero understood where the viceroy was leading. It was rare that Junípero met his intellectual equal; the idea of it filled him with a sensation like lust.

"That is an interesting idea, Your Excellency. I trust you also have read about our search for the Bay of San Francisco."

"I have."

"You may also know that the Visitor General, Don José de Gálvez, assured me that when that bay was finally located, a new mission would be created there, in honor of Our Seraphic Father San Francisco."

"I discussed this very subject with Don José before he left us for Madrid . . . "

A moment of silence, as the two men considered their next moves. It was a kind of bureaucratic quadrille, a dance of the two most powerful men in New Spain.

"You realize it would be expensive to launch another expedition, Your Excellency."

"I am well aware of the expense of exploration, Father Serra."

"Of course you are."

"Let us suppose your 'arm of the sea' is in fact the Bay of San Francisco."

"That is a bold conjecture, Your Excellency."

"I am prepared to be bold, Father Serra."

"And I admire your boldness . . . "

The viceroy stopped pacing, and the men stared at each other for a moment.

"Assuming you can find an outlet," Bucareli said, "and I know there must be one, for I doubt your man was describing a lake—how would you feel about establishing not one but two missions on its shores?"

Junípero could not believe what he was hearing, but he was careful not to reveal his surprise.

"And the names, Your Excellency? What would be the names of the missions?"

"The first would be San Francisco, of course. It must be so, for reasons we have discussed. The second might have any number of names; however, I did some reading on the matter, and I suggest that we name the mission for Santa Clara."

"Ah!"

"The two would be a perfect match, I feel."

"You know your Franciscan history, Your Excellency."

"Actually, I was schooled by Jesuits . . ."

And so went the rest of audience, concluding with Bucareli's signature on an official order removing Governor Fages. Of course the real news, the part that captured Junípero's imagination all the way back to California, had nothing to do with Fages.

"I went in hoping for permission to establish one more mission," he told me, "and emerged with a mandate for two!"

"And there are funds?"

"The usual disbursement. Two thousand pesos each. I spent the entire amount before I left México. I have commissioned the finest vestments, the most intricate *reredos,* freshly cast brass vessels . . . Nothing less for the mission of Our Seraphic Father. Can you believe it, Paco? At last!"

THE ONLY DISCORDANT notes in those harmonious months at Carmel came from a pair of letters Junípero brought me from México. The first was from my sister, informing me that our elderly parents had passed away:

The firemen's speculation is that mother left a candle-lamp burning in the drawing-room, and that the wind had blown the curtains across the flame. By the time the neighbors smelled the fire, the smoke had already filled their lungs. I blame myself, Paquito . . . I should have insisted that mother and papi live with us. Several times I offered—papi especially had become quite frail of late—but each time they refused, saying they did not wish to be a burden. I will never forgive myself. The only consolation, I suppose, is that they passed together . . .

I had been prepared for this news. I had warned myself long ago that when this day came, I would feel helpless, unable to perform that most basic duty of the priest-son, the singing of the requiem Mass. I was reminded of this every time one of my missionary companions received grim tidings from home. Fray Junípero's own sainted mother, for example, had passed the year before, and he had received the news while he was in México. His Reverence went into the hills to mourn, spending a night alone amongst the rattlesnakes and ironwoods, and returned the next day with a renewed focus on his work.

But that was Junípero: I doubted that my own mourning would result in a sharpening of anything, let alone missionary zeal. On the contrary, I wished more than ever to be home in Mallorca, and not by means of dreams or meditations but in the flesh. I wanted to see my sister's children take their first communion in the Palma cathedral. I wanted to smell the *maquis* on the dry breeze of summer, to gather salt flakes from the tide pools. I was mourning, you see, not only for the loss of my parents but for the loss of myself. In all the world there was only one place where I was not an invader, nor a guest, nor a colonizer, nor a missionary—and that place I would never see again.

With Junípero's help, I performed the requiem in absentia.

"Come, Paco," said His Reverence said afterwards, "the sting of death is painful indeed, but you have brought great glory to your parents."

"Yes, it was a beautiful Mass."

"Not the Mass," he waved his arms, "but all of this! You have honored them by your work."

This was of course what Fray Junípero told himself, but I was not sure I agreed. I was confident that I had commended the souls of my parents to God, but I could not believe they saw my work in America as just compensation for losing a son.

"Our mission is a tribute to God," I said meekly. "And perhaps to our parents as well."

Junípero shook his head and clucked, as he often did when he was disappointed. Probably he felt I was being too hard on myself.

As distraught as I was over the loss of my parents, I was even more upset by the second letter:

My dear Paco,

Please accept my sincerest condolences on the passing of your mother and father. I took leave from the convent to attend the requiem Mass at Santa Eulália. It was very well attended, you should know, as your parents were deeply admired by the entire parish. Your absence, of course, was felt by all.

I have had no letters from you in such a long time that I began to fear you were dead. But then your mother received a letter from your friend Don José de Gálvez (who is returned to Madrid, as I am sure you know) informing her that you were very much alive and hard at work on the frontier. When Don José's words were read aloud at Sunday service, the congregation erupted in spontaneous applause. Know that you labor in proxy for many more than yourself, Paco. Don't ever forget this.

I have some news that I know will disappoint you. I have decided to leave the Poor Clares. I am still with the sisters as I write, but by the time you receive this letter I will have rejoined the laity. Paco, this decision weighed heavily on me; it is the result of many months of contemplation and prayer. I have determined that the cloistered life is not for me. Unlike you, I will never have the opportunity to see other shores so long as I remain a nun. Further, I am not sure that I wish to renounce the secular world the way we are asked to do here. There are aspects of nonreligious life that I cherish very much, and others that I may wish to explore in the future.

Forgive me if this news wounds you. But understand that although I will no longer be your sister in the cloth, I shall always remain your—

Here she wrote *wife*, but crossed it out, then tried to conceal the mistake with inkblots.

—sister.

At first, I was astonished at the coincidence of her thoughts with mine: half a world apart, we had both questioned our choices, both regretted the abandonment of cherished parts of ourselves. But as I sat with the letter, I realized that her choice was fundamentally different from mine. While I mourned my home, she was still living there. For her, there was nothing to mourn. For her, it was not too late to change course.

This brought me real, crippling sadness. In my mind, we had been two of a kind, a latter-day Francis and Clare, bonded closer than any blood relations, closer even than man and wife. If she left her vows, this perfect order crumbled. My will to work, to conquer, to persevere—which had grown so strong with our correspondence— shrank to nil when I thought of losing her.

I took a pen and paper that very night and composed my reply:

My dear Encarna,
I urge you to reconsider your decision to leave the convent. I too have had my doubts about vocation, about travel, and about the sacrifices we must suffer to remain true. Add to that the hardships I have faced in California—yes, I almost died; you were correct to

worry!—and what results is the strictest test one can imagine, a crucible of immeasurable heat. But my dear Sor Guadalupe, I prevailed! I survived with my faith intact. And so will you.

I will give you one example of the rewards of perseverance. The viceroy has commissioned us to create two more missions in the north—on the shores of a great bay named for San Francisco. Fray Junípero has asked me to accompany the expedition to scout sites for the missions. You recall how in the past His Reverence has overlooked me for duties like these? In the end, I had only to wait my turn.

Please remain at the convent one more year. Promise me you will. I will pray for your change of heart and await your reply.

With love, I am,

Your cousin,

Francisco Palóu, OFM

FURTHER INSTRUCTIONS FROM Don Antonio Bucareli made clear that we were to waste no time in settling the Bay of San Francisco. A letter addressed to the new governor, Don Fernando de Rivera y Moncada, instructed the civil authorities to establish a royal presidio there as well, preferably at the mouth of the estuary, which would be located by a minute survey of the coast between thirty-seven and thirty-eight degrees north latitude. Considering the superior skill of Spanish mariners—and the fact that His Majesty's Manila galleon had skirted the coast every spring for two hundred years, *en route* to Acapulco—it was no small embarrassment that the mouth of the bay had never been spotted by sea. One could attribute this to Alta California's impenetrable fog, but Bucareli had heard enough excuses: he wanted the outlet found. No more failures would be tolerated.

Once again, the goad came not from México but from Moscow. The Russian threat in America remained heavy on the mind of His Highness King Carlos—a weight that only increased after his trusted advisor, Don José de Gálvez, returned from California to his place at the King's ear. One imagines that Don José needn't have said much to inspire our apprehensive Majesty to action. Knowing the Visitor General's affection for our undertaking, one can be sure he said that and more.

The sea expedition would proceed in the packet *San Carlos,* recently come to port at Monterey. Among the usual necessary items (flour, wine, tobacco, etc.) the packet had also delivered Father Fray Vicente Santa Maria, a colleague of many years who had accompanied our missionary party into Old California. Fray Vicente had been appointed chaplain of the *San Carlos,* and had an excellent rapport with its skilled but tempestuous captain, Don Juan Bautista de Ayala.

I was to accompany a second northward expedition, this one traveling over land and led by Governor Rivera himself. Men at the presidio who had been north assured me that the distance to the great Bay was short; we would be back in Monterey within a fortnight. Nonetheless I burdened our mules with twice the recommended provisions, including several large skins of water. My memory of the starving times was so keen that I was loath to risk any kind of privation.

"You will take Rigoberto?" Fray Junípero asked.

We were standing in the corral, where Rigoberto and Juan Evangelista stood whispering into the oversized, indifferent ears of the mules.

"Rigoberto," I called across the yard. Chickens scattered at my voice. Rigoberto looked up nervously, the mule's ear twitching back and forth before his face like a fan.

"Let him be, Paco," said Junípero. "Perhaps the asses will learn to pray. Walk with me. There is something I want to tell you."

We went to the garden beside our dormitory, which buzzed now with the busy industry of insects. The previous winter I had transplanted half a dozen of the wild roses which grew in the valley and pruned them so that they would bear large flowers in the fashion of Spanish garden-roses. From that desperate, starving season, the roses had been my only success. It was in one way satisfying to see them flourish as I hoped they would; but they were also a bitter reminder of the lives I had fought to save but lost.

Fray Junípero loved the rose garden. He had recently ordered the neophytes to build him a wooden bench amongst the flowers, which he employed, in true imitation of Saint Francis, as a kind of outdoor study.

"Sit," he said when we reached the bench. "Enjoy the perfume of your labors."

"I will sit," I said, "but I doubt I can enjoy . . . " My voice trailed off, lacking the energy to explain.

Never one for throat-clearing, His Reverence started in right away. "I have heard from Juan," he said. "He is not well."

"Oh?" My voice rose in genuine concern. "I hope it is not the fever."

Junípero shook his head. "I wish it were. No, he complains of the sun. It seems our brother's constitution is sensitive at both extremes."

I gave a shallow, ambiguous nod. A moment passed in silence, and then I said, "What will you do?"

"About Juan?"

"Will you send him to México? I would even suggest sending him home to Palma, if the sun did not shine so brightly there as well."

His Reverence looked up and caught my eye. "I have summoned him here," he said. "I know you will disagree, Paco, but I believe that the best treatment for Juan is constant attendance."

"But Your Reverence—"

"It is best."

"Best? How can you say it is best when you already know how he fares in this climate?"

"I have made my suggestion, and Juan agrees. He arrives a week from now."

I said nothing.

"He asked me to tell you sooner," Junípero said. He placed his hand on mine. "But I know how his suffering upsets you."

In the yard a mule whinnied.

"You should go," said Junípero. "Rivera is waiting."

"You are sending me away."

"Is that what you believe?"

"To make room for Fray Juan. I thought it was a favor, but no."

"In the past, Paco, you have complained of being left behind. In Old California for example. I assumed you would want to be in the vanguard this time."

"I want to be with you! That is my only wish."

"It is mine as well," he said soberly.

"Then why do you send me away?"

Junípero spread his arms like an actor, his dark eyes alive with a kind of optimism. "I will be reminded of you!"

I realized he meant the roses.

"A fortnight," he said. "We shall meet again in a fortnight."

I stood up and picked my way through the roses to the plaza, where Rigoberto held our mules. The neophyte was no longer whispering prayers but only following me with his wide-set, inky eyes. I did not know how much he had heard, but I could see that he was frightened. Only later, at the crest of the hill overlooking the mission, did I allow myself to look back. Fray Junípero was exactly where I had left him, seated on the bench in the roses. But now his face was hidden, buried between his knees.

THERE ARE TREES in Mallorca: jagged cypresses and palms taller than the spires of the cathedral. But these are mere blades of grass compared to the behemoths I saw in the mountains north of Monterey. There were trees as thick around the base as the aft hull of a galleon, and so tall that their branches disappeared into the clouds. Regarding one fallen specimen, I remarked that one might carve a sailing ship from its trunk in one piece, as the heathens carve canoes from pines. The thick bark was spongy and filled with splinters; however the heartwood (if one could reach it) was dense, resilient, and a deeper red than cedar. I could not imagine a finer material for roof beams—an opinion I shared with Governor Rivera. "It is too bad," I said, "that our saws are too short to cut the trunks."

"There is plenty of fallen wood," the governor replied. "Note that in the journal, Valdez." I had taught the governor's boy to speak and read Castilian and to write in a beautiful, elegant hand. Now he drew a pen from his sack and opened his book. *"Hemos observado la madera en la tierra,"* the governor dictated. *"El árbol se llama palo colorado."*

I stopped him. "You will call it *palo colorado?*"

"Palo alto, palo de las nubes—do you know its Latin name?"

"This is the first I have seen the species."

"Then it shall be *palo colorado.* Red wood."

In the hollow where we had stopped for lunch, our words died in the foot-thick bark of the trees. I felt as though my ears were filled with water. The governor seized this pause in our progress to doff his hat and run one of his smooth hands through his hair. The oily black tresses fell onto his shoulders like strips of meat.

"Are you close with Father Junípero?" he asked me. It struck me as a reasonable topic of conversation; Rivera was only recently governor, having replaced the deposed Fages. Understandably, he did not wish for the colony to fail on his watch, and he knew that success required good relations with the Father President of the missions.

"He was my teacher in Mallorca," I said.

"Is he that much older than you?"

"No, only more intelligent."

"Yes, the monks in San Diego said the same thing. I must confess I was surprised when I finally met him." He said this wistfully, as though we were discussing a vintage of Rioja or a new play in Madrid.

"Is that so?" I was curious to hear the soldier's impression of Fray Junípero. As a rule, His Reverence did not mix well with the military.

"I was expecting a much taller man, for one thing. His wrath is legendary, but I find that he only scampers about and makes noise. Your Junípero is a terrier. Ultimately his size confounds his ambition."

"With all due respect, Don Fernando, you mistake stature for size."

"Why should I not believe that he is harmless?" said the Governor, his eyes now suddenly alive. "My predecessor, Don Pedro, cannot even bear to speak his name. But why? Whom has Fray Junípero harmed? Who is this beast you all fear? I wonder, should I fear that I left Monterey in his care?"

"You have nothing to fear on that account, Don Fernando."

"Then why the lame tongue? Even you hesitate to describe him. You who know him best of all."

"I know him, yes, but—"

"You have a long history. And just then, your eyes shifted as you said it. What is this madness?"

"It is not madness, Don Fernando, only respect."

"Respect? I respect my superiors, but not to the point of trepidation. I can tell you, for example, that His Excellency the Viceroy is a righteous and upstanding administrator, but that he plays cards like a child and dotes too much on his wife. Look—do you see my hands? They are not shaking. I can even speak freely of His Highness, the King of Spain, without a twinge of fear. One would think your Father Junípero were two men: on one hand the tyrant whom you and your brothers describe, and on the other, the harmless friar I've come to know in Monterey. Listen, if God can be three, then Fray Junípero can easily be two."

Don Fernando smiled at this small sacrilege.

"What do you think of that, Father?"

"That is heresy, sir."

The governor smiled, pulled his hand through his hair one more time. "I meant no harm by it, Father. I am a good Catholic."

I frowned with due severity—as he must have expected I would—and prepared for his request of absolution.

"Forgive me, Father," he said, eyes wide in what he believed to be his most pious expression. "I have sinned against God."

"I cannot offer the Sacrament now, Your Excellency. You will have to wait for this evening."

Just then, there came a shout from one of the sentries, and the clicking of pistols being readied. One of the donkeys brayed and was hushed by his neophyte handler. We all turned to the noise and saw a party of half a dozen brown-skinned natives. They had emerged from the trees like vapor.

The sentry shouted over his shoulder for Don Fernando, keeping his gun trained on the Indians.

"Lower your arms!" commanded the governor. All traces of levity were erased: his face was now severe, humorless. "Lieutenant, bring the beads. Just a handful. I don't wish them to know what we have."

The Indians, I saw, had brought gifts of their own. As was the custom in their society, all meetings, whether of friends or foes, commenced with gift-giving, normally in the form of food. These had prepared a basket of red and yellow raspberries and a quantity of dried fish. Like the *costanoans* of Carmel, these men were marked all over with tattoos. However, the markings were only partially visible on account of the red clay they had smeared over their exposed arms and legs. I would learn later that this was a defense against insect bites, but at the time it seemed a kind of war-paint.

"*Buenas tardes,*" said Don Fernando, bowing low. The Indians' headman stood a yard in front of his men, as was their custom. "We come in the name of His Most Catholic Majesty King Carlos III of Spain, who offers you this gift as a token of goodwill."

Don Fernando turned to his lieutenant and received in his cupped hand a measure of glass and ceramic beads, such as might be procured anywhere in Europe for half a copper. At the sight of the beads, the younger heathens stamped their feet. Their leader, however, remained perfectly stern. He called for his own offering, which one of the mud-smeared boys brought forth. The headman said a few words in his language.

Don Fernando took the berries and gave them to the lieutenant, who ate two or three, gingerly, as a demonstration of trust. Now the governor put out the fist containing the beads, and the headman cupped his hands beneath like a bowl.

Before releasing his fist, Don Fernando turned his head and met my eyes, as if making sure he had my attention. In fact everyone in both parties was rapt: there was no sound but the swishing of the pack animals' tails.

"Take these in the name of Fray Junípero Serra," said Don Fernando to the headman, "who will soon be your master." He unclenched his fist slowly, so that at first just a few beads escaped, then a few more, and finally the rest. Behind the headman, the other heathen stomped and grumbled, as though the sight of so many beads—which were in fact their only currency and symbol of wealth—had made them forget all propriety. And when the headman's trembling hands faltered and spilled a portion of the gift, they lost their heads. The five muddy boys, clothed only in loincloths, dove to the earth and scampered after the tiny bits of clay and glass, which danced in the pine duff like fleas. It was a sad reprise of the scene in Rigoberto's village, when the women had trampled one another over a similar offering.

The melee was broken only by a fantastic explosion, so near that I flinched. I smelled powder. Before me, the heathen boys sprung up like raccoons caught scavenging the midden. They looked left and right with beady black eyes, but they were still only for a moment, until one noticed the headman lying prone in the duff, bleeding out through a hole in his abdomen. One boy uttered a word which the others repeated, and like a school of fish they turned and moved, melting into the forest between those giant trees. *Palo colorado.* Red wood.

With reluctance I returned my attention to our party. One of the men had been hasty with his gun, I was sure, and Don Fernando would be obliged to punish him for it. The other men, henceforth, would fear to pull their own weapons, even in a needful situation, which could endanger the expedition.

But none of this was to occur, for the killer had been none other than Don Fernando himself. The smoke from the shot hung around him like an aura. His face and the front of his riding costume were speckled with blood. He made no attempt to wipe himself, but instead went about fastening his pistol into the pouch at his belt, pulling the strap through the buckle like he was saddling his horse. He did this very deliberately, with the sternest expression one can imagine.

All our eyes were upon him. All our ears rang from his shot. "You," he said to the lieutenant. "Find a spade."

When none of us moved—too frightened, too stunned—he raised his voice at me: "Are you so naïve, Fray Francisco? I would expect you to understand. You of all people, who knows how the Kingdom of God must expand."

I had no special love for the dead chief. Unbaptized, his soul would not enter Eternity, but neither would the souls of his kinsman, unless they were brought first into the flock of Christ. Which would be impossible without proper civil authority . . . I understood the governor's logic. And yet it seemed unnecessary to spill blood. "There must have been another way," I said.

"Do you think I relish this duty, Father? It is not a simple task to kill a man, even if he goes about dressed like a beast. But you must agree that it is better to cut off the head so that the body might be saved."

"Might the body be saved?"

"That is your business, Father, not mine."

Now the men were active all around us: a young soldier gathered himself and unlashed a pick from his saddle. Another took down a spade. Together they approached the body of the chief. The blood was already attracting flies. "Now they will run," said Don Fernando in the same full-throated voice he used in giving orders. "Now they will know that greed is not our way, and that our punishments are swift and final. We do not crawl on all fours. We are men of reason."

The governor shouted this as though he intended his words to reach the boys gliding through the forest. But even if his voice penetrated that dark maw, they would not understand. What was reason to them? It was neither violence nor faith, neither joy nor sadness. What animal knows reason? Indeed few men know it. But few men are much more than animals, no matter their pedigrees.

THE WITNESSES TO Don Fernando's murder of the headman must have spread the news of our coming, for we did not encounter any other natives as we traced the coastal ridges north. There were in places the signs of recent habitation—smoldering coals in fire pits, fresh dog scat—but the heathen did not allow themselves to be seen.

A conspicuous silence rose among the members of our party, which Don Fernando attempted to correct by ordering his men to take needless precautions.

"Walk behind the mule train, Moraga," he instructed his lieutenant. "And load your gun."

The men complied, but soundlessly, as though they knew the only danger on the trail was their own leader.

Eight days from Monterey we reached our goal. Below us roiled a great stormy channel perhaps a league across. This was the end of the peninsula. Don Fernando took a sighting and determined the latitude to be thirty-seven degrees and forty minutes.

"My chart suggests the end of land should be farther north," he said to me. "Will you do me the honor of a second opinion, Father?" There was no malice on his face as he handed over the tarnished brass sextant. I took the instrument but did not yet raise it up.

"With respect, Your Excellency, there can be no doubt that the land ends here." I gestured toward the bluff, which was especially steep on the oceanward side, dropping from a height of several dozen fathoms over precipitous cliffs to a narrow, rocky beach, thence into the churning sea. On the bay side, the land sloped more gently toward the water, giving up the bluff's elevation over a much greater distance. In the east, on the opposite shore of the bay, past several large islands and at least two smaller ones, the hills rose like golden dunes.

I raised the sextant and sighted the horizon. The sunlight was diffuse, but I soon found the disc in the mirror, lowered the shades, and took the measure.

"Thirty seven degrees forty minutes," I said.

"So it is established."

"So it is."

Rivera gave directions for his boy to note the second sighting. Then he said, "You are still upset, Fray Francisco. It is plain on your face. For Heaven's sake, why must you cloak your thoughts like a judge? Look around you—this is not the court of Spain. This is not even Christendom! What is the use of hiding your true sentiments here? Do the birds pretend? Do the deer?"

"We are not animals."

"No, but we are, I hope you admit, less encumbered by propriety here."

"There can be no civilization without propriety, Don Fernando."

"I quite agree. It is why I shot the headman, in fact."

"That was not propriety. That was only wickedness."

The governor smiled. "There! See how the color has returned to your cheeks? It was worth the shot just to see your color improve."

"Do you call yourself a Christian?" I asked.

"Don't be naïve, Father. Christians have killed."

"In the name of propriety?"

"Without force—and by force, you can be sure I mean killing—Mother Spain would still be under the heel of the Mohammedans. And who recaptured Córdoba? Who freed Sevilla? Mind you, Father, it was not just any Christian but a *saint* who waged that war—my namesake, San Fernando, the King. Would you dismiss the restoration of the Holy Catholic Church in Spain simply because blood was shed in the process?"

"You did not have to kill that man."

"I did, and you will thank me for it. Some night, when the wolves are howling in the canyons, and the fog is so thick you cannot see your hand in front of your face, much less an intruder over your shoulder—on those nights, you will be grateful."

"Never."

"You do not need to agree. I have no need for your approval."

In all my years in the cloth, I had never excommunicated anyone. In my opinion, the soul was a regenerating entity, which could be healed no matter how far it had decayed. The loathsome Don Fernando forced me to reconsider my stance.

"I cannot respect a man who murders for his own pleasure," I said.

"Now padre, we both know that is not true."

Just then the governor's lieutenant arrived, out of breath, sweat pressing his black curls against his temples. "Your Excellency," he panted, "the other party has arrived."

"Just now?"

The young man shook his head. "The scout found a cross on a hill not far from here, and a decorated stone. And under the stone was this—"

From his purse the lieutenant produced a leaf of parchment folded in three and closed with the great seal of New Spain. The governor broke the wax with his thumb.

"It is from Fray Vicente," he announced after scanning the first few lines. "They came to anchor on the bayside four days ago."

"To anchor?" said the lieutenant. "There are no ships at anchor."

Don Fernando read quickly. "The heathen came with berries, *atole,* and so forth. Our men spent two nights on the beach. Then on the morning of the third day, there was an ambush. Two soldiers were killed, and Captain Ayala was wounded superficially."

"Does it say who was killed?"

The governor did not look up. "It does not."

"And now? Where are they?"

"It says they went home, Moraga."

"Home?"

"Yes, home. To Monterey."

The young lieutenant made the sign of the cross. "If that place is our home," he said under his breath, "God help us all."

HOLDING IN HIS hand the cautionary words of Fray Vicente, Governor Rivera ordered the expeditionary party to round the peninsula and bear south along the bay shore. We continued perhaps a league beyond the beach where our sister party had been ambushed. Then our leader turned to the hills.

"We shall make our camp on high ground for safety," he explained.

I myself did not believe location would afford us any safety, no matter where we sited camp. The heathen would spring from the dark and kill us while we slept, if that was their intention. This was their country, not ours.

I did a calculation in my head, subtracting days to determine if the ambush on the beach might have been precipitated by the murder in the pass. The two locales were separated by at least two days' walk. The heathen here and there were not likely of the same tribe, and thus communication would have been difficult. All the same, no word travels faster than danger, and nothing breeds alliance like a common enemy.

We pitched tents along a narrow creek ten minutes' walk from shore. Reeds and flowering bushes grew along the banks of the riverbed, but there was only a thin ribbon of water flowing below. According to our chart, the place had been named by a previous expedition for Our Lady of Sorrows, Nuestra Señora de los Dolores. It seemed to me the recent violence against our men (and also perpetrated by them) made the name especially appropriate.

I cleaved to La Dolorosa, finding succor in her anguish. I knew that at that very moment, as I made camp in the absolute farthest reach of the Empire, clearing brush alongside a royal governor who took innocent lives for pleasure, my brother Fray Juan Crespí would be returning to Carmel. To a happy reunion with our master.

Suddenly a fortnight seemed too soon to return.

I found the governor sitting atop a flat rock, smoking his pipe and taking in the view of the bay. The flicker of campfires was visible on the *contra costa,* two or three leagues across the water.

"This is a fine site for a mission," he said. "You might find a more substantial creek, but other than that—"

"I intend to stay here," I said. "When the party returns to Monterey, I will remain behind."

"They expect us back in a fortnight."

"I understand, Your Excellency, but don't you feel that in light of the attack on Captain Ayala, we ought to establish fortifications in this quarter as soon as possible?"

"Listen to you! Are you now a general as well as a friar?"

"Sir, I am willing to consecrate this site tomorrow. I believe that the sooner we begin civilizing these barbarians, the better our chances for permanent control of the region."

It was a shameful exploitation of the governor's worst fear; namely, that he should fail to secure this harbor on behalf of His

Majesty. I did not even need to mention the Russians—they loomed behind my words like fur-capped phantoms. As for his suggestion that I was speaking like a military officer, I can say only that the words came easily; the military is not the only society that speaks in code.

"You will require a guard."

"Yes, sir. Two soldiers will be enough. I will also have Rigoberto. We will sleep in tents until the chapel is constructed."

Don Fernando craned his neck to take a more careful survey of the surroundings. "What do you think about this spot for the presidio?" he said.

"You know more about such things, sir."

"Correct." His eyes gleamed as he realized the opportunity. If he stayed here instead of returning to Monterey, he might speed the establishment of the royal presidio by several weeks or even months. In his mind, he was already composing the dispatch to the viceroy.

Of course, he did not want to accede too easily, lest it appear that the idea had been mine and he had only signed on. "Still, Fray Francisco, our orders were to find the sites and return."

"Orders, sir?"

"Yes, orders."

"But sir—you are the governor."

This was too much for his boastful heart to bear. He removed his hat and swept his fingers through his oily locks. "Indeed I am," he said.

"Sir?"

"It is decided, then. By order of the Royal Governor of California, we shall remain here indefinitely."

"As you wish, sir."

NINE

THE NEXT DAY RIGOBERTO and I began preparing to consecrate a new mission, named for Our Seraphic Father San Francisco
de Asís. We constructed a cross from crude lumber and set it in a
post-hole one of the soldiers excavated near the creek of La Dolorosa. Next we gathered a barrow full of head-sized stones, which
Rigoberto arranged around the base of the cross. A semi-rotted
length of fallen redwood served as altar. Upon its strange, spongy
bark I spread the linen altar cloth Junípero had purchased in México with the viceroy's purse. Carefully I unpacked the brass chalice
and paten. Rigoberto had polished both before our departure from
Monterey, and they had held their shine. Especially in this wilderness, where there was no metallurgy in evidence anywhere save
the objects brought by our party, it was remarkable to see the brass
vessels smiling in the sun, awaiting their sacred contents.

Fray Junípero had insisted I bring a full bottle of wine, despite my
misgivings about keeping wine around thirsty soldiers. "They will
look after themselves, Paco," he had said, and he had been correct:
the silver arch of a flask was as common a sight on our marches as
the swish of a mule's tail. Governor Rivera especially was fond of

his refreshments and drank liberally all day from a flask of port he replenished nightly from a jug.

Finally I uncrated the bell, cast especially for this purpose by His Majesty's royal foundry in México City. There is nothing orthodox about founding a mission with a bell—Saint Paul does not speak of bells in his letters to the Christian enclaves in Asia Minor—but it was the one bit of tradition upon which Fray Junípero insisted absolutely. Rigoberto climbed an oak and hung the bell from one of its thick arms. A rawhide thong dangled from the clapper, weighed down not by beads, lest they become objects of contention among the natives, but by a large oyster shell, through which Rigo had chipped a hole with his knife.

Late in the afternoon I wandered among the soldiers hewing logs, stripping bark from saplings, digging foundations for the new buildings of the settlement, and reminded them that the hour was nigh: God's hour. They put down their tools and followed, weary as beaten hounds from their labor.

I found Governor Rivera in his tent, log book in his lap, writing the official account of the day.

"Your Excellency, sir, I request the honor of your presence at our Mass."

He looked cockeyed at my request, as though trying to divine its hidden menace. But there was none; in those moments I was free of bitterness, jealousy, and all other plagues of the heart. I felt the grace of God lift my soul above all injuries, real or perceived. The air buzzed with the beating of a thousand hearts, not just those of my countrymen, but the birds in the trees, the furred beasts in the fields, and somewhere, hidden yet to us, the heathen people of this country.

"In nomine Patris, et Filii, et Spiritus Sancti, amen."

"Amen," returned the congregation of filthy soldiers and neo-phytes. There were no pews, of course; the worshippers knelt on the earth. It was dusk, and the air was filled with mosquitoes. From the

bay shore rose the stink of fish and backwaters. Somewhere in the hills behind a coyote cried. Another answered from the next ridge.

"*Dominus vobiscum.*"

"*Et cum spiritu tuo.*"

I led my rag-worn flock through the Psalm and the Scriptures, the Gospel and the homily, and behind them, the vermillion sun kissed the hills. From the paten I removed a tortilla—still more bran than maize—and broke bread as Christ had done. From the bottle, I poured wine. Then raising first the dish and then the chalice, the miracle of the Eucharist transpired anew, our humble offerings transfigured into the body and blood of Christ.

After Mass, the men began drifting toward the mess, eager to consume whatever fare the cook had managed to scrape together. I called them back, for we had not yet performed the most important task. Standing beneath the gnarled oak, I took the clapper-cord and drew it back and forth, as wide as my arms would allow. At first there was only the whisper of a ring, but as my arm revolved, it grew louder until the bell rang clearly with each revolution. Every man in the camp stopped and admired the note. Even in the crudest fellow, this sound brought forth the memory of home, for no matter where one is in the Catholic world, he is never far from a church bell. And now the dominion of God had been stretched, by our effort, to include this dark place.

"Come, you heathens!" I called into the woods, just as Fray Junípero had at Monterey. "Come and hear the Good News of Christ!"

The coyotes howled in the canyons, frenzied by the grace of God. There could be no doubt now that the heathen people heard our call, but we would have to wait till morning to confirm it.

WHEN WE WOKE, the mission bell remained on the oak branch, just as we had left it the night before. However the pull-rope had been transformed: in the night, feathers of all colors and sizes had been affixed so that the cord looked like the tail of a bird. I approached with caution, but Rigoberto strode up confidently and bent down beneath the bell. He held up a dark parcel which had been left on the ground, swaddled in willow leaves.

He held the mass under his nose. "Rabbit meat," he said.

"A gift?"

"Or a sacrifice. I remember when your people first came to the valley, the elders of our tribe mistook the mounted soldiers for spirits." He had told me this story before, how the tribe's scouts described a race of demons riding large-headed antelope with tails of long straight hair.

"Have they seen us?" I asked.

"They may be watching us now."

I heard pride in Rigoberto's voice. Ever since the murder in the hills, he had been unusually quiet. I knew that he was torn between two allegiances—one built on blood, the other on faith. Don Fernando's wanton murder of the headman, and the subsequent ambush by the tribesman, had shown that neither side was averse to killing men, although both claimed to be.

The air was opaque from our cooking fire and a persistent morning fog. Downhill, through the trees, the bay looked like a dull slab of clay. If there were heathen nearby, they would emerge only if they wished to be seen. They could not be flushed like game; Fray Junípero had tried that when he arrived at Monterey. The heathen sat hidden, perplexed by the ineffective hunting techniques of the pale-skinned spirits. They would leave offerings of dried meat and seed cakes for several days, until their curiosity became too much to bear and they showed themselves.

I realized that I would have to be a fisherman, not a hunter. The pull-cord would be my line, the bell my hook.

"Take the feathers down," I told Rigo. "Give the rabbit to the cook, but do not tell him where you found it. Tell him you caught it yourself."

"Yes, Father." His fingers hesitated as he unraveled the bands of sinew which fastened the feathers to the cord.

"The governor should believe we are alone."

Rigoberto nodded. Artifice did not offend him. The *costanoans* were primitive in many ways, but they were every bit as cunning as white men. They gambled and fought, and sought to outmaneuver one another at every opportunity. Rigoberto told me that his aunt once suspected her husband of being unfaithful, so she dressed up her brother in women's clothes and sent the boy to the sweat lodge. When the man made his advance, the boy stabbed him in the leg with a sharpened stick. The husband never strayed again.

After morning Mass, I relaxed with Rigoberto in the shade of a hasty *ramada* one of the soldiers had constructed of redwood boughs. Work had stalled on the dormitories, because Governor Rivera was having second thoughts about his choice of sites. "This place is neither here nor there," he complained. "It is neither the highest point in the vicinity nor convenient to the shore. We can do better." That morning he took a detachment of men north to find a site overlooking the mouth of the harbor—"a location for a proper fort," as he called it.

Rigoberto looked down at his hands, where he was knotting his fingers together nervously.

"Is something bothering you, my son?"

"I am embarrassed to tell you, Father."

"Think of this as confession," I said. "In lieu of a booth, we have this sail." I reached up and shook the ribs of the shelter. A shower of tiny flat needles dropped from the dry redwood. Rigoberto smiled briefly.

"Do you remember, Father, the first time you came to my village?"

"Of course. You took me to the sweat lodge."

"But before that, do you recall meeting any members of my tribe?"

I raised my brow. "I remember that the women were less than gracious in the presence of beads."

I meant it as a gentle chide, but Rigoberto frowned. I worried I had offended him.

"Do you recall any of the women in particular?" he asked.

"I remember the headwoman. And her young assistant."

Rigoberto's eyes grew tall. "You remember her!"

"The headwoman? Of course."

"No—the young one."

"Was that her daughter? She was very helpful as I recall."

"Yes, she is the daughter of the chieftess." There was a peculiar tone in his voice, a kind of hopeful lilt. "You are kind to compliment her."

"Do you know her well?"

"She has been as close as a sister all my life. But she is not my sister. She is only—like a sister." He tilted his head in frustration. "I cannot explain."

"I see. If I were to hazard a guess, I would say that you fancy her."

"Fancy, Father?"

"You love her."

Rigo blushed, returned to worrying his hands. "Not as I love God."

"Do you wish to marry her?"

"That is for you to decide, Father."

This was the custom in our missions. Just as we did not allow the neophytes to go about in animal skins, we insisted on proper courtship leading to marriage, as we would expect of young people in Spain. To this end, male and female neophytes lodged in separate convents on the mission grounds, and except when they were released for Mass, meals, or chores, the girls were kept secure in their dormitory under lock and key. By this system we had promoted civilized contact between the sexes—and avoided the senseless fornication one finds in the villages.

Selfishly, I had not considered the possibility that Rigoberto might want to start a family. He was certainly mature physically, but he had shown no interest in a secular life. I had assumed he would follow me into the sacred Order of Saint Francis.

"Are you ready to be married, Rigoberto?"

"When you determine I am ready to marry, Father, you shall tell me the time and date."

"And the girl?"

"You will choose her."

"Very well. The convent at Mission San Carlos is filled with good candidates, I should think."

"Yes, Father. I would happily accept a union with whomever you choose."

"Would you?"

"I defer to your wisdom, sir."

I paused. "Rigoberto, you know that to marry a heathen girl, you would have to leave the Church."

"That is not my intention. I love God with all my heart, just as Jesucristo commands."

"I know you do. But unless the girl renounces Satan—"

"She intends to be baptized in Christ."

"Yes, but when, and by whom?"

"She will go to Fray Junípero the morning after the tenth moon. That is the fourteenth of July, by the proper calendar."

I was stunned. "When were you going to tell me? We left Monterey a month ago. You must have arranged all this in advance."

"Forgive me. I did not wish to put my personal concerns before those of our party. But now that the mission has been consecrated . . ."

He had been planning this moment for days. Maybe even longer.

"How long have you been meeting this pagan girl behind my back?"

"Your Reverence, I assure you that our courtship has been chaste. Her mother, the chieftess, has given her blessing. All that remains is for you to give yours. If you lend your support to our union, I know that Fray Junípero will allow it."

I thought of Encarna. About the sweetness of impossible love. Before I knew what I was doing, I said, "I was once in love."

"Father, I had no idea."

"How would you have known? This was in Palma, when I was younger. Her name was Encarnación Mora. She was a cousin of mine."

It felt wonderful to say these words. Almost like truth.

"Did you want to marry her, Father?"

"Very much. I imagined that we would live out our days in Palma. I would work in the harbor-master's office, and she would raise our two children."

Rigoberto smiled. "Two children?"

"Yes, we had everything planned."

"If you don't mind my asking, Father—what happened?"

"That is a fair question."

I realized that my eyes had filled with tears.

"Father, I did not mean to upset you—"

"It was not God's will. She joined the convent of Santa Clara. And I came here."

I wiped my face with the sleeve of my cassock.

"About your girl," I said. "Are you sure she is the right one? There are pious girls already in the convent, already baptized."

Rigoberto did not possess the arrogance to insist. But I gathered from his silence that there would be no substitution. He did not simply wish to be married; he wished to marry the headwoman's daughter. There was no one else. I understood the difference better than anyone.

"If you will only lend your blessing," he repeated, "I am sure Fray Junípero will consent. His Reverence trusts your judgment."

"If that is true," I said, "why did he send me away? Now I am alone in this new province, and Fray Juan Crespí sits in my rightful place beside our master . . . "

This made Rigoberto uncomfortable. He knitted his hands more furiously than ever.

"You are correct that I have Fray Junípero's trust," I said. "It is good to be trusted. But I did not leave my home for trust. I left to be with Junípero."

Rigoberto lowered his head. "I understand, Father."

But how could he understand? He had never traveled farther than forty leagues from his home. How could he comprehend lives like ours—lives spanning decades and half the Earth?

"I will consider your request," I said.

"No, Father," he said. His eyes brightened suddenly. "I will earn your blessing."

JUST AS AT Carmel, the first heathens to visit our camp during daylight hours were children: two boys, perhaps ten or eleven years old. They had painted their naked bodies head to toe in swaths of red, yellow, and blue. One boy was several inches taller than the other and had a bone through the septum of his nose. The shorter one boasted no adornment other than the paint.

When they emerged from the thicket, I was in the *ramada* making entries in my journal. The governor had decided to separate the presidio and mission settlements, as at Monterey, and had delegated Lieutenant Juan José Moraga to direct construction of both sites. Don Fernando himself had returned to Monterey. With him went Rigoberto, who volunteered to carry my expedition journal to Fray Junípero. "It is better that I deliver the book myself," Rigo had argued, "in case His Reverence has any questions." I knew that the neophyte had other business in Carmel besides my chore, but I reasoned that no additional harm could be done. I had all but made up my mind to give my blessing to his marriage, so long as the girl was baptized as he promised.

Now, in the presence of the first Bay Indians, I regretted letting Rigoberto go. Although he did not speak all the dialects of the region, he had become skilled at negotiating the differences. Alone, I would have to communicate by signs.

I closed my book as silently as possible and rose to my feet. I did not smile, for we had learned in Carmel that to show one's teeth was taken as a threat and not a greeting. I raised one hand, palm facing the boys, and said softly, *"Amar a Dios."*

The taller boy stretched his arm across the chest of the other, holding him back. Because they did not run away immediately, I guessed that they were not here on their own account, but had been put forward by their fathers or the headmen of their tribe. However dangerous it seems to a Spaniard to send children as scouts, there was a certain logic to it: children were less threatening in the eyes of hostile parties, and thus less likely to be struck down. This was particularly true when the invaders hailed from the spirit world.

"I greet you in the name of the Father, and of the Son, and of the Holy Spirit. I am Brother Francisco Palóu."

The boys said nothing, their bodies taut as cats stalking prey.

I pointed to the wooden cross. "This is the symbol of our faith. You will know us by this sign." I drew a cross in the air with one hand. Although they were several yards away, the boys flinched with each wave of my arm, as though they expected flames to erupt from my fingers.

Without turning my back to the boys, I went to the trunk where I kept the Eucharistic vessels. I circled the trunk, opened the lid, and removed the bundle of feathers Rigoberto had taken from the bell-cord. "Do these belong to you?" I asked. I pointed to the boys, each one in turn, and then to the feathers.

Keeping one arm on the chest of his brother, the older boy pointed to the bell. He spoke a few words in his tongue—an amalgam of clicks and gutturals.

"Yes," I said, gesturing alternately to the feathers and the bell. "You left these here." I bowed slightly, making sure the boys remained always in my peripheral vision.

I returned to the trunk, put the feathers inside, and removed a bar of chocolate. I broke off two corners.

"Are you hungry?" I lifted the chocolate to my mouth and panto-mimed eating.

The boys did not answer by voice or sign.

I took a careful step forward. Then another. When I was just a yard away, I reached out with one of the pieces of chocolate. The younger boy made a move for it, but his brother stopped him. Realizing that the duty fell therefore to him, the older boy stepped forward and opened his mouth. I put the chocolate on his tongue. He did not chew; in fact, he left his mouth open. As the chocolate began to melt, his tongue turned slick. I reached out the other piece to the smaller boy, but the older brother held him back. The little boy protested, and in return got thumped on the chest with his brother's fist.

"Swallow it," I said to the older boy. "It is sweet." I closed my eyes slowly and reopened them, trying to express the pleasure of chocolate. To demonstrate, I popped the second piece of chocolate in my own mouth, chewed, and swallowed. "*Delicioso.* We call it chocolate."

Just then there was a noise in the brush and the boys whipped their heads around. It was only a bird, but the boys decided that they had seen enough for today. The older one spat out the chocolate sludge and wiped his tongue with his fingers.

I grabbed the leather thong and rang the bell once. "When you hear this," I said, "you may come and listen to the Good News of Christ. The Lord welcomes everyone in his house. Bring your par-ents, bring your aunts and uncles, bring anyone—"

But the sound of the bell had frightened them. Deer-like, they bounded into the thicket and disappeared, bare feet only skimming the ground.

RIGOBERTO RETURNED FROM Monterey on a Tuesday afternoon, having left Carmelo Sunday morning after Mass. Because

regular commerce was now required between Monterey and our settlement on the Bay of San Francisco, scouts had beaten out a more
expeditious route than the one I had taken with Governor Rivera.
The new path cut through the wide valley south of the bay, over a
shallow mountain pass, and into the alluvial plain of the Río Salinas.
The trip now lasted just two days. However even this new trail could
not explain why a messenger arrived so fast on Rigoberto's heels. It
was Juan Evangelista—Junípero's boy. He was covered head to toe
in dust, and his face bore dark circles under the eyes, as though he
had not slept. Rigoberto had not known Juan Evangelista was coming
north; otherwise he would have waited so they could make the journey together.

"Juan Evangelista," I exclaimed as the neophyte limped into
camp. "You look half-starved. Come sit by the fire." Rigoberto took
his friend's mule, and I made chocolate for the three of us. "Tell me,
Son: what is the matter?"

"You are requested to come to Carmelo," the boy said. "Fray Juan
has taken ill."

"What is this? Rigoberto came from Carmelo this noon. He said
nothing of an illness."

"It began suddenly," Juan Evangelista said. "Fray Junípero
thought at first it was a digestive imbalance. The doctor from the
presidio gave calomel, but His Reverence's color has now left him
completely."

"How long ago was this?"

"I left Carmel yesterday, Your Reverence."

"You walked through the night."

"Yes, sir. Fray Junípero said you are to depart at once, with no
delay. As I left he was already preparing oil for anointment."

The chocolate was ready, but I no longer wanted it. When Rigoberto returned from the paddock, I asked if he had noticed anything
awry with Fray Juan.

"No, Your Reverence. He remained in his cell most days, but

when I saw him at Mass, he looked healthy. The time at San Diego improved his color, I think."

"I agree," Juan Evangelista said. "The sun was good for Fray Juan."

"And now his color is gone?"

"His complexion is like whey."

"Does he have a fever?"

"I do not know, Father. Fray Junípero only told me to come and get you—"

"Rigoberto," I said. "Saddle our mule."

But then I stopped myself. I knew how this incident would end: Juan Evangelista and I would hasten to Carmel, the poor neophyte making the grueling overland journey for the second time in a week, and when we arrived, Fray Juan would be holed up in his cell. His health would have returned but not his nerve. He would apologize profusely, and I would turn around to come home.

"Wait," I said. "This is madness; we should spend the night here. In the morning, when Juan Evangelista is rested, we will go."

"His Reverence gave strict instructions," the boy protested. "Do not dawdle, he said, bring Fray Francisco at once."

"He says this every time," I pointed out. "Have you ever known Fray Junípero to give an uncertain order?"

The boy's liquid black eyes beseeched me. "Your Reverence, this is not the same. His Reverence would have come to you himself, were Fray Juan not in such danger. I assure you, Father, the situation is grave."

The truth was that in my short months by the bay, I had made peace with Fray Juan Crespí. At some point I realized that it was ridiculous to harbor resentment against such a pathetic enemy. If this were a contest—a lifelong contest for the affections of our master—he had won the prize. Though I was the more trusted disciple, he enjoyed the proximity to the great soul. But at what cost? He had sacrificed his dignity. I no longer felt the bite of envy when I heard his name. Instead I felt pity for a colleague who had shown great promise but lost his way. Only rarely did I revisit the enmities between us. I regretted sharing them with Rigoberto, because I knew they did not reflect my better self. I had even started exchanging letters with Juan, now that he was back in Carmel. He knew that I bore him no ill will.

Still, as I watched Rigoberto spread hay on the ground for Juan Evangelista's mule, I wondered how many times I would be made to scramble on his behalf. There seemed to be no end to the inconveniences he was capable of causing those around him. But they were only inconveniences; what monster would miss his companion's last breath because the trip was too inconvenient?

I went that same night, but in the end it did not matter. By the time we arrived in Carmel, Fray Juan Crespí was dead.

I FOUND JUNIPERO naked and prostrate on the dirt floor of the mission chapel. I gathered that he had recently been violent with himself, because none of the neophytes knelt nearer than a leg's length away. The air was redolent with candle smoke. All the tapers in the mission's stores had been deployed around the altar and in the niches of the carved-wood *reredos*—at least two dozen in all. I had not seen two dozen candles burning together for many years, and the effect was powerful. The painted statues of Saint Anthony, Saint Joseph, and Our Seraphic Father San Francisco shone with the lurid colors intended by the artisans who had released them from wood. Their graceful postures—an arm outstretched, fingers gently unrolling—exaggerated, by contrast, the anguish of the earth-bound friar.

The mourners stirred when I entered with Juan Evangelista, and Fray Junípero lifted his head. "You are too late," he wailed.

"I know. The sentries told me."

"You could not have come quickly enough, I am afraid. God issued his call to Fray Juan and took him promptly."

I made the sign of the cross. "May he rest in peace."

Junípero called for his cassock, and it was brought to him. As he dressed, I saw in the candlelight the old scars on his back. He looked like a mangy dog, white skin showing through in the patches where his body hair had stopped trying to grow.

I sat with His Reverence in the mission's parlor, a double-sized chamber next to the friars' sleeping quarters. This is where we received the governor on his weekly visits from the royal presidio, as well as any foreigners whose ships came to anchor at Monterey. It was an incongruously ornate room, housing all the gifts bestowed by visitors over the years. There was, for example, a set of ivory and ebony chessmen given to Fray Junípero by the captain of His Highness's Manila galleon. Fray Junípero loathed chess and kept the pieces locked in a small china hutch which had been the gift of another visiting mariner. We sat in carved armchairs—fashioned by neophyte carpenters after a gift in the presidio. A boy brought chocolate, but neither Junípero nor I felt like refreshment.

"I knew this would happen, Paco. Even before I released Juan Evangelista to bring you back, I knew the news would reach you too late."

"It is not your fault, Your Reverence."

"He was as fit as an ox! Then suddenly the spirit drained from him. One evening I noticed that he was pale, and I asked if he was ill. He said no, of course. But one could have passed a hand behind his back and counted the fingers."

"Had he been well otherwise? The neophytes say he had color in his face since returning from San Diego."

"He had color, yes, but rare was the day I saw him out of his cell except at Mass."

"He was melancholy."

"But Paco, a melancholy man does not simply wither and die!"

"God's plans can be inscrutable."

Junípero gave me a look that seemed to say he had his doubts about this statement, even if he could not dispute it theologically.

"What I mean, Your Reverence, is that we cannot pretend to know why God has called our brother home, but we can be sure he is in Paradise."

"Yes, that is assured. It is unlike me to dwell in the past, but I cannot help revisiting the events of the last few days."

"You loved him, Your Reverence. It is only natural to remember."

"Yes. But I am afraid this is something else. An obsession, perhaps. I think of everything I did those last days, everyone I saw, looking for connections, for hints that he was not well. It could be just as you say—that God only wanted Fray Juan to come home. I felt certain God would take me before Juan, simply because I was older and had once been his superior. Did you not feel the same way, Paco?"

"I was never his superior, Your Reverence. And he was, as you may recall, two years my senior."

Junípero brushed this off. "There are years, Paco, and then there is age. They are not the same thing."

It seemed as though His Reverence was going to pay me a compliment. My ears grew warm in anticipation, but then he struck off in another direction. "Do you know your neophyte came to see me?"

"Rigoberto?"

"Yes, Rigoberto Palóu." His eyes swelled as he said the name. "He delivered your journal of the expedition with Governor Rivera. Very thorough work. Quite disturbing in parts. Though I cannot say I am surprised."

I assumed he meant the incident on the ridge, which I had related in detail. Fray Junípero had walked to México City to remove one governor; I was sure he would do it again if the crimes were sufficient.

I expected that he would press for more on Don Fernando, but instead he returned to the neophyte.

"Yes, Rigoberto Palóu. He had the strangest request, which we discussed briefly. And then without so much as a rosary, he took his leave."

No doubt this request concerned the baptism of Rigo's heathen girl. But I was surprised that he had gone to Fray Junípero so soon. I had yet to give my blessing to the marriage, and I had been sure he would not approach Junípero without it.

"He rushed off," Junípero went on. "He was so eager to return. He reminds me of you in so many ways, Paco. Logical, dependable, hardworking . . ."

"He is a good boy. I am glad to have him with me in the north."

Junípero opened his mouth as though he were going to speak, and then closed it. A long silence ensued, during which we were alone with our thoughts. Finally Junípero said, "Do you think your neophyte might have brought some disease with him from the north country? There is bad air in the marsh, you know, and foul smells and insects. Do you think that perhaps in his pack, or in some of his traveling provisions, the boy harbored a type of vermin? There remains the question of how it might have passed to Fray Juan, but—ah!" Junípero's face flashed. "Yes, of course—the two of them shared a meal while I was absent in Monterey one afternoon. It might have been then, but one can never be sure of these things. Before he left, Rigoberto came to see me—but I have told you this already. I can still recall his face: his skin was ashen, his lips trembling slightly. Something was amiss with him. Do you suppose he was ill?"

That was one interpretation. An icy shadow came over my heart as I thought of another. "When Rigoberto came to see you," I said, "did he speak of Father Crespí?"

"We may have spoken about him, but Fray Juan was not our subject."

"He did not mention any arguments between Juan and me?"

"Let us not speak of such things now. Our brother deserves better than to have us dwell on past ills."

"Of course. It was disrespectful of me even to mention it."

We prayed, and we did not stop until two days had passed, as is our tradition in mourning the departed. I sang Mass, served the Eucharist, heard the confessions of His Reverence and half the neophytes at the mission. In other words, I performed the duties required of me. But all the while, my thoughts were in another place, coalescing around the idea that Rigoberto, far from keeping Juan's illness at bay, had somehow caused it to descend. Like Junípero, I revisited the past few days, recalling how in one conversation Rigoberto had divulged his plan to marry and I had shared my frustration with Juan Crespí. "No, Father," he had said. "I will earn your blessing."

Might the boy have thought he could earn my favor by murdering Fray Juan? As the mourning wore on, I realized I had made a grave mistake in judgment. In granting Rigoberto permission to travel to Carmel, I had set in motion a plan to kill my brother. Ignorance was no excuse; I was responsible for the boy's behavior, whether or not I understood his intentions. He went to Carmel as my surrogate. Indeed, as Fray Junípero had pointed out, he and I were very much alike. He was loyal, dependable, hardworking. He even shared my name. Everything he did reflected on me. If there were one man in the world I might consider an extension of myself, it was he. His actions, therefore, were as good as mine, and also his sins.

I TRAVELED BACK to Mission San Francisco under gray skies and steady rain. The trail was washed out at every stream and gully, every *arroyo seco* now an angry, gushing vein. My escort and I struggled to find the notched trees in the mist and fog, and several times we found ourselves lost among the giants. Once, my sandals slipped in the mud and I found myself helpless among the logs and leaves. I put out a hand to push myself up and caught instead an enormous yellow slug, long as my foot. Its stippled skin was covered in a viscous liquid that I could not remove from my fingertips no matter how I tried.

Against my will, the soldier took me up on his horse. He said we had lost enough time as it was, and with God as his witness he would not stand to lose a friar down a slippery canyon wall. I resisted all comforts, refusing even to wring my clothing when the rain stopped. The cassock clung to my back like a second skin, heavy and cold. In the evening, the escort pitched only one tent and insisted that I lie next to him to regain my heat. I waited until he fell asleep and then made my bed outside, next to the embers of the small fire where he had warmed our dinner. I deserved every discomfort God could devise for me, and I was determined to find them all. By the time we reached the bay, I was delirious with fever.

"Satan is a worm," I whispered in the soldier's ear, "a yellow worm, and he is here among us!"

"Hush, Father," said the man. He shrugged his shoulder to adjust my weight. He had lashed me to his torso, as I was no longer able to sit erect on my own.

He took me to the Presidio of San Francisco—at that point a wooden structure of a single room and several covered porches, hardly deserving of the royal standard rippling proudly on the mast— where the men laid me in a cot and called the doctor to my bedside. The fellow appeared to me like a faun, raising his cloven feet to my temples and forehead, and pressing diligently upon my stomach and spleen. I drifted in and out of consciousness. I recall that during one of the doctor's ministrations, I sat upright, tossing off his hooves. "Let me die!" I cried. "Let me die, as I let my brother die."

"Fray Francisco, you are not well. Rest your tongue."

"Yes, yes. Better that I should take this with me to Hell. No need to trouble Fray Junípero."

The soldiers exchanged worried looks, but the doctor, who had seen his share of febrile ravings, reassured them. "He will not remember what he says, and neither should you. Priests stray farthest of all when they are ill. I do not know why."

"Perhaps the press of discipline?" suggested one of the soldiers.

"Or all the confessions they have to hear . . . At any rate, he must remain in bed until the fever subsides. No matter how he protests, keep him here."

I had no desire to leave the presidio, because a return to the mission would require that I confront Rigoberto, and I could not predict how I might react when I met him. If in my fever-altered state an innocent doctor could appear as a goat, I could only wonder what form a murderer might take.

I should have known better than to take solace in distance; loyal son that he was, Rigoberto appeared at my bedside within hours of my arrival at the presidio. At first he was only a dark presence in the corner of the room, mumbling over his rosary. When he saw that I was awake, he rushed to my side. "Father, I thought you would never return. Fray Vicente sang a novena, and when that did not produce you from the trail, I insisted that he begin another. We were halfway through the second when word came from the presidio . . . "

The neophyte's eyes, ovoid in the manner of all the heathens, had shrunk to slits, the yellow irises barely visible within. His skin had turned rough, and it hung about his neck like drapery. When he turned his head and his cheeks caught the light from the doorway, I saw that his face was covered with reptilian scales, thousands of them, arranged in neat rows. A wicked forked tongue darted in and out of his mouth, shivering in the air at each stroke. I heard a groan, then realized I myself had made the sound.

The doctor heard me and rushed back into the room. "Everyone out," he commanded. He pressed his hooves into Rigo's side.

Neither remarked upon the other's strange form. A moment later the room was still, even the doctor having taken his leave. I heard the barking of seals, and in the distance, a long way off, the song of heathen women grinding acorns into flour.

AFTER A WEEK'S convalescence, I returned to my mission on the creek of La Dolorosa. Mission Dolores, the mission of sorrows. It seemed only right to call it by that name, considering how its residents had failed to follow the perfect example of San Francisco.

My companion Fray Vicente Santa Maria greeted me warmly and shared good news: the boys who had begun to visit before my trip to Carmel now came to Mass every day. Fray Vicente rewarded them with beads and cups of maize flour, and every day they carried these offerings back to their *rancherías* in small baskets ornamented with feathers. My companion reported that several times during Mass he had seen other figures huddled in the brush. He assumed these were the boys' parents, or perhaps their older siblings.

So great was his joy and excitement that it was suppertime before he asked about my trip. He wished to know the readings His Reverence had chosen for the requiem Masses. I gave them, and described for him the elaborate *ofrenda* that the neophytes had constructed to honor Juan. It began with a cross of rough timber and grew day by day as the heathen brought baskets of food, wreaths of flowers, and feathered garments of all kinds. Even the heathen sent tribute: a bleached deer skull, a necklace of bears' claws threaded on sinew. At one point we were summoned from the chapel to the mission gates, where a half-dozen heathen men were standing with feet together and arms pointing straight out to the sides, in imitation of the cross.

Fray Vicente was pleased by my story. "Satan's grip is slipping," he pronounced.

I glanced quickly at Rigoberto, then back. "Let us hope you are correct."

"There can be no doubt, Your Reverence," interjected the neophyte. "When one considers the progress made here in just a fortnight, and the continued success of Mission San Carlos . . . "

"Oh?" I said. "Has there been progress at Carmelo?"

Rigoberto bowed his head, and for a moment I felt sorry for him. Then I remembered the image of Fray Junípero, prostrate on the packed-earth floor of the chapel, mourning our dead brother. I remembered how His Reverence struggled to understand how his *condiscípulo* could have faded away so quickly. And how close he had been to the truth.

"Fray Vicente, may I have a word alone with Rigoberto, please?" It was an unusual request, to dismiss my brother in favor of a neophyte, but Vicente sensed my urgency. He bowed and took his leave.

In the twilight, Rigoberto's skin glowed crimson. I had found it difficult to forget the vision of him as a snake. Now his face shone with a kind of conspiratorial glee. Or perhaps I was imagining that as well?

"Father, tell me," he said anxiously, "did you speak with Fray Junípero? About what we discussed—did you speak to him on my behalf?"

I marveled that he could think of himself at a time like this, with my brother dead by his hand.

"I spoke to His Reverence, but not on your behalf. Nor would you want me to. Not after what you've done."

"What have I done?"

"God help you if you cannot confess."

"I promise I have done you no ill, Your Reverence."

"Yes, quite the contrary."

"I have done nothing wrong!"

NICK TAYLOR • 227

"That is true. The wrong was mine. I should never have shared with you my history with Fray Juan."

"Forgive me, Father, but how does your history with Fray Juan bear on me?"

"I should have closed my heart to you."

"But Father, the Lord says, 'harden not thy heart' . . . In the Psalms first, and again in the epistle to the Hebrews—"

I shook my head, ashamed at what I had wrought. This boy, this Indian boy, who could quote Scripture like a seminarian, was he to be the model for the others? What about the boys who were now regular visitors here? Would we perpetuate our error?

"I can see that I will never have your blessing," Rigoberto said somberly.

"My blessing? You are lucky I do not hand you over to the Governor for hanging!"

"If I have sinned, Father, let me be punished. But please tell me what I have done."

"You thought that if you murdered Fray Juan, I would be grateful. You hoped I would bless your union with a heathen girl. That may be a logical course of events in the *ranchería,* Rigoberto, but not in the civilized world. We do not take one another's lives. That is for God only. If you do not understand this most basic lesson of our faith, then I have failed you. As a teacher and a father, I have failed you."

The boy looked as though I had slapped him across the face. He said, "Father, you are mistaken. Look into my heart, you will see I have done nothing wrong." He fought tears, as a man will when his world collapses about him. "Whatever I must do to convince you, I will."

"Go away from here tonight," I said. "I will have to live forever with what I have done; let me at least not be reminded by seeing your face."

"If that is your desire, Father."

"There is nothing I desire less, but it must be so."

There was a brief moment when neither of us spoke. I would revisit this moment hundreds of times in what remained of my life, each time with a different regret.

"If it is the will of God, I will go," the neophyte said soberly. Without so much as a tear, he dashed into the woods, disappearing into the fog.

TEN

IN THE HILLS THE coyotes fought their loneliness. Never fear, I told myself, he will return in the morning. He will remember that Christ forgives all sins. Perhaps I needed to remember this as well. Yes, I was a poor imitation of the Lamb of God—this I would freely admit to my son when he returned.

All night I rolled on my cot. I rose at the pinking of the eastern sky. The camp was silent. Where I might have seen my son laying sticks for the fire, now there was no one. The place on the earth where he normally made his bed was undisturbed except by dew. I followed the sound of leaves into a thicket, hoping that like the curious *indios,* my neophyte might have left a sign, some feathers or a carving, anything to make his presence known, even as he remained hidden from view.

Peeling back the branches, I found no evidence of man. Instead I found a deer, a young buck whose antlers were still covered in velvet. The animal stamped the ground with a foreleg, protesting my intrusion.

"Amar a Dios," I said weakly.

The deer's wet nostrils quivered. I stared into his eyes, dark and innocent, pupils olive-wide. For a moment we regarded each other in silence. Fog sprung from the animal's nose in regular bursts.

I had acted in haste, governed by anger. By envy, the sharpest tine on Satan's fork.

"Dear God," I prayed aloud, "take a message to my son Rigoberto. I do not appeal often to your mercy, O Lord, but I have made a grave mistake."

Have you?

The voice issued from everywhere and nowhere like an echo. I turned quickly to see if Fray Vicente had come out to the fire ring looking for his morning chocolate. There were no bodies anywhere to be seen; nothing but to the buck in front of me, which oddly had not stirred at the noise.

"Who is there?" I said loudly. At the sound of my voice, a couple of sparrows chirped and fluttered from the bush. But the buck did not flee. He stood still as an oak, his eyes intent as ever.

Father Francisco, why have you cast me out?

I recognized the timbre of Rigoberto's voice, the slow and careful enunciation.

"Rigo? Is that you?" I expected my son to burst from the manzanitas, open-armed and smiling, all forgiveness. But again, I saw no movement in the trees. My knees trembled as I began to understand what was happening. I remembered the sweat lodge, the vision of Fray Junípero. This time, however, I had ingested no herbs, inhaled no toxic fumes.

You know me, Father.

"Yes, Rigoberto, I know you. I hear your voice."

Because I did not know where to address myself, I faced the buck as I spoke. Every now and then he twitched an ear, as though discouraging some winged insect, but otherwise he did not move.

You knew my character, Father, yet you rushed to judgment.

"I acted in haste, my son. Forgive me."

You have no evidence that I killed Fray Juan.

"That is true. I have only my suspicions."

Of all people, Father, why would you suspect me? I loved Fray Juan. I loved all of God's chosen people. Most especially, I loved you.

"And I you, Son." My eyes began to water. "Please, Rigo. Please come home."

That is not possible. I am far away.

"Surely you can turn around."

It is too late. You must accept what you have done.

"I accept it! No matter how it pains me, I accept it. I will do penance a thousand times over."

This is not confession, Father. There will be time for confession, but not now.

"When? When may I unburden myself?"

I must go. Good-bye, Father.

There was a noise behind me, the clinking of metal and the popping of a rekindled fire. I saw Fray Vicente's boy bent over the pit. We were separated by not more than ten paces, but he appeared oblivious to my conversation.

I returned to the buck, but found that it had vanished.

"Boy," I called to the neophyte. "Where is Fray Vicente?"

Startled, the neophyte looked up from his work. "Father Francisco!" he cried. "Forgive me, I did not mean to disturb your prayers."

"My prayers?"

"You were sitting so peacefully. I assumed you were deep in meditation, and I did not wish to interrupt you. Would you like a cup of chocolate?"

I tried to appear composed, though my heart was in knots. "I—yes, thank you. Is Fray Vicente awake?"

"Not yet, sir. Would you like me to wake him?"

"That is not necessary . . . "

I occupied myself with cleaning the altar vessels while the neophyte made chocolate. When the beverages were ready, Fray Vicente strode into the clearing, summoned by the aroma.

"Morning, Brother."

"Good morning," I said.

Vicente accepted a cup of chocolate from the boy. He blew over the lip and looked around the camp. "Where is Rigoberto?" he asked.

"Did you sleep well last night? It was especially cold, I think."

"Did he go to the presidio?"

"That's right, he—" I started to prevaricate, but stopped myself. As my companion, Fray Vicente would have to know the truth. "Rigoberto is not here," I said. "He left last night."

"For the presidio?"

"I do not know where he went."

"To Carmelo?"

"Perhaps there, but my feeling is that he has left us for good."

"Oh? That is a surprise."

I searched my brother's face for clues, for any sign he knew the truth.

"Yes, I was surprised as well," I said carefully. "He told me that he was . . . that he had been doubting his faith."

Fray Vicente sighed and held the steaming bowl of chocolate between his palms. "Better that he left us now, before the new tribes come around. I would hate to hold out a doubter as the example."

"Rigoberto was a pious boy!" I was surprised at the indignation in my voice. "He feared the Lord with great conviction."

"That may be so, but he made his choice. It is a shame how many recidivists one finds among the heathens. Did you know that at Mission San Antonio, Father Lasuén was forced to excommunicate a group of neophytes who had been holding pagan rituals in the family lodgings? It seems they also attended Mass, but that kind of behavior cannot be tolerated."

"Of course not."

"Honestly, Brother, I was not prepared for how difficult it would be to break these *indios* from the pagan faiths. Why do they cling to such fallacies? Can you imagine worshipping eagles, for example? Or deer?"

"Indeed," I said. "It troubles the mind."

AT THE FLEDGLING mission campus, we felt Rigoberto's loss in our hands as well as our hearts. With so much work to be done, it soon became clear that we needed another neophyte laborer. Fray Vicente recommended that I send to Carmel for Teófilo, who had been Fray Juan's boy. He was married now, but there was no other neophyte more qualified to serve us here.

"I would prefer that Fray Junípero not know why we need Teófilo," I explained to Fray Vicente. "Rigoberto may return, and then we will have worried His Reverence needlessly."

Vicente nodded and said he understood, but I could tell that he thought I was being overcautious. "You are right," he said, "Junípero is not a young man anymore. His heart may be fragile for all we know. He certainly would not tell us if he were ill."

And so it was done: Teófilo arrived within the month. Soon after, we performed our first baptisms. The two young visitors allowed Fray Vicente to pour water over their heads in exchange for a double helping of beads and masa harina. The boys laughed and licked the drops that fell from their noses. After the ceremony we showed them to the wood-frame dormitory just completed by Lieutenant Moraga's crew. It was a pathetic little house by the standards of Mission Carmelo, a wooden peg in the door serving in lieu of a proper lock, but it would easily accommodate the boys. We gave them proper clothes and told them their Christian names—Alejandro Serra and Daniel Santa Maria. At first they were delighted by the attention lavished upon them, but when they realized that the wooden planks in the house were for sleeping—that this would be their home—they grew apprehensive. By signs they indicated that they wanted to deliver our gifts to their families. I pitied them, and told them we would leave their baskets in the clearing near the cross. Their parents could fetch the baskets if they wished. We gave each boy a blanket and locked the dormitory. Their cries lasted only a few hours before they fell asleep.

A week later, the adults of the tribe came to call. They looked more or less like the heathen of the Carmel Valley, with bone ornaments stuck in their lips and ears and elaborate scarifications over their backs and shoulders. As in Carmelo, the women had enough natural decency to cover their breasts and nether regions, but the men went about quite naked. We gathered from their signs that they had come with a double purpose: first to view the boys who had never returned to the village, and second to secure more of the provisions they had become accustomed to receiving from us. We showed them the dormitory, where the boys—now ill with a cold—lay indolent on their bunks. The heathens refused to come closer than two or three fathoms from the building, and when they began to make gestures resembling eating, we understood that seeing the boys had perhaps been only the secondary purpose of their trip.

I measured four bowls of corn flour into their baskets—the same small, tightly woven vessels the boys had used—and gave them also a small pouch of assorted glass beads. Unlike the natives we had encountered on the ridge with Don Fernando, these took our gifts with grace and reserve. The one who stood at the front of the group produced a seed cake wrapped in willow leaves, which he handed to me with a benediction of some kind.

I said, "I thank you in the name of the Lord Jesus Christ."

The headman said nothing. The bone stretched his lip into the shape of a shovel, so that he looked to be frowning.

"Christ welcomes all to His Church with the promise of everlasting life . . ."

We had learned it was best not to confuse the heathen with

theology, particularly not at first contact, but I still believed that a convert ought to have some idea what he is about to accept. I had once voiced this concern to Fray Junípero, who only smiled and said, "Did you understand the bishop's words when you were baptized, Paquito?"

"Fray Vicente," I said, "would you please bring the font?"

As with the boys, we indicated that we would give double rations in exchange for this favor. Teófilo dipped the tin bowl in the sack of corn and allowed a stream of the yellow flour to cascade from its rim. The heathen were mesmerized by the almost vulgar plenitude, and they came forward without a struggle.

One by one, I drizzled the water of the Sacrament upon their heads, baptizing each in the name of the Father, and of the Son, and of the Holy Spirit. When all four had been saved, we put the corn in the basket and showed them to the dormitories. As they came to understand our intention, the heathens began grunting and waving their arms. We called the sentries from the garrison. Seeing the resistance, the soldiers rushed in and threw ropes around the neophytes' necks. With every thrash, the ropes cinched tighter. One of the neophyte woman fought so valiantly against the restraint that she lost the ability to breathe and fell down. After allowing a moment for the lesson to take hold, the soldier loosened the noose. The woman resumed normal respiration, but now she was silent and still.

Our catch stood at six.

SPRING CAME TO the Bay of San Francisco, the hills once more fresh and green, but Rigoberto did not return. Though I gave the appearance that I had moved on from the loss of my first and best neophyte son, in fact I had not. Every time I walked alone in the woods I strained my ears for voices, for animals who lingered too long after hearing my footsteps. My son did not present himself to me, but I was not content to wait: I devised a plan to search the villages—all the pagan *rancherías* in New California, if necessary—using Teófilo as my agent.

The first time I asked Teófilo to go into the heathen country, he had been at Mission San Francisco only a week. It was before the first adults had come for baptism in the Lord, and I cloaked my request in the guise of reconnaissance. "Go and see where they have their camps," I instructed. "Find the highest ground and mark the *rancherías* on this." I gave him a tracing of the most recent chart of the area.

As I expected, Teófilo performed his task with thoroughness and alacrity, arriving home three days later with the sheet covered in markings of trails and habitations both current and abandoned. I began to spend time with him alone, fostering the intimacy required by my plan. I learned that he was a devoted husband and a devout Catholic. When I could be absolutely sure of his trustworthiness, I took him into my confidence regarding his predecessor.

"Your brother Rigoberto ran away from God," I explained. "Under the influence of Satan, he chose to return to the wilderness."

Teófilo's face paled. I had not meant to frighten him, but I wanted him to understand that Rigoberto had not been excommunicated.

"Where is he now?" Teófilo asked. "Has he gone far?" Then an instant later: "I can find him, Father. With your permission, I would like to try."

Had the scene been scripted by a playwright, it could not have unfolded more profitably for me. I had no need to put the fire of God in this disciple's heart; he had kindled it there himself.

"But you have so many responsibilities here . . . " I wheedled.

"I will be quick! No one knows this land like I do."

"That is true. But with the recent baptisms, I do not see how we could afford to let you leave."

"Are you afraid I will fall prey to Satan as well?"

"It is a tragedy to lose one son," I said. "There is no word to describe losing two."

"Father, please allow me to go. There will be no danger if I hide myself."

"I see you will not be deterred. You may go. But please do not stray too far."

Now Teófilo began making frequent trips to the villages, extending his range each time. By the third trip, he had wandered as far south as the next station, the new Mission Santa Clara de Asís, and by the fourth, all the way to the Pueblo of San José, a civilian plot settled by Lieutenant Moraga and several dozen brave families from Sonora. In all instances, there had been much to report—at Mission Santa Clara, a newborn calf had been abducted by a mountain lion; near the pueblo, twenty acres of green wheat sprouts were ruined by insects in a single afternoon. But none of the news concerned Rigoberto.

Teófilo's fifth and sixth expeditions took him to the other side of the bay, where he reported the native population was even thicker than on our peninsula. "The shell mounds are inconceivably large, Father, like chalk mountains in the marsh. And the smoke from the villages is so thick you would think you were in Hell."

The weeks wore on, and then it had been six months since Rigoberto disappeared. I knew that by now he might be anywhere—San Diego, Sonora, even México. The weak flame in my heart, flickering so long, now threatened to snuff out. Worse still, I had no companion to whom I could turn for sympathy. Fray Junípero did not know Rigoberto was gone. Fray Vicente knew it, but not the reason why. How it would have appalled San Francisco to see one of his brothers, whom he wished to protect from loneliness, so isolated by his own mendacity!

Finally one evening Teófilo announced to me that he would go to Carmelo. "We have searched everywhere else," he said. "Rigoberto must have gone there."

"You will not," I said, and I was firm. Carmelo was Teófilo's home; he would be recognized there. Also, no amount of will would keep him from visiting his wife. And if he went to Mission San Carlos, even surreptitiously, Fray Junípero would know.

After a brief argument, Teófilo backed down. He agreed to remain at Mission San Francisco, where his presence, I promised him, was indispensable. He took my praise with characteristic modesty, avoiding my eyes as he tamped the earth with his foot.

Why must we continue to believe that native people have simple minds? Again and again we "people of reason" misjudge them. Because the *indio* prizes beads as the Spaniard does gold, we conclude that he is unsophisticated in other ways as well. Nothing could be further from the truth. I appealed to Teófilo with the kind of empty flattery that would not have fooled an infant in Spain; why did I think it would persuade a grown man in California?

In the end I was the fool, for the next morning when I woke, Teófilo was gone.

FOR THE FIRST few days of Teófilo's absence, I maintained to Fray Vicente that the neophyte was only spending time in a village, making contacts and spreading the Good News of Christ. This was roughly the excuse I had given for Teófilo's previous trips. When he had not returned a week later, I said he had gone to another village. Then another. Eventually my explanations became implausible. Fray Vicente was not surprised when I gave him the truth.

"He has gone to find Rigoberto," I confessed.

"To find him, you say?" My companion wiped snuff from his nostril. "I would have thought he went to join him. Answer me this, Brother: supposing Teófilo finds his quarry, how will he return Rigoberto to God? You say Rigoberto's faith was damaged even before he left us. It would seem unlikely that he has changed his heart."

I could not bear to give Fray Vicente the truth. "Between us," I said, "I think he wished to see his family."

"Likely both are lost, to God and to us." He waved his hand. Sadly, it was the attitude of most missionaries that the loss of some souls was inevitable, like sand between our fingers, but that we ought not worry about it, so long as the majority remained. And to be sure, our dormitories were filling rapidly: in the month since Teófilo's departure, twelve more natives had been saved in the healing water of Christ.

But I took no solace in the baptismal rolls. I knew in my heart that two of our most promising soldiers of God had gone astray because of me. The logic was irrefutable: had I not spoken ill of Fray Juan to Rigoberto, he would not have made his murderous error; had I not sent him away, there would have been no need for Teófilo to follow. My influence had been nothing short of disastrous for these two men. I was a plague. I might be damned for keeping the truth from Fray Vicente, but how could I expose him to the pestilence in my heart?

"Let him go, Paco," said Fray Vicente. He took another pinch of snuff, lifted it to his nose, and inhaled. "Give your attention to the work we have here. Our rolls are growing. The Father President will be impressed. If Teófilo comes back, so much the better. But the worst is over, my friend."

As it turns out, the worst was not over, although the next catastrophe came in the form of a blessing. Six weeks after his departure, Teófilo returned. He had become rather adept at stealthy movement and stole into my quarters without waking the guards, the neophytes, or even Father Vicente, who lay dozing on the cot next to mine. He roused me with a quick jab to the ribs and then put his palm over my mouth. "Follow me outside," he whispered.

My heart hammered as I rose and found my sandals. Teófilo crept out before me, filling the doorway with his shadow. I tried to imagine why he had felt it necessary to steal into camp unannounced; he had never taken such a precaution before. Perhaps it was because of the length of his absence. Or—and I now allowed myself to hope for the first time in weeks—perhaps he had some news of Rigoberto.

Perhaps even more than news. As I neared the door, I saw a second shadow beside Teófilo's. I stepped into the chill night air.

"Father—" Teófilo's voice strained. "Father, this is my wife, Maria Lucia, and our son, Juan Crespí."

A short but handsome native woman, dressed in the simple homespun of the mission neophytes, stood clutching a bundle to her chest. She bounced the child slightly, almost imperceptibly. She did not smile at me, but only stole a quick glance at my face before resting her attentions on her husband.

"Forgive me for waking you, Father," Teófilo said. "Please do not be angry with me."

I said nothing. He gathered my mood. And I gathered all I needed to know of him: that he had stolen his family from Mission San Carlos. Perhaps he had spent the six weeks in avid pursuit of Rigoberto, or perhaps he had only been plotting escape. In any case, he had not found my son.

"Father, I did not intend to come back here. It is only because Maria Lucia insisted. You see, there is a piece of news she felt she must share—"

"Rigoberto?" The word escaped my mouth.

"No, Father. I could not find him anywhere. I checked all the villages from here to Carmelo, and further south as well—"

"But the Father President . . . " said the wife in their tongue. Her face had turned sour, and she looked as though she might cry.

"Be quiet," whispered Teófilo.

"Why don't you tell him?"

"I will. Be patient."

"This is no time for patience!" Maria Lucia redoubled her bouncing, and the boy whimpered in his sleep. Had I heard correctly that his name was Juan Crespí?

"Forgive her, Father. She is only concerned for Fray Junípero."

"Why is that?"

"His Reverence has taken ill, it has been four weeks—"

"*Five,*" corrected the wife.

"He tells everyone he is mending, but he has been too weak to sing Mass."

This was startling news. Junípero was remarkably hale for a man of his age, but he had been hobbled by the chronic irritation of his left leg. He had treated the wound from time to time with a shepherd's liniment of tallow and herbs, and to the amazement of the presidio doctor—though not to anyone who knew Junípero well—the crude cure had always reduced the infection. However he had always, even on the days of his worst suffering, stood at the altar to sing Mass.

"Is it the leg?" I asked.

"It is that, but now he has other complaints as well."

"You say he complains? That does not sound like Junípero."

"He does not complain in words, Father, but the suffering is plain on his face."

"You have been to see him, then?"

The neophyte cast his eyes down. "Not I, Father. My wife. She saw him before she—that is, before we—"

"Enough," I said. "Go."

IN THE WEEKS that followed, I learned that Junípero had recovered somewhat from the impairments reported by Teófilo's wife. He sang Mass, heard confessions, and administered the temporal affairs of the mission. In the spring, he traveled south to establish, at last, the Mission of San Buenaventura.

His letters had begun to resemble a journal, as though he were writing not to me but to posterity. Informing me that Governor Rivera had been killed, he tried to be impartial, or even patriotic ("the heathens came in the night, in the manner of assassins"), but I knew he must have rejoiced to see God's justice done. Hell, he always said, reserved a special place for colonial governors.

In his letters too there were passages where he drew aside formality

in favor of a surprising intimacy. For example, after a long description of the proceedings at the founding of San Buenaventura, including the names of all present (and the ranks of the military men) he
inserted the following:

> Paco, if I died today you would be the one I missed most, for we
> have been closer these many years than if we had been brothers
> in the flesh. It is my greatest wish that you understand my special
> affection for you. Please do not think ill of me, despite my many
> failings in this life.

He went on to perform the verbal equivalent of an altar-top flag-
ellation. He had always been obsequious in closing his letters *(Your
most unworthy friar*, or *God's most wretched and undeserving priest*, or
Yours in penitence, etc.), but our Order places a high value on humility, and usually I read these lines as nothing more than convention.
However in these new humiliations I detected an urgency not present in his earlier writings. What were these "failings," I wondered,
which might make me think ill of him? Certainly he realized that
by this point, decades into our acquaintance, I had settled on my
opinion of him—"warts and all," as the English say. Without question he was a great man, but it seemed that in his old age he had
become suddenly bothered by the compromises required for greatness. A man cannot be both great and pure, not even a man like Fray
Junípero. I had thought he understood this choice.

He began to hint, in these intimate postscripts, that I ought to
come to Carmel, that he might not have long to live: *If I live to renew
my vows once more on the feast of Our Seraphic Father*, he would write.
Or, *Anointing a sick neophyte boy this morning I considered that I myself
would receive the oil before long* . . . The appeals were uncharacteristically pitiful, and I was moved by them. However I was determined
not to visit Carmel until it was absolutely necessary. I feared that
seeing His Reverence in the flesh would cause me to revert to my

meek novice self—the Francisco Palóu of forty years ago, who went to pieces before his mentor, simply out of awe for his intelligence and the force of his convictions. As long as I could monitor his health through impartial observers, I would remain by the Bay of San Francisco, mulling my own "failings in this life."

And there were many. Late that winter I had a letter from Encarna:

My dear Paco,

I received your letter from Monterey. It brought me great relief to read with my own eyes that you are alive and well. I appreciated your encouragements regarding the convent, but by the time your letter arrived I had already left the Order. As of this writing, I have been a laywoman nine months, and although I still have occasional doubts, I believe it was the right decision.

This past October, I was married to a man named Antonio Villegas. He is a widower, a good Catholic, and only a few years older than you. He works as a clerk in the district court in Palma. Like me he spent time in the cloister but felt it was not his life's calling. His late wife bore him two beautiful children, a boy and a girl, who are now grown and healthy. They have become my children as well, for God has willed that in the autumn of my life I should become a mother. I hope that you will share my joy in this unexpected blessing.

I know how this news must hurt you, Paco, but I felt it was better not to hide. We are not young anymore; I would hate for one of us to pass to Eternity with untruths between us. I hope you can find it in your heart to wish me well. I certainly wish you continued success in your important work.

With best wishes, I remain,
Your devoted friend,
Señora Encarnación Villegas

Never had my work seemed less important. What difference did seven missions make? Or eight or nine? What were the rewards of a thousand baptisms or twenty thousand? I knew the answers, for Junípero had drummed them into my head since I was a boy, and for a while they were enough. But what if our missions failed? What if the fever snuffed out every neophyte on our rolls? What would we have to show for our "important work"?

Encarna at least had found companionship. Though it broke my heart to admit it, I did wish her well. I was angry when I read the letter the first time, for all the reasons one would expect. She had been the Clare to my Francis, and I assumed it would be ever thus. But looking back, I saw that she was only continuing the theme of her previous letters. In fact her heart was changing from the moment I met her, as it realized, gradually, that it could never achieve what it desired as long as it was trained on me.

I had felt that way about Fray Junípero Serra. I chose the man to be my lifelong mentor when I was only a boy. I followed him to the edge of civilization, but we never enjoyed the closeness I imagined for us—the closeness which I felt we deserved after so many years laboring apart.

In a way, the greatest gift His Reverence could have given was to send me north to the Bay of San Francisco. Only in isolation was I able to find my peace. Only here, tending my own flock and tilling my own unworked soil, would I understand that my master would never love me as I loved him. Sometimes affections are mismatched, as Encarna discovered. His Reverence preferred the company of Juan Crespí; I had only now, at sixty-one years of age, accepted that fact.

I read Encarna's letter many times, searching for its lesson. I knew I could not simply leave the Franciscan Order as she had. There are some choices one must live with forever—particularly those which lead to the other side of the world. Therefore I could not change my circumstances. But I could change my heart. I admired Encarna's courage in confronting her demons—in leaving the Order, in marrying late, and in writing to tell me she had done these things. I would do well to follow her example.

Thus when His Reverence's next letter came, I read the usual breathless news with fresh eyes: *There has been a packet ship! The governor is a fool! You must come and see the roses, Paco!* Between the lines, the request was the same as always: His Reverence wished to see me. This time I put aside my fear, my shame, my lies. Folding the letter, I calmly gathered my belongings, called for an escort, and set out on the trail for Carmel.

I TOOK A leatherjacket soldier, two boys, and enough mules to haul back supplies. I have described the journey and our reception in Carmel. You recall that we found Fray Junípero in grave condition—much worse than I expected. His skin was gray, his pulse weak. His throat whistled even when he was not speaking. You recall our vigil in the half-finished mission chapel: the swell of music from the choir of neophytes in the plaza; Junípero's proud demonstration of the chapel's stone sanctuary, where he wished to be interred beside Fray Juan. You recall how we made our way to the virgin confessional, and how at the last moment the chore was reversed, so that I took the penitent's side of the booth.

His Reverence stifled a cough with a bloody rag. "You are a practical man, Paco. You were a practical boy, and now you are a practical man. All those years ago, when you appeared in my class, I knew that we would be companions for life, for as you know, my spirit is like yeast, foaming and ever expanding, while yours is like . . . some kind of anti-leavening powder, I don't know what. I am old and ill, and my vocabulary fails me. But do you really believe that Juan was cursed? Is that your explanation for his illness?"

"Better men have been run down by Satan," I said.

"To be sure. But Juan's faith was unassailable. And his health was good! How can it be that a week later he was with God? Men in good health do not simply wither and die."

If His Reverence's vocabulary was blunted, his guile was keen as ever. I realized that he would never accuse Rigoberto of the murder, but would rather guide the interview so that I would be forced by any comment to reveal what I knew. It was precisely the technique one would expect from a man who served in the Holy Office of the Inquisition when he was fresh from seminary.

"Rigoberto was a good boy," I said weakly. My tone was level, my stare unflinching. I did not even notice that I had used the past tense.

"Rigoberto? How does this concern Rigoberto?"

"Let us quit this dance," I said. "You wish to know whether my boy killed Fray Juan. Every time we discuss the subject of Juan's death, you mention his name. I am not a fool, Your Reverence."

Junípero rose up. "Pardon me?"

"We are old, Brother, and your time here is short. The answer to your question is yes. Rigoberto poisoned Fray Juan. He wished to marry a heathen girl, and he thought he could earn my blessing that way."

"By murder?"

Had I stopped here to consider the shape of our conversation, I might have pared the words that followed. But once I began my confession, it felt unstoppable.

"One evening after we arrived at the bay, Rigoberto and I revealed our hearts to each other. He explained his intention to marry, and I shared with him . . . " It was like opening an old chest of clothes, closed in another chapter of life, which spills dust and mildew everywhere, along with ill associations. "I shared with him that I envied Fray Juan living here with you. I told him that my only wish in life had been to be your companion, to follow you through Spain or wherever God may lead. He said he understood. Then he said he would earn my blessing for his marriage. I had no warning other than that. I had no idea what he would do."

"And you are sure this is what happened?"

"Your Reverence, Rigoberto left the mission nearly a year ago."

"He is gone?"

"I hoped he would return. That is why I never told you."

"But you are sure he poisoned Fray Juan. You have evidence of this."

"He was guilty. Why else would he leave?"

Junípero considered this for a moment, nodding his head gently. I thought I heard him mumble a prayer. "It saddens me about you and Juan," he said. "I hoped you had found peace."

I wanted to tell him that we had; that I was comfortable with my life at Mission Dolores. As proof, consider that I did not envy Fray Junípero's new companion at Carmel, the Reverend Fray Matías Noriega. But how would this revelation be useful to Junípero? Fray Juan would still be dead.

"You know," said Junípero, "I had my own trouble with Juan. It always surprised me that you thought I favored him over you."

"I do not wish to reopen old wounds, Father."

"I understood your grievances, Paco. All of them—from that trifling oratory contest in the convent to the assignments in Old California to my choice of companions here in Carmelo. You must understand, Brother, that in each case I could not have acted otherwise. As the agent of God's dominions, I had no choice."

It was one thing for Fray Junípero to advise me to forgive Juan. Tolerance, forgiveness, forbearance—these are fundamental virtues. With respect to Juan Crespí, I had been deficient in all three. I have never denied these failures, and I never questioned the appropriateness of Junípero's advice. However I was much less willing to accept this new argument. As much as I tried to remain calm, I felt the old familiar bile creeping into my blood.

"How can you say that you had no choice?" I cried. "You might have left the Jesuit missions in the hands of Lasuén. Or even Fray Matías! You thought enough of him to bring him here as your companion."

Fray Junípero shook his head. "Regarding Lasuén, you are correct—he might have served as Father President of the Jesuit missions, had he been older and more experienced. Since then he has proven himself a capable administrator, and I expect he will serve God in this country for many years to come. At the time, however, you were the only one I trusted—"

"I have heard this before."

"But regarding Father Noriega, you are mistaken. He is here not because I favor him, but because I could not in conscience pair him with another man from our College. When a mission field is as difficult as ours, with the provisions as unreliable and the natives as unpredictable, a friar has every reason to run away at the first opportunity. When one adds the loathsome Fray Matías, the man's exit is assured."

"You say he is loathsome?"

"You do not know Fray Matías. He mutters obscenities under his breath while others are speaking to him. He does not bathe regularly, nor even perform the most rudimentary tasks of personal grooming, for example scraping nits from his hair. Further, his complexion is untidy—"

"You would damn him for his complexion?"

Junípero's face turned sour. "Listen, Paco. Before Fray Matías came to Carmelo, he was nearly killed because of his ill judgment. He was serving as chaplain for a sea expedition, and he took an unhealthy interest in one of his seaborne companions, a young member of the crew. I shall not contaminate your ears with the details, but let us say that it was only through my intercession that Fray Matías's life was spared."

He paused to let me digest these words.

"Naturally, I could not send him back to México, where his crimes might be repeated. If any man should be harmed by him, it should be me. As Father President, that is my duty. Thus I have not allowed Fray Matías to leave my supervision since he arrived. I tell you this only because of our longstanding confidence, Paco. And because we are here—" He rapped the wooden frame of the confession booth.

"I trust the details of Fray Matías's history will not proliferate after I am gone."

"Of course not."

"You see, the post of companion to the *padre presidente* has never been an honor. I have never chosen my companions; rather, they have always chosen me."

"That may be true of Fray Matías, Your Reverence, but surely not of Juan . . . "

"Matías Noriega cost the Lord no souls but his own. Fray Juan, however, jeopardized all the souls in this country. His negligence put this mission at grave risk and almost caused its ruin, as you well know. I ask you, my friend, who posed the greater danger to the Kingdom of God?"

He took a deep breath—as deep as his tattered lungs would allow. "These missions must not fail, Paco. We must not allow them to fail. If we have done our work correctly, they will stand for centuries, bringing light to this benighted land. This is God's plan. But the continued service of Fray Juan Crespí was an obstacle in the path of God. That is why he had to be destroyed."

"I did not know what Rigoberto intended to do—"

"You have not heard me, Brother. Your neophyte did nothing. I killed Fray Juan."

The voices of the neophyte choir drifted in from the courtyard. Words caught in my throat. I had in the ledger of my mind a careful accounting of crime and recrimination, of slights and retributions, which I had laid out at great pains over the past months. The balance at the bottom of the ledger had not turned out in my favor, but at least it had been certain. In a sense, I was comfortable with my culpability in the death of Fray Juan. I had never thought myself a saint. Rigoberto's betrayal was only another in a long history of sins. But this changed everything: all my calculations were now null and void.

"But Your Reverence," I pleaded, "you once said that when

Rigoberto came to see you, just before Fray Juan took ill, he looked—what was your description—ashen-faced? You said something was amiss with him. Well, you were correct: something was amiss with Rigoberto. The shame of what he had done was too much to bear."

Junípero raised his wrinkled palm. "The neophyte did come to see me, Paco, and he was just as I have described."

"Then you see, he was guilty—"

"The subject of the visit was most vexing to him. It concerned the Christian name of his bride. He wished for me to baptize the girl Encarnación."

My heart stopped.

"Encarnación Palóu, she would have been called. He did not wish for me to tell you, because he was unsure how you would receive the news. Frankly, I did not understand his concern; I told him Encarnación was a fine name, and that you would certainly not object to it."

"You kept this from me?"

"At his request. But now that the boy has vanished, I see no reason not to share it."

"You are a monster."

"Paco, please . . ."

"All this time, you wanted me to believe that Rigoberto killed Juan!"

"Come Paco, be reasonable. I have confessed that I poisoned our brother; why would I blame a poor neophyte?"

"Marriage was to be his reward! After all his years of service to this mission, to my mission, to his fellow neophytes . . . It was the least we could do for him. And now—now he has nothing."

"You have a kind heart, Fray Francisco, but you must think of this logically. One fish has slipped through our net, but thousands remain, and millions more will be caught in time. Because of our labor, the reign of God has been established in New California.

Hundreds of years from now, the Good News of Christ will still be spoken here. That is your accomplishment, not the marriage of a single neophyte."

I thought of the human fertilizer Junípero had turned under the soil of his vineyard. Juan Crespí was only the latest in a roster that included the first Father President who perished at sea; the neophytes Rigoberto and Teófilo; even Teófilo's wife, for whom His Reverence loomed as large as any lacquered saint. All were lost to us—not in the name of God, as Junípero would have me believe, but in the service of his ambition. There may have been others, too, other "obstacles" whose names I never knew and never would. As it stood, no official of Crown or Church would ever know the name Rigoberto Palóu. Nor would anyone know his wife, named for my Encarna. Nor would God know her, for the girl had never been baptized in the saving waters of Christ.

"I only wish that Fray Juan had served us better," said Junípero wistfully, as though he had not just a moment before admitted murder. "When I am gone, Paco, take Brother Juan's diaries and have them published. The journals from the first voyage with Governor Portolá will be especially useful in recruiting new friars. I have heard there is reticence among our brethren to embark for this place, and it is a pity. This is our brother's chance to make amends."

"Fray Juan is not the one who should be making amends," I said.

Junípero's eyes narrowed. "I did what was required of me. Of course I made mistakes. That is why I am here. Is this not a confession? Are you not my confessor, Fray Francisco?"

"For thirty-four years I have served God in that capacity."

"Then you must let me confess!" He took hold of the wooden booth and shook it with surprising strength.

"Calm yourself; the children are near."

"Do you wonder, really, why I removed Fray Juan? Or why I split you apart from that neophyte you loved so well?"

"Tell me, Father."

"Do you think you are the only one capable of envy, Fray Francisco? I never wished to send you away. My wishes were the same as yours—to live together in tranquility and companionship. But we were called to higher duty! When we sailed from Mallorca, do you think I knew that the success of our enterprise would depend on the two of us remaining apart, sometimes by hundreds and hundreds of leagues? My son, had I known that, I might have defied my God! I might have rejected his call!"

His eyes blazed with rage, with frustration, with loathing.

"You are not well," I said. "I fear your time is near."

"Indeed, Paco—nearer than you know."

I heard a rustling on Junípero's side of the confessional, as though he were lifting up his cassock. A blade winked in the candlelight.

Faster than I thought possible, I was on the other side of the booth. Junípero held the knife at arm's length, the point aimed inward. His eyes were closed, his lips busy with prayer. I charged into the narrow stall and knocked him back. Our combined weight tipped the confessional so that it fell against the stone wall of the church. Our candle tumbled and blew out.

In the dark I fumbled to find the weapon. Junípero's hands balled into fists. He made an effort to free his legs from under me, but he was weak with disease. He began to cough. I raised myself to my knees. All of a sudden, I felt his hands grab my face. He pulled me close. I smelled the sickness on his breath, the odor of death. In my ear, he whispered, "Lord have mercy on me." Then he took my right hand, and then my left, and wrapped them around his throat.

WHEN THE NEOPHYTES had placed Fray Junípero's body on his cot, I bid them leave us. "His Reverence is very near death," I said. "He wishes to be alone with his confessor."

"Please, one more blessing," said Juan Evangelista, who had started to cry. "Let me see his face one last time."

"We must allow His Reverence to make his final reconciliation with God."

The pious neophytes could not deny this appeal, and they left the cell slowly, the whole group stealing glances over their shoulders as they stooped under the doorframe and into the corridor.

Of course, Junípero was already gone. He had made his final confession, and whatever reckoning he deserved was already being served at the gates of Paradise.

I knelt before the corpse and arranged the crucifix on his chest. Without the sharp black eyes to enliven his face, he looked old. Thirty years of mission work will age anyone, but His Reverence had kept his fatigue a secret until just before the end. Now relieved of the burden of life, his skin had gone pallid, his lips gray, his hair thin and dull. Though I had witnessed it myself, I could not believe that this corporation of bones and skin and gristle had walked from Monterey to México and back; had dictated terms to viceroys and governors; had brought an entire heathen civilization into the flock of the Lord.

I would bury him, as he requested, next to Fray Juan Crespí. The markers on their graves would note their dates of birth and death, and a keen observer might notice that both hailed from a place called Mallorca, born a scant ten leagues apart. The two would cross oceans and continents, traveling to the farthest reach of Christendom before dying in even closer proximity than they had been born.

It was a poor summary of two lives. Despite enormous accomplishments, they would be little known to posterity. Aside from dates in various ships' logs and perhaps a sheaf of letters in the missionary college of San Fernando, the story of the *condiscípulos* would be written only in the shifting dust of California. Our missions here were as precarious as the reed huts of the pagans—no matter how Fray Junípero wished them otherwise. In a year's time they might vanish, and with them all traces of God.

This, I realized, would be Junípero's greatest sorrow—greater than the loss of family, friends, or colleagues, greater still than the loss of his own life.

Kneeling before my fallen master, I understood that the role of guardian had now passed to me. When I emerged from the cell and informed the congregation of his death, I would be declared the new Father President of the New California missions. My first inclination was to duck the responsibility, to pass it to Lasuén or some other man better suited to lead. But then what would I do? Where would I go? I could move to México and wait for death, spend my remaining days in bitterness and delusion. (Yes, my erstwhile roommate Fray Eugenio had shown me the end of that story!) Or I could return to Mallorca. Mother, forgive me: it would have been possible after all. But there was nothing for me in Spain. My parents were gone, and my sisters were occupied with their own lives. Even Encarna had found a life that suited her better than the illusion I was offering.

I knew I must remain in California. Though not a conqueror like Portolá, nor a diplomat like Don Gálvez, nor a zealot like Fray Junípero, I was useful. I was a clerk, and I knew my powers. I could not impel the colony to survive by force of will or by saintly example, but I could recruit the next generation of *condiscípulos*. Among these might be included—who could know?—a second Junípero, a Linus to his Peter. Without new labor, our vineyard would wither and die. But Juan's diaries could not serve as the lure. Junípero had been wrong about that. In Juan's accounts, there was simply not enough to admire or to fear—not enough of the raw material of hagiography.

And a hagiographer I would be. I thought of what had compelled Fray Junípero to America: the vision of San Francisco Solano with the violin at his feet, risen from the finger-slick pages of the *Lives of the Saints*. I realized that if we hoped to compel young men to New California, we would need our own Solano. But it could not be the story of Juan Crespí. In fact the identity of the Apostle of California had been clear before we left Mallorca. No sin or flaw or "failing" could negate what he had done. All our labors had been in his service. Some of us had even given our lives.

His Reverence had been prescient when he asked me to be his confessor—there in the dusty *ramada* by the side of the Veracruz road. He predicted I was to be his conduit to the Lord, his route to grace and glory. This would be more accurate than any of us could have imagined. I would open my heart to the Holy Spirit, and with words—the only tools I ever mastered—I would create the portrait of a saint. I knew the story minutely, for I had been the subject's confidante all my adult life. Like any good clerk, I would wash the facts, removing ambiguities like a winnower picking pebbles from beans. I would present Junípero Serra not as he was but as we needed him to be. Young men would read my account and declare: "Where trod the feet of Saint Junípero of California, there shall I follow!" His story would call them forth by the thousands, these new Isaiahs, and fresh hands would populate our continent. They would arrive as fast as ships could cross the seas. The reign of God in this land would be assured, our children saved, and our sins washed away.

I had always been the one left behind. Now I understood why.

I made the sign of the cross and bowed my head—one last private moment with my master. Then I threw open the door and shared him with the world.

ENDNOTE

After the death of Junípero Serra in 1784, Francisco Palóu served less than one year as Father President of the Alta California missions. He was replaced by Father Fermín Lasuén, who went on to establish nine more missions. By 1821, when México gained its independence from Spain, there were twenty-one Franciscan missions in Alta California, spaced approximately one day's walk from one another.

In 1785 Father Palóu retired to the College of San Fernando in México City, where he spent his days working on a biography of Serra. This book, the first published by a California author, was printed in México City in 1789. Father Palóu intended the book to be read by prospective Franciscan missionaries in Spain, but copies soon spread to other audiences in Europe and to the rest of Hispanic America. The calls to canonize Father Serra began almost immediately and have continued to this day. In 1988, Pope John Paul II beatified Junípero Serra—the third of four steps in the canonization process. For Serra to achieve the final step to sainthood, his supporters will need to demonstrate that at least two miracles have been achieved through his intercession.

Father Palóu remained at the College until his death in 1789. He assumed a leadership role in the Franciscan community in México City but was reportedly ineffective and mentally unstable. One of his successors, Fray Tomás de Pangua, wrote to the viceroy that it was "unfortunate that the guidance of the community fell to a superior who was not only advanced in years but who had already arrived at his second childhood and could do nothing but cry and lock himself in his cell out of fear."

Spanish officials remained concerned about Russian encroachment, but by 1812, when the Russians established their first permanent settlement in California (Fort Ross, in present-day Sonoma County), Spanish Alta California already consisted of nineteen active missions, four presidios, two civilian settlements, or pueblos, and numerous smaller religious and military outposts. The Russians stayed at Fort Ross only twenty-eight years before retreating to their Alaska colonies.

Modern scholarship suggests that when the Franciscans arrived, there were between 150,000 and 300,000 native people living in Alta California. By 1832, when the Mexican government began to dissolve the missions, the friars had performed nearly 90,000 baptisms. Three-quarters of the neophytes died of disease and were buried on mission grounds.

Roman Catholicism remains the most popular faith in California, with over 11,500,000 adherents—more than the entire population of Spain during Father Serra's lifetime. Today approximately 27,000,000 Californians, or nearly three-quarters of the state's population, live within a day's walk of one of the Franciscan missions.

FURTHER READING

Berger, John. *Franciscan Missions of California*. New York: Putnam, 1941.

Crespí, Juan. *A Description of Distant Roads: original journals of the first expedition into California, 1769–1770*. Trans. Alan K. Brown. San Diego: San Diego State University Press, 2001.

DeNevi, Don, and Noel Francis Moholy. *Junípero Serra: the illustrated story of the Franciscan founder of California's missions*. San Francisco: Harper & Row, 1985.

Engelhardt, Zephyrin. *San Francisco or Mission Dolores*. Chicago: Franciscan Herald Press, 1924.

Geiger, Maynard. *Franciscan Missionaries in Hispanic California, 1769–1848: a biographical dictionary*. San Marino [Calif.]: Huntington Library, 1969.

La Pérouse, Jean François. *Monterey in 1786: the journals of Jean François de La Pérouse*. Berkeley: Heyday Books, 1989.

Margolin, Malcolm. *The Ohlone Way*. Berkeley: Heyday Books, 1978.

Neuerburg, Norman. *Saints of the California Missions*. Santa Barbara: Bellerophon Books, 2001.

Palóu, Francisco. *Historical Memoirs of New California*. Trans. Herbert Eugene Bolton. Berkeley: University of California Press, 1926.

———. *Life of Fray Junípero Serra [Relación histórica de la vida y apostólicas tareas del venerable padre Fray Junípero Serra]*. Trans. Maynard Geiger. Washington, DC: Academy of American Franciscan History, 1955.

Starr, Kevin. *California*. New York: Modern Library, 2005.

Sunset Books editorial staff. *The California Missions: a pictorial history*. Menlo Park [Calif.]: Sunset Books, 1964.

ACKNOWLEDGEMENTS

Many thanks to Malcolm Margolin, the only publisher in America who knows Junípero Serra's birthday. Thanks also to Gayle Wattawa, my editor, and the rest of the intelligent and dedicated staff at Heyday.

Thanks to my agent, Jennifer Carlson, for editing numerous drafts of the manuscript and for insisting that I find a way to include women in this story. Bob and Benjie O'Connell also read an early draft of the book, and I am grateful for their suggestions.

Big thanks to my *condiscípulos* at San José State University: Andrew Altschul, Paul Douglass, Cathleen Miller, Alan Soldofsky, Samuel Maio, and especially Persis Karim, who suggested the publisher.

It's fair to say that I wrote this book because I attended Catholic school for twelve years, but it would have been a much different book without the influence of the Jesuits at Loyola High School in Los Angeles. Thank you to the Reverends Tom Carroll, Jerry Lindner, and Tom O'Neill for their guidance and encouragement at a crucial time.

Thank you to my parents, Diane and Paul Taylor, for dragging me to church on Sundays, and to my sister, Megan, for enduring it with me.

Finally, thank you to my wife, Jessica, for her friendship, love, and support, and to our daughter, Violet, for inspiration and for correcting my Spanish.

ABOUT THE AUTHOR

Nick Taylor is the author of the novel *The Disagreement*, winner of the 2009 Michael Shaara Prize for Excellence in Civil War Fiction. Raised in Los Angeles, he attended the University of Virginia, where he earned an MFA in fiction writing. He is currently a professor of English and Director of the Martha Heasley Cox Center for Steinbeck Studies at San José State University. Visit him on the web at http://www.readnicktaylor.com.

Photo: gregkochphoto.com

HEYDAY
into California

About Heyday
Heyday is an independent, nonprofit publisher and unique cultural institution. We promote widespread awareness and celebration of California's many cultures, landscapes, and boundary-breaking ideas. Through our well-crafted books, public events, and innovative outreach programs we are building a vibrant community of readers, writers, and thinkers.

Thank You
It takes the collective effort of many to create a thriving literary culture. We are thankful to all the thoughtful people we have the privilege to engage with. Cheers to our writers, artists, editors, storytellers, designers, printers, bookstores, critics, cultural organizations, readers, and book lovers everywhere!

We are especially grateful for the generous funding we've received for our publications and programs during the past year from foundations and hundreds of individual donors. Major supporters include:

Anonymous (3); Alliance for California Traditional Arts; Arkay Foundation; Judy Avery; James J. Baechle; Paul Bancroft III; BayTree Fund; S. D. Bechtel, Jr. Foundation; Barbara Jean and Fred Berensmeier; Berkeley Civic Arts Program and Civic Arts Commission; Joan Berman; John Briscoe; Lewis and Sheana Butler; California Civil Liberties Public Education Program; Cal Humanities; California Indian Heritage Center Foundation; California State Parks Foundation; Keith Campbell Foundation; Candelaria Fund; John and Nancy Cassidy Family Foundation, through Silicon Valley Community Foundation; Charles Edwin Chase; Graham Chisholm; The Christensen Fund; Jon Christensen; Community Futures Collective; Compton Foundation; Creative Work Fund; Lawrence Crooks; Nik Dehejia; Frances Dinkelspiel and Gary Wayne; The Durfee Foundation; Earth Island Institute; The Fred Gellert Family Foundation; Fulfillco; The Wallace Alexander Gerbode Foundation; Nicola W. Gordon; Wanda Lee Graves and Stephen Duscha; David Guy; The Walter and Elise Haas Fund; Coke and James Hallowell; Stephen Hearst; Cindy Heitzman; Historic Resources Group; Sandra and Charles Hobson; Donna Ewald Huggins; Humboldt Area Foundation; JiJi Foundation; The James Irvine Foundation; Claudia Jurmain; Marty and Pamela Krasney; Guy Lampard and Suzanne Badenhoop; Christine Leefeldt, in celebration of Ernest Callenbach and Malcolm Margolin's friendship; Bernard and Josie Le Roy; Thomas Lockard; Thomas J. Long Foundation; Judith and Brad Lowry-Croul; Michael McCone; Nion McEvoy and Leslie Berriman; Giles W. and Elise G. Mead Foundation; Michael Mitrani; Moore Family Foundation; Richard Nagler; National Endowment for the Arts; National Wildlife Federation; Native Cultures Fund; The Nature Conservancy; Nightingale Family Foundation; Northern California Water Association; The David and Lucile Packard Foundation; Panta Rhea Foundation; Alan Rosenus; The San Francisco Foundation; Greg Sarris; William Somerville; Martha Stanley; Roselyne Chroman Swig; Swinerton Family Fund; Sedge Thomson and Sylvia Brownrigg; TomKat Charitable Trust; The Roger J. and Madeleine Traynor Foundation; Lisa Van Cleef and Mark Gunson; Patricia Wakida; John Wiley & Sons, Inc.; Peter Booth Wiley and Valerie Barth; Dean Witter Foundation; The Work-in-Progress Fund of Tides Foundation; and Yocha Dehe Community Fund.

Getting Involved

To learn more about our publications, events, membership club, and other ways you can participate, please visit www.heydaybooks.com.